SURVIVE

THE SURVIVAL SERIES

AMBER R POLK

Cover design by John Sullivan
All Rights Reserved.

ISBN- 978-1506119830

*To Michael for always loving and supporting me
and to my children, I love you more than life.*

Survive

CHAPTER ONE

I snapped the stem of the last ripe apple from the last tree on the last row furthest from my house. Closing my eyes, I lifted it to my nose, thinking of how my father used to lift me up over his head to grab an apple from the very same tree. Shaking myself from the memory, I ripped open my eyes. There wasn't time left to reminisce about the past. Figuring there was a good chance we wouldn't make it through the winter if I didn't hurry my ass up, I tossed the apple into the half-full wheelbarrow in front of me.

As if Mother Nature herself wanted to taunt me, a cold wind whipped around my legs and worked a chill up my body. I watched the leaves dance in the air all around me, wishing my body was as carefree and light as they were.

Fantastic. My life sucked so incredibly bad, I envied a freaking leaf.

With a sigh, I slung the strap of my shotgun over my shoulder.

Fall was in full swing and winter wouldn't be far behind, so I bent my head and moved toward home.

Home.

I had been living in Tulsa when what everyone called "the plague" hit the United States, but immediately returned to the orchard. I had been raised just outside of a minuscule town of Jasper, Arkansas to be with my parents, and naïve me thought I would be there weeks, maybe a month or two at the most. I had no way of knowing I would never go back to my old life, because my old life no longer existed.

While waiting out the sickness in the quickest and slowest two weeks imaginable, the plague ended up taking both of my parents and two thirds of the former United States population with them. More than likely, it killed most of the world's human race, but I may never know. I wasn't sure if I really *wanted* to know. More than anything, I was grateful my brother came home from college the day before me. Had he waited one more day, he might not have made it at all.

Without Jacob, I would have nothing or no one.

The plague hit without warning and killed the carrier with horrific pain within a week. No one had enough time to figure out what it was or how it was contracted before it spread out of control. Bloodshot eyes, high fever, and vomiting were the signs I knew to watch for.

In the beginning, the news stations seemed excited about the devastation trampling throughout the Middle East and quickly spreading through Europe. As the plague moved closer, the news anchors went from panic, to the station going static, to nothing when we lost power and it never returned. We were in the dark and on our own.

One day the world would recoup. It probably wasn't going to end up being the same world we had before, but anything would better than the day to day struggle to stay alive like we were doing now. I just hoped we survived long enough to see it happen.

"Roni," I heard my not so little brother, Jacob, yell as he trotted down the thin path between the trees. My name is Veronica, but he never grew out of calling me by my nickname. When he was right in front of me, his hands were rested on his hips. "Thought I told you not to go out this far without me."

Rolling my eyes, I pushed past him. "Did you find any more jars?" I asked, ignoring him. He brushed me aside and picked up the handles of the wheelbarrow and started home.

"Got about forty from June Miller's old place. Found more blankets and kerosene, too."

"That's great," I nodded. "I can go with you next time and look for some more jars."

Jacob ran a hand through his tousled, dirty blond hair he had inherited from our father and nodded, even though he didn't like the idea of my tagging along. He would just have to get over it. He was only twenty-two and nearly four years my junior, yet he thought he had to protect me at all times.

Yeah, it was kind of sweet, but flipping annoying.

We needed to gather as many supplies as we could—as quickly as we could—so he would just have to get over his need to be alpha male and let me help.

Once we reached the house, we transferred the apples from the wheelbarrow to buckets and took them to the kitchen in relative silence. We worked the same routine we had had since we were old enough to carry buckets. Working on this orchard was second nature to both of us.

By the time I became a hate-the-world teenager, I detested anything to do with the orchard. Now, I was glad my mom made me spend hour upon hour learning how to can foods.

My parents would be happy to know we were applying what they had taught us as kids to keep us alive.

A whisper of a memory began to form, but I hushed it back into a dark corner of my mind.

Winter was coming and I was going to make damn sure we survived to see spring.

Having used up the majority of our pre-plague sock of canned foods the winter before, our lives depended on how much we could harvest and hunt this season. We didn't survive the plague just to starve to death. I wouldn't allow it to happen.

Once we put away all the supplies and washed up, I pulled out a chair and plopped down. I had been on my feet all day and my legs and arms ached in agony. Recalling the ridiculous amount of money I used to spend on workout classes in order to feel this much pain, I asked myself, *why the hell had I ever wanted to make myself feel this way?* Then I remembered the sweets that existed back then and how big my ass would have gotten *without* the class.

Jacob leaned his back against the kitchen counter, resting a palm on top, and downed a bottle of water in a few gulps then pointed the empty bottle toward me. "Can you can meat?"

"If we can eat it, I can can it." I rubbed my temples with my thumbs, hoping some of the pain would abate.

"Candy canes. Can you can candy canes?"

"What?"

"Can you?" he smirked.

"You're such a dork," I answered. I tossed a hand towel at him and smiled. He chuckled before picking up an apple and eating half in one bite. "I'm going to do a quick walk around before it gets any darker. I'll be back by dinner time."

I stuck my tongue out at his back as he walked out of the house. I never really enjoyed cooking, but doing it every day without much variation made me hate it with a passion. Jacob was just about as useful in the kitchen as a slab of bacon in a vegetarian camp and he wasn't enthusiastic about learning. What I wouldn't give to be able to pick up the phone and get a pizza delivered. At the very least, I wished I knew how to make cheese. I was pretty sure that was primarily milk and I didn't have a cow hanging around anywhere.

There was a time I thought I was being trendy and healthy by eating a salad and fresh fruit every day. Now, I would give my whole left leg for a candy bar. It had been over two years since the unexplained plague hit and I was sure all the factory made, artery clogging goodness was bound to be long gone by now.

I wasn't quite ready to give up hope on that just yet, though.

I went to the pantry and pulled out a jar of stew and sat it on the table. I wasn't at all hungry and Jacob could manage heating up his own food. All I wanted was to soak myself in a bath and fall into a coma in bed.

There were things I was still thankful for and having a well for water was definitely one of them. We were fortunate our dad had purchased two generators for the well, to use during tornado season. It took more fuel than we liked, but we always turned the generators off when they weren't being used. With the well, it kept us hydrated, I was able to cook with it, wash laundry with it, but in my opinion, the best was taking a nice, long hot bath. There was a bathroom downstairs, but it was only equipped for a shower; therefore, if we wanted a bath we had to heat the water on the cast iron wood burner downstairs and make multiple trips up and down the stairs to fill it up.

Though my body was tired and achy, I made the many trips up and down the stairs. It was so worth it. Stripping off my clothes in eager anticipation and gingerly easing my way into the steaming water, I laid my head back to rest on the cold porcelain, letting the hot water seep into my pores and redden my skin. I dreamed of the day I could fill the bath enough to cover my belly when I laid back.

Closing my eyes, I let out a deep breath through pursed lips. What I wouldn't give to have a sweet, sexy man rubbing my tired shoulders. If I were truly honest with myself, I wouldn't even care if he were sweet at this point. A sexy asshole would work just as well for what I wanted from him. His mouth would be too occupied to talk, anyway.

Yeah. I could handle a sexy asshole just fine.

I washed my body and hair before shaving my legs. I wasn't sure why I bothered with it anymore. It wasn't like there would be anyone around to feel them, but I just couldn't go all native and not shave. Even if I was crawling into bed alone at night, I still had to feel them.

I let out a self-pitying sigh.

The urge for sex seemed to grow as time passed. I had always heard if you haven't had something in so long, then you forget what it was like to ever have it in the first place. I called bullshit. It wasn't that I had much sex before the apocalypse. I could count the amount of men I had on two fingers, but I remembered what it was like and the chances of ever having sex again were pretty slim.

Too bad my last sexual experience was with my prick head of an ex-boyfriend, Harvey Baker.

These days, my boyfriend was tucked inside my nightstand and before long, even the batteries I snagged here and there on supply runs were going to give out.

Then what would I do?

Maybe I was an idiot to think of such things when people were dead or dying all around, but it was important to me. During the day, I worked hard from dawn to well past dusk, worrying about my brother, the food supply, and crazy gun toting idiots who wanted everything we had. Every now and then, I let myself pout and be needy.

Right then I felt incredibly needy.

Standing, the chill in the air gave me goose bumps, effectively causing stubble on my legs. I wrapped a towel around me before stepping in front of the mirror. There was a fear one day I would look into the mirror and see a lifeless shell of my former self. I feared that there wouldn't be anything feminine or attractive about me anymore.

I remembered, in school, seeing photos of the women of the Oklahoma dust bowl and how worn and hard the women looked from days upon days of nonstop backbreaking work. I didn't want to look like that at all.

7

My *worst* fear, when looking at my reflection, was that I would see signs of the plague. Luckily, today wasn't that day. My eyes were still green, not blood shot, which would be the first sign I was infected. The same long brown hair laid in wet ropes over my shoulders and around the tops of my arms. My thin cheeks were pink from the steam of the bath and the dim light of the candles stacked on the countertop made my skin glow and look more tan than it actually was.

I threw each leg up on the counter, one at a time, applying lotion to my semi-smooth legs and arms before putting on anti-aging night cream. I didn't care what kind of world we lived in, I had no desire to show signs of premature aging. After towel drying my hair, I braided it down my back and put on my pajamas and made the short trip across the hall into my bedroom. My only sanctuary.

I sat on a flower patterned wingback chair in the corner of the room. Placing a vanilla scented candle on the nightstand, I opened a romance novel I had been reading a little of every day, for almost a month. Obviously, I was a glutton for punishment.

Especially if it was a Scottish Highland Laird dishing out the punishment.

Clanking came from the kitchen. No doubt Jacob was leaving a mess I would have to clean up the next morning. I could already hear his excuse that he already turned off the generator so he couldn't clean up. *The little shit.* I continued to read until I heard him go to his room and close the door.

Setting down the book, I blew out the candle and made my way to bed. Lying on my back, I stared at the ceiling in boredom. It only took minutes to hear the sounds of Jacob's snoring. I couldn't help but smile. He had snored like a dying elephant since elementary school. I used to throw fits as a preteen that I couldn't sleep because all the racket he made. My parents finally bought a big box fan for my room to drown out the noise and I could get a peaceful night's rest. These days, I didn't think I could manage falling asleep without hearing the rhythmic sounds of his snore.

Just as my body relaxed and I began to fall asleep, the chickens began rustling around outside, not quite making a racket, but not settled, either. It was probably a fox, I assumed yanking the blankets back and going to the window. The moon illuminated the yard and the chicken coop. I couldn't see anything and the chickens were settling down so there couldn't be a fox. The chickens would be in near hysteria if there was one. Just as I was about to let the curtains fall into place, I saw a shadow at the edge of the yard. A human shadow. I froze, my hand going straight to my chest. I had to act quickly. There was no telling how many of them were out there. I ran to the nightstand and grabbed the 9mm that was kept loaded and ran to my brothers' room. God, I hoped he hadn't locked his door. I twisted the knob and quietly pushed open the door in relief. I rushed to his side and shook him until he startled awake, fist already pulled back.

"Jacob, it's me," I said, taking a quick step back.

He ran a hand over his face, "What the hell, Roni," he said.

"Shh!" I chastised, holding a finger over my mouth. "There's someone outside. I saw someone in the yard."

In a split second, he was up and shoving his feet into boots. "You stay in the house no matter what. Shoot anything that isn't me that tries to come in."

"How am I supposed to know it's you or not?" I asked.

He stopped at his door and looked at me like I was a lunatic. "I don't know. I don't have time to come up with a secret knock."

With that, he was out the door and without making a sound, out of the house. I cursed under my breath and on the balls of my feet, tiptoed down the stairs, handgun in tow. I centered myself about ten feet away from the front door, holding up the gun like I had seen in so many movies. After about ten seconds, I felt like an idiot and my arms ached. The house was pitch black, but I knew it like the back of my hands. I went to the kitchen window, heard a curse, and someone darted across the yard again. I wasn't sure if it was my brother or not, but whoever it was, they were large. There was no way I could just sit in the house and wait to see if Jacob was going to come back or be killed out there alone, protecting me. I went to the kitchen door, slipped on a pair of house shoes, and quietly snuck out the backdoor.

Pressing myself against the side of the house, I tried to calm my breaths while taking in my surroundings. My heart raced in my ears, making it difficult to hear anything around. Why couldn't I be one of those people who could come up with a plan in the spur of the moment? I bit my bottom lip. *If I were a bad guy, where would I be,* I contemplated. Hell, I didn't know. What I needed was a vantage spot. Somewhere I could look around without being seen. I looked up at the towering oak tree about thirty feet in front of me and centered just about right to see most of the yard.

Decision made, I took off, keeping to the shadows, and made my way to the tree. I tucked the gun into the waistband of my pajama bottoms, flung off the house shoes and gruntingly started up the tree. Stopping about halfway, I positioned myself on the same branch I had sat on too many times to count while growing up.

I couldn't have been there more than a few minutes when I heard a loud thud and my brother yelled before cursing up a storm, then everything went completely silent. Fear gripped me by the throat. I was about to climb down when I saw a large figure, larger than Jacob's, come racing across the yard in my direction. Scared and majorly pissed, I waited until he was almost under the tree before I let out a roar from some inner Amazon warrior inside me as I jumped from the tree and landed on top of the man, effectively knocking him flat to the ground. My forehead knocked the back of his head and for a moment, all I saw were stars. I pulled myself up and straddled him, whipped out the gun, and pushed it between his shoulder blades.

"I swear to you, if you hurt my little brother, I'm going to beat you even *more* stupid before I shoot your dumb ass."

CHAPTER TWO

Jacob!" I yelled, trying to keep the panic from my voice. I made quick work of patting the man down, trying not paying attention to the multitude of muscles beneath his clothes. I had to be very careful—from the size of him, he could easily overtake me. "I'm going to get up and you're going to slowly stand up ten seconds after I do. You will *not* turn around."

Slowly, I made my way off him, still holding the gun to his back until he was completely standing in front of me. Dear Lord, he was a big man. I had to tilt my head back to see the top of his head. I wasn't small for a girl, measuring in at five foot eight inches, but he literally towered over me. Jacob was a big man himself and this guy was taller.

"*Jacob!*" I yelled again, this time not caring if this man heard my panic.

"Veronica," Jacob said, coming up behind me. He was out of breath, but not enough to hold back his frustration. "I thought I told you to stay in the house. Are you ever going to listen?"

The boulder that had been crushing my chest rolled off when I heard his voice. "Damn it Jacob! I thought you were dead!"

Jacob stomped past me until he was standing in front of the man I held still with my gun. The two men, both huge, stared straight at the other. "Who the hell are you and what the hell are you doing here? Are you alone?"

"I'm alone," a deep husky voice told us. Chills ran down my spine and straight to my girl parts. That was the kind of voice people used to pay good money to hear on the other side of the phone.

I rubbed my arm unconsciously. "Can we at least go inside? My arm is getting tired and it's cold out here."

Jacob looked past the trespasser and to me. "Are you freaking kidding me?"

"*No*, I'm not kidding you." I rolled my eyes, wishing he could see. "We can still hold a gun on him while we're sitting down at the kitchen table."

I could have sworn I heard the man chuckle and I glared at his back. Jacob ran a hand through his hair. He gave the intruder a wide berth as he walked around him and next to me. As he took the gun from my hands, my hand immediately dropped. I really needed to rest my arms more if I wanted to be able to ever use them again.

"Lead the way," he said with a mock bow, pointing the gun at the man and his free hand toward the house.

Grabbing my house shoes, I avoided looking at the intruder or Jacob as I stalked to the house and opened the door. I hated it when Jacob treated me like I was helpless. I just so happened to be the one who tackled the guy *and* I was the one who held him there until Jacob arrived. Did he even say thanks? Of course not, because I wasn't being the good girl and doing as I was told and staying in the house.

Bullshit!

As soon as I got inside, I hurried to the shotgun and slung it under my arm while I waited for them to walk in behind me. When they did, I had a difficult time keeping my mouth from smacking the hardwood floor.

He was beautiful.

Not cute. Not handsome. Not good-looking. Nope, he was *hella* beautiful. Beautiful in a manly, soak your panties in seconds kind of way. In a way that made a woman want to feed him grapes and beg to be a part of his concubine.

Jacob pulled back a chair and the man sat down, placing his forearms on top of the table. He seemed alert, but not in the least bit intimidated by the situation or us. I looked up to his face and found him inspecting me. I deduced he probably wasn't thrilled to be taken down by a girl, but his eyes weren't angry. They looked hungry. Hungry for what, was the question. I cleared my throat to keep from choking on my tongue. It wasn't until my nipples got hard did I realize I wasn't wearing a bra. I quickly threw my arm over my chest, watching one side of his full lips quirk into an almost grin. My face burned with embarrassment.

"I'm, um, going to run upstairs real quick." I was already moving up the stairs before I finished what I was saying.

Once I made it to the bedroom, I lit a candle, sat the shotgun on top of the bed, and looked down at my grass-stained pajamas bottoms and yanked them off. I threw on a bra, a t-shirt, and a pair of yoga pants. After throwing on a bra, t-shirt, and yoga pants, I removed the braid in my hair and ran my fingers through it before blowing out the candle and heading downstairs. I wasn't sure why I wanted to look decent in front of this man. He could very well be a killer for all I knew. No, he wasn't a killer; he didn't have that killer vibe.

Not that I actually knew what a killer's vibe would feel like.

I thought it probably felt evil.

When I left the room, I could hear both men talking, but couldn't make out what was being said. I reached the bottom of the stairs and they both went silent and looked at me. Feeling much more confident with my girls locked in tight, I turned to Jacob.

"Who is he?" I asked Jacob, trying to ignore the man watching me with such intensity. I pulled out a chair furthest from the stranger and sat down with the intended grace of a ballerina, but stumbled over my own foot and slammed into the seat with a thud.

Oh my God, how embarrassing!

My eyes wide, I stared at Jacob who was looking at me bewildered. Jacob shook his head and picked something up from the table.

"His name is Lucas Greslon, twenty-eight years old. He's from Colorado from what his license says. He says he doesn't want trouble." Jacob slid the card across the table to me. It looked real enough, not that I would know if it was a fake. I never managed to get a fake ID when I needed it. I was right about his six foot three and two hundred give pounds. *And all muscle*, I thought, sliding the ID back across to Jacob.

"And what's he doing here? On our property?"

"I was just looking for a place to sleep for the night and saw you had a barn," Lucas assured me. "I was only passing through."

I turned my head to Lucas and inspected him. His hair was either dark brown or black and close to his head on the sides and maybe an inch or two on top. His features were strong with a hard chin, high cheekbones, and a nose that wasn't too wide or long for his face, but still manly. Even in the dim light of the single candle on the table, his eyes were deep silver. They were almost predatory without being menacing. His formerly full lips were set in a thin line. He wore a dark blue t-shirt with a ripped collar. I wondered if that rip was from when I jumped out of the tree like a lunatic or if it was from an earlier skirmish. Trying to see past his obvious good looks to his character, I could see honesty behind his eyes along with something else I couldn't quite put a finger on. He seemed to be telling the truth, as far as I could tell.

Jacob tapped his fingers on the table and let out a sigh. "Where are you headed, Lucas?"

Lucas pulled his gaze away from mine and faced Jacob head on. He definitely didn't have issues looking people in the eye. It was unnerving to say the least. "Nowhere in particular, and you can call me Luke."

He was in an awkward place, with awkward people, and seemed to be taking the questioning well enough. I didn't feel threatened by him. If anything, I felt a low hum of weariness from him. Danger just wasn't there and I always

16

had a good sense of people. I trusted my gut. "Are you thirsty?"

His eyes moved to me swiftly, his eyebrows pulled together like I had asked him if he wanted to jump on the next train to the moon. "Yes, I am."

I stood and poured him a glass of water from a pitcher, setting it in front of him.

"Thank you," he said, pulling the glass to his lips and taking slow, steady drinks until the glass was empty. At least he had some manners.

Without asking, I took his glass, refilled it, and handed it to him again. I turned to sit back down and Jacob was glaring up at me. "What? Do you want a drink, too?"

"No," he said, exasperated. "Just, sit down."

I sat, but not before lightly smacking Jacob on the back of the head. Jacob rubbed his head, more to make sure his hair wasn't sticking up than from pain. He took a deep breath and looked at Luke. Before he could say anything, Luke began talking.

"Look, I'm really sorry I trespassed and scared you. I'm not here for sinister reasons. I was just looking for a safe place to sleep for the night." This time he looked straight at Jacob. "If you let me just sleep in the barn tonight, maybe a small meal in the morning, I can help you with anything around the house tomorrow."

Jacob leaned back in his chair, still pointing the gun toward him, but kept his finger off the trigger. The silence seemed to drag on forever. On one hand, I didn't think he was really a personal danger to us, but on the other, where was he going and how had he made it alone? I didn't really know what the world was like out there now. The most I had seen of the outside world was a town about a twenty minute drive away. Jasper had been an All-American small town before and last time I saw it, it was desolate and the few people that remained were fighting for supplies in the middle of the streets. I couldn't imagine what it was like in the more populated areas.

No one willingly trekked across country these days, so why was he?

Just before Jacob's mouth opened to say something, I stopped him. "You can stay the night."

"Roni, you're killin' me!" Jacob yelled and smacked the table with the palm of his hand.

"Well, *you* weren't saying anything," I said, shrugging my shoulders.

"I was going to tell him he could stay, if you would wait a damn minute."

"Okay, go ahead," I waved a hand toward Luke.

Jacob stood. "It's a little late now."

I stood too and looked at Luke. "By the way, I'm Veronica, and this is my jackass little brother, Jacob. Are you hungry?"

****

After I fed our guest, Jacob took a sleeping bag out of the hallway closet and waited for Luke to follow. Luke considered me before saying, "Thank you for everything."

I avoided looking at him by wiping down the counters. "We wake up early, so you better get some rest."

He watched me for a second more, then turned and followed Jacob outside. I walked to the living room and looked at the grandfather clock against the wall. It was a little past midnight, though it felt like we had been up all night. The days were getting darker, earlier. Just another indication winter wouldn't be far away.

No more than ten minutes later, Jacob came into the room and sat down on the couch. "So."

"So, what do you think?"

"I really don't know," he said, with a long yawn. "I don't trust anyone, but I *do* think he just needed a place to sleep."

I nodded in agreement. "Did he hit you with something?"

"No, why?"

"All that racket you were making out there, I thought you were being killed. Plus you have a big red mark on your forehead."

He eyed me sheepishly and his neck turned red. "I ran into the clothes line. Hurt like hell."

I couldn't help but laugh at him. Once I got it out of my system, I stood. "I'm exhausted. Are you sleeping down here?"

"Yeah," he said, lying back and closing his eyes. "See you in the morning."

"Night."

Upstairs, I tiptoed to the window in my room and peered at the barn. I noticed Jacob had put a chain and padlock around the doors. *Not a bad idea*, I thought before letting the curtain fall back into place. Climbing into bed, I realized it had been months since we had spoken to another person. Tomorrow was going to be an interesting day.

The next morning, I was up with the chickens—literally. I took a few more minutes than normal picking out a pair of jeans and a form fitting t-shirt. Most of my jeans were a little too big since I had lost so much weight, but not enough to have to wear a belt yet. After brushing my hair into a low and loose ponytail, I put on a little mascara and lip gloss. *I'm not trying to look good for him*, I kept telling myself. Every now and then I would try to look a little nicer just to change the monotony. I rolled my eyes at my own sorry excuse. I knew *exactly* why I was trying to look decent.

I went downstairs and nudged my snoring brother awake with my foot. "Go unlock our guest, let him take a shower while I feed the chickens, and gather some eggs for breakfast."

Pulling a knit cardigan over my shoulders, I waited for Jacob to get up before heading out. "You might want to give him something to wear, too, and he can wash his clothes before he leaves."

"Want me to share my toothbrush with him too?"

"No, I already set out an unopened one on the bathroom counter, smartass." I smiled overly bright at him and picked up a bucket.

First things first, I went to the garden and picked the wilted leaves from the lettuce to feed to the chickens along with a handful of chicken feed. Looking around, I decided it was time to pick the carrots and it looked like a few of the pumpkins were ready, too. I needed to learn to make pumpkin pie. Maybe we could have one for Thanksgiving dinner in a few weeks. This Thanksgiving, like last, we had so much and so little to be thankful for.

The chickens ran straight to me as soon as I opened the pen. They weren't typical pets, but I enjoyed them. I even named the little buggers and could swear they knew when they were being called. I fed them, then while they were occupied, went to the coop and picked the eggs. From the twenty chickens we had, I got almost a dozen eggs. Considering the weather was getting cooler, that was far more than I expected.

Trying to not be obvious, I watched as Jacob let Luke out of the barn. He strolled out and stretched his arms behind his head, causing his shirt to come up enough to see his well-formed abs underneath his tanned skin. I swallowed hard against the sudden dryness in my mouth. Jacob said something and they both walked toward the house. As they passed by me, Luke glanced in my direction and nodded with a lift of one side of his mouth. A gust of wind blew a few strands of hair over my face causing me to inhale a chunk of my hair. By the time I was able to remove the hair and catch my breath again, they were already walking through the front door.

I busied myself for a few minutes before taking the eggs inside. The shower downstairs was on and Jacob was nowhere to be seen. He had to be freezing in the shower, but something was better than nothing, the way I saw it. I tried not to imagine him naked in there, but failed miserably. The man was hot, and if I didn't imagine his hard, naked body glistening with beads of water then there was something *seriously* wrong with me.

By the time I had the eggs fried and the hash browns made, both men came into the room. I often wondered if men had some sort of sixth sense that told them when food was done, because it never failed for Jacob. Jacob kissed me on the cheek and I patted the top of his head.

"Thanks, Sissy," he said as he made his plate and sat down.

I set out three glasses of apple juice and held out a clean plate to Luke who stood toward the back of the kitchen with his arms crossed over his chest. "Get as much as you want."

He walked up next to me and took the plate, my skin tingled with him being so close. Not to mention my nipples felt like swords trying to break free of my bra.

"You eat first and I'll take what's left."

I took a small step back to get some distance, "It's okay, there's plenty."

He didn't move and I finally gave up, "Stubborn, aren't you?"

He half-grinned, showing straight white teeth under his full lips. If this man had a flaw, I had yet to find it. I made my plate and sat down. Luke put food on his plate and sat across from me. I tried to remember my manners and take small bites, unlike my darling little brother who was scarfing his food down like it may disappear at any moment.

"Do you like the juice?" I asked, trying to think of something to say to break the awkward silence.

Luke turned the half-empty glass on the table. "It's the best juice I've ever had. Did it come from the apples here?"

"Thank you and yes," I said, smiling. "We're about appled out, but it's better than nothing."

"I could never get tired of apples," Jacob said, pushing his empty plate away from him. He leaned back and looked at the ceiling. "You should eat her apple pie. It's the best thing I've ever eaten in my life."

"It's not all that great, he just likes food," I said, waving a hand.

"I would love to try your apple pie," Luke said seriously and drew his brows together in thought. "I can't remember the last time I had pie."

"We've been out of flour for about a month now or I would gladly make one." I took my empty plate and set it in the sink full of soapy water.

Luke stood and put his plate in the sink, remaining next to me, yet again. Our upper arms brushed against each other, momentarily giving me chills, before I took a small step to the side to keep the distance between us. I had real fears that if he touched me too much, my body was going to spontaneously combust. Having seen and even dated hot guys before, no one—not one of them—had made me tingle just from being close. And the way he was always watching me was another first. The thought of being stared at would normally creep me out, but with him, it felt like he was trying to memorize everything about me. It was different, but it was oddly nice.

Jacob cleared his throat. "Ready to get to work?"

"What are y'all working on today?" I leaned a hip on the side of the countertop and looked to Jacob.

"Figured we would start getting the hay down on the base of the last two rows," Jacob said, resting both hands on the back of a chair. "If there's time after that, we will work on the wood or anything else you can think of."

I tilted my head at Jacob and raised my eyebrows. Either he hadn't noticed or wasn't bothered. He was taking him awful close to the one place we wanted to keep secret, although it couldn't be seen unless someone knew what they were looking for. It was a large cellar our dad had put in years ago for when tornado warnings came through and the people in the orchard didn't have time to make it back to the house. It currently held gallons upon gallons of gasoline for the generator and truck, and a survival kit for each of us in case we ever had to leave for good. There were also a few handguns out there as another precaution.

Basically, it was our safe house slash getaway plan.

It was the most important plan we had.

Luke's eyebrows drew together quizzically at Jacob's answer, so I explained. "The younger apple trees' roots need protection in the winter so we put hay around the base of them for insulation. It works really well, actually."

He rested his hands on his hips and nodded. "Makes sense."

"You guys go ahead. I'm going to take care of a few things first then I'll be out there. I'll bring drinks when I come." Taking a dish rag out of the sink, I wiped down the table.

Jacob came to my side and kissed my cheek before whispering in my ear. "You okay with him still being here?"

My eyes moved until I found Luke. He was purposely looking away, giving us space.

I nodded. "I'm good."

"'K," he said, taking a step back and turning to Luke. "Let's go."

Luke followed behind him, but watched me as they left the house.

I was finally alone with my thoughts. There wasn't really anything I needed to get done. I just needed a second to breathe normally before going out and facing those eyes again.

It had been so long since we had real interaction with anyone besides each other, I wasn't sure if I was imagining his attraction to me or not. I didn't have to wonder if I was attracted to him—I freaking *was*! Even if he was as attracted to me as I was him, there wasn't anything good that could come out of it from my point of view. He would be gone by the end of the day and I would just have to live with the memory of those eyes and that body.

And oh what memories those would be.

Letting out a self-pitying sigh, I apologized to my lonely lady parts for getting them excited for nothing. I filled a plastic gallon container with water and stacked three cups in a bag and headed outside.

The easy walk across the yard and through the orchard felt good and calming. The sun shone bright between the clouds in the sky, warming my body against the chill of the wind. I closed my eyes and raised my face to the sun. The crispness of fall air always energized my body and soul. This used to be my favorite time of year and I still thought it was beautiful, but now, it was more of a warning of what was to come.

When I opened my eyes to start walking again, I noticed Luke about fifty feet ahead, observing me. His stood still, with a square bale of hay in his hands like he stopped mid-motion to watch me. I didn't know what to do, so I looked down and tucked a strand of hair behind my ear. Thank God he was fifty feet away and hopefully didn't see my face as it no doubt turned red. When I glanced back up, he had begun moving again, like he hadn't stopped, and I made my way to them.

"You guys thirsty yet?" I sat the jug of water and cups on the ground.

"Thanks, Sis," Jacob said, pulling off his gloves and getting a drink.

"Luke?" I asked.

"No, I'm good," he said, without stopping.

I bet you are, I thought as I watched him layering the hay around a tree. Every visible muscle in his body was tight and well formed. He wasn't overly muscled like a body-builder, but it was clear he took the time to work out and stay in shape. And what a wonderful shape that was.

Down, girl, I told myself.

Jacob nudged me with his arm. "Seriously?"

Flames moved up my neck into my cheeks. Jacob had caught me and I would probably never live that down. I just hoped I didn't have streaks of drool as evidence on my chin.

26

I turned to Jacob and shrugged before walking to the hay. The square bales weren't huge, but I had trouble picking up one of them, so instead I dragged it down the row on the opposite end of where the men were working and got to work.

"Take my gloves," Luke said, coming up behind me, causing me to jump. I threw a hand on my chest. He gifted me with a sexy-as-hell half grin. "I'm sorry. Didn't mean to scare you."

"Oh, it's okay. Guess I'm just not used to having another person out here." I waved a dismissive hand toward him. "You keep them. I hate wearing them."

Looking past Luke, I could see Jacob working but not taking his eyes from the two of us. My sweet little, big brother probably didn't care for Luke being so close and alone with me. Honestly, I wasn't sure how I felt about it, either. Not because I feared for my safety, but I feared I might do or say something exceptionally asinine.

His head tilted slightly to the right as he looked down at me with his gorgeous, full lips. "That has to be hell on your hands. Why don't you let us do this then?"

I chuckled. "I've been doing this since I was able to walk. Don't worry about me, but thanks, really." I bent and used wire cutters to cut the wire holding the hay together. I glanced up at Luke, who was still watching me curiously, before he turned and strolled back to Jacob, giving me a great view of his jean clad ass.

There were words said between the two men, but they were far enough away and kept their voices low so I couldn't make out what was being said. After a few minutes, I heard both of them laughing and the pressure on my chest I hadn't been aware was there, eased.

For the next few hours, the three of us worked in relative silence. Every now and then we would stop for a drink, but would quickly get back to work. When we were all on the last row, I couldn't help but repeatedly look in the direction of the cellar to make sure it couldn't be seen. Jacob had caught me a few times and shook his head *no* in warning. I guessed my constant checking would make it more obvious that there was something out there.

"Luke, did you know to make one apple, it takes the energy of about fifty leaves?" Jacob asked out of the blue.

"No, can't say that I did," he said, standing.

"Luke, did you know Jacob didn't know that until I told him?" I said, picking up a small stick and tossing it at Jacob's arm and missing by a good foot. Jacob stuck his tongue out at me. I stuck mine back at him.

Our maturity never ceased to amaze me.

Luke laughed.

"Did you know that my sister is a brat?" Jacob said.

"If my brother wants to eat lunch he better take that back," I said in a sing-song voice while smiling.

As if on cue, his stomach growled. The man's stomach was that of a bottomless pit. My eyebrows went up a notch, waiting on his apology. Luke stood with both hands on his hips and a smile on his face. His smile seemed genuine and a little weary, like smiling wasn't something he wasn't used to doing very often.

"Did you know my sister is the most amazing and beautiful person in the world?" he asked Luke.

Luke looked down to me and nodded, "I would have to agree."

Jacob's eyes narrowed slightly then turned to me and clapped his hands together. "Go make me some food, woman."

I turned my head away so Luke couldn't witness the girlish grin slapped on my face. Jacob probably wasn't expecting any sort of a reply from Luke and I sure as hell hadn't expected him to agree. Although, he was probably just being polite, it made my stomach drop like I was at the edge of the Grand Canyon and a horde of zombies were closing in.

"Give me about twenty minutes to get something ready."

On the trip back to the house, I kept thinking about the way his eyes seemed to see everything around him. And man, his lips looked so flipping soft. I wanted to reach out and touch them and feel them on me. I was being absolutely absurd and needed to get over myself and if he wasn't so damn sexy I probably could have. Maybe if he had been an asshole, it would help? Then I could probably get past his panty melting looks, but he had to go and have manners and a smile that dampened my panties in three seconds flat.

After I fed all of us a quick lunch of my version of fried rice, the guys went back to the orchard and I decided to stay close to the house. If I stayed out there any longer I would feel like the temptress Eve and might end up asking Luke to take a big ol' bite of my juicy red apple.

29

So, instead of condemning all women for all of eternity—I decided to do my most hated and tedious chore as penance—laundry. That alone took up a good two hours of the day, but I managed to get everything we needed out on the line. Including the clothes Luke had worn the night before.

I picked up the old wicker basket and turned to see Jacob jogging toward me. I stopped and waited for him to reach me.

"Everything okay?" I asked, worried.

"Yeah, I wanted to come talk to you about something."

"Where's Luke? You didn't leave him by the cellar, did you?" I asked, frowning.

"No, we're about to start on the wood." He halted a few feet in front of me and looked behind him, presumably where he had left Luke. "I wanted to see how you felt about him maybe staying another night?"

I wasn't entirely sure how I felt about it, really. When he said the words, my stomach dipped at the possibility, but then again, if he stayed another day that would mean I would have another day to suffer through looking and not touching. Sometimes it was just better to rip the Band-Aid right off than to slowly pull.

"He'll stay in the barn," he said when I didn't answer, "and I already told him you're hands off and I'll kick his ass if he even looks at you in a way one of us doesn't like."

I didn't know if I should be mortified or laugh my ass off at the thought.

"Please tell me you did *not* tell him that," I moaned and closed my eyes. "Jacob, I am so going to kick your ass."

"Why?" he asked, with a shrug. "We've got more done today than I could've done in three days by myself and you have so much you still have to do around the house to get ready. If you don't want him here, that's no problem, I can tell him to go. I just thought another day could be a lot of help."

I nodded in agreement. "I don't mind at all. I think it would be good for all of us. He probably could use a few good meals and doesn't seem to mind working for us and we could definitely use the help. Just don't be threatening him about me. I'm a big girl and I don't think he's interested in me like that."

Jacob rolled his eyes and put his weight on one leg. "You *do* realize he has a dick, right?"

"Yes," I said, my voice higher than usual, "I *know* that."

"*And* you have boobs. He's interested. But he won't do try anything if he values having any teeth when he leaves."

I outright laughed this time and pushed him in the shoulder. "Go away."

"So you're really good with it?"

"Yep."

He nodded and turned back toward the front of the house. "Love you, Roni."

"Love you, too, Jackass."

Resting the basket on my hip, I watched as Jacob called Luke over and spoke to him. Luke put his hands on his hips and glanced in my direction before nodding. They turned and walked toward the barn. I let out a long, slow breath. Looked like he was there for another night. That would be another restless, sleepless night, but I was sure the extra help would be worth it in the end.

At least I hoped so.

CHAPTER THREE

The night before had been eventless. I had kept to myself inside the house and once dinner was made, I had excused myself upstairs and decided to take my sweet time straightening up the bedroom. I waited until I heard Luke head out to the barn before I went back downstairs to straighten up the kitchen.

Now, the three of us were seated at the small kitchen table and I was cranky as hell since I kept waking up wondering if Luke was sleeping okay. I shouldn't have been worried if he was sleeping at all, much less if he had been comfortable and warm. When I finally dragged myself out of bed and came down to make breakfast, Luke had greeted my bedhead self with a cheery "good morning" like he had the best sleep of his life.

Asshole.

I was sleepy and sexually frustrated.

Not a good combination.

"I'm going to take Lucas and do a supply run. You will be able to stay and finish canning," Jacob said, putting his empty bowl of oats in the sink.

I shoved a spoonful of oats into my mouth to keep it firmly shut. I had really wanted to go, though it didn't make sense now that he had Luke to go with him. I *did* need to get the canning done, but I was tired of being stuck at the house all day for months at a time. A change in scenery would have been nice every now and then.

"I'll make you a list of things to look for," I told him once I swallowed. I glanced up and Luke was watching me *again*. "So, what are your plans, now? Where will you go from here?"

He set his fork down and cleared his throat. "Keep moving, I guess."

I nodded, unsure what that meant since it was vague as hell. "You don't have an ultimate destination?"

"No, I don't. I figure I'll keep moving until I find somewhere safe and where I can make it." He picked up the glass of apple juice and down it at once. "Maybe we can find you some of that flour today for your apple pie."

"Speaking of that, I better go make that list." I scurried out of the room and made a quick list. I could use some tampons, but hell would freeze over before I put those on the list while Luke was there. I handed the list to Jacob and went to pack them water and a lunch.

"Hairspray?" Jacob shook his head.

"Only if you see some, if you don't, then you don't."

I crammed bottles of water into a duffel bag and topped it off with two cans of soup and a handy-dandy can opener.

Ten minutes later, we were all outside. A multitude of worries came to mind when I handed Jacob the bag. I looked at his wrist to make sure he was wearing a watch. "Have plenty of bullets?"

"Yeah." Jacob opened the truck door and tossed in the supplies before climbing in and closing the door. Luke was already in the truck, glancing back and forth between them and the orchard. I guessed he was trying to give us some privacy.

"What time will you be back?" I asked when Jacob rolled down the window.

"By five. We're going to have to go further out this time. Pretty sure we've taken all we're gonna get around here," he must have seen the fear in my eyes, "Don't worry."

I nudged him in the shoulder. "It's my job to worry."

"Yeah, yeah. Do me a favor and stay close to the house 'til we get back."

It was his turn to worry. We had this same conversation every time he went on a run.

"Yeah, yeah," I mocked him, then leaned over to look at Luke directly. "Watch his back."

He nodded with a set in his jaw that told me he intended to.

Looking back to Jacob, I said, "I love you."

Without a bit of embarrassment, he repeated the sentiment before driving away. I stood and watched the truck until it was no longer in view. It always felt like a piece of me was gone when he left. He was the most important person in my life. Taking a deep breath, I looked around. Mercifully, there was plenty of work that needed done to keep me busy so I didn't drive myself half insane until Jacob came home.

The first half of the morning, I took my time weeding the garden and picking anything that was ripe. I planted a small row of garlic since it needed done before the first snow and played with the chickens. I unenthusiastically ate a cup of instant beef flavored noodles for lunch while flipping through a magazine for the millionth time. Looking at the clock, I rolled my eyes.

How could it only be eleven o'clock?

Groaning, I stood and gathered all the apples from the day before and began peeling them. We had a pantry big enough to be a small room in the back of the house we had lined with canned foods, the vast majority being canned apples. I knew as each day went by, our stock would rapidly dwindle.

While humming every Pink song I could think of, I began the long process of canning.

I managed to have enough leftover apple slices to bake enough for three people to have chips. My hand paused mid-air, holding an apple chip at the end of a pair of tongs. *Enough for three people?*

Had I been making Luke his own bag?

Dropping the chip into the bowl, I thought a bag of chips would be a nice parting gift for him for his journey. That had to be what I had been thinking. Wasn't it? Of course it was. Yet, if he was to stay for a while, it would really help out around the farm. We were behind on cutting firewood and I knew how difficult it was for Jacob to do all the heavy work. I tried the best I could, but I wasn't a man and just couldn't physically do the same work as him. Luke would be able to help with that. I saw how strong he was and between the two men, we could possibly even get ahead.

Deciding I would have to wait and discuss the possibility with Jacob, I started losing light in the kitchen and lit a candle. My eyes flickered to the kitchen window, realizing the sun was starting to go down. I whipped around to the antique grandfather clock in the living room.

It was five-thirty. They were thirty minutes late.

Immediately, my chest constricted and my palms began to sweat. Pushing a kitchen chair out of the way, I went to the living room again and stared at the clock. It seemed to be working correctly. I flung on a sweater, slipped on a pair of boots and went outside.

What could have happened? *Anything and everything*, I thought, running a shaking hand through my hair. What if he hurt Jacob or even killed him to keep the truck? We took him in, gave him a place to stay for a couple of nights, made him breakfast and he could have hurt the only person who mattered to me.

I made the asshole apple chips.

Apple chips!

We knew absolutely nothing about this man. Had I trusted him with my baby brother's safety because his eyes were so silver and his face was so beautiful? Was I really *that* shallow or hard up?

And what if it wasn't him at all?

What if they were both gunned down by madmen? I wanted to run and not stop until I found Jacob. I did run, but only to the end of the driveway before I was out of breath. I inhaled long gulps of cool air as I looked left and right at the cracked, paved road. Nothing. There was nothing in sight. I closed my eyes and begged God to please bring Jacob back to me.

I couldn't live without him.

I stumbled back to the house, realizing for the first time I was holding the shot gun. I didn't remember grabbing it, but somehow it made me feel marginally better. Sitting on the porch swing with a view of the driveway, I tapped my fingers on the shotgun resting in my lap, trying to calm myself down before I hyperventilated and passed out.

Anything could have gone wrong, and I tried to convince myself it didn't necessarily mean the worst. Maybe they got a flat or ran out of gas or even found a brothel. If they were late, because they were out getting laid, I would kill them both when they got back.

The sun was now all the way down, but my body was frozen in place and time. How could I let him go away with a stranger? How could I have trusted my entire world with a man I had only known less than forty-eight hours?

How stupid could I be?

Jacob had always told me we had to learn to live in a world that had lost its humanity, but I always laughed at him. Maybe he was right? Maybe we were the last of what was left of the world *before*? All I knew was without my brother I wouldn't want to be in this inhumane world.

I would rather be put out of my misery.

Hearing the unmistakable sound of a roaring engine, I jumped out of the swing and raced to the yard. Headlights were barreling down the driveway. The lights bounced from the high speed and ruts in the ground. Not positive it was Jacob coming down the drive, I ran to the cover of a tree, raising the gun. When the truck came to a screeching halt in front of the house, I thanked God Almighty that my brother was home. That was until the driver opened the door. It wasn't Jacob behind the wheel and I didn't see my brother anywhere.

It was Luke.

Terror sprang to life in my blood as I took a step forward, still pointing the gun at him. "Where's Jacob?" I yelled, my voice shook as did my arms and legs. He jumped and when he saw the gun, he held his hands up. "What have you done with my brother?"

"He's been shot!" Luke yelled. "He's in the truck, we have to get him out now and in the house."

"Oh my God. Did *you* shoot him?" I asked, running to the truck, trying to keep my hands steady as my world was crumbling around me.

"God, no," he turned to the truck and started pulling Jacob out. "I need to get him in the house."

I threw the gun down and ran to the other side of the truck and yanked the door open. Jacob laid still with his shirt covered in blood. My hand flew to my mouth. "Oh my God."

Jacob started groaning as Luke pulled him from the other side. As soon as he had Jacob to his feet, Luke yelled at me. "Hold the door open for me!"

I ran up the steps and held the door open while Luke half pulled, half carried Jacob up the steps and into the house. He tossed him on the couch and a slew of profanity came from Jacob. Oddly, hearing that made me feel better.

I lit a lantern and set it on the coffee table before turning back, afraid of what I was about to see.

"What happened?" I asked, falling to my knees in front of Jacob. I lifted his shirt, but couldn't find where all the blood was coming from.

Luke pulled out a pocket knife and started cutting Jacob's shirt from him. "I'll explain what happened later. Right now you need to help me take care of Jacob."

Luke was so calm. *How the hell could he be so calm?*

"Okay, what do I need to do?" My hands were on my cheeks, not knowing where else to put them.

Luke pulled the shirt away and blood oozed out from just beneath Jacob's right collar bone. I felt the blood drain from my face and my hands began to shake. Luke grabbed my face with both hands and put his face close in front of mine until I had to look at him. "Veronica, he's going to be okay. The bullet went all the way through. We just need to get the bleeding stopped and cleaned so it doesn't get infected. Okay?"

I nodded my head, not trusting myself to speak without vomiting all over him. There was confidence and truth in his eyes. My brother was going to be okay.

"Can you start a pot of water to boil?" He still had my face in his hands, but I nodded again. "That's good. I need some clean rags and rubbing alcohol."

He searched my eyes and I don't know what he saw, but he gave a brief nod and let his hands fall. My head started to turn to Jacob, but Luke stopped me with a hand on the shoulder.

"Go get the supplies."

On autopilot, I went to the kitchen and started the water. Running up the stairs, I went to the linen closet and pulled out every towel I could find. Once I found the rubbing alcohol under the sink, I raced back downstairs and held my full hands up for Luke to see.

"I need you to take one of those towels, tear it into strips, and put them in the boiling water." he said, coming around the couch and taking the rubbing alcohol and a towel from me. I did exactly what I was told and returned to the living room.

"What else?" I asked, watching Luke put pressure on the wound from both sides.

"It looks like the bleeding has slowed down." He glanced up at me. "Do you have a sewing needle and thread? And maybe some pain meds?"

"Yeah." Running back up the stairs, I returned to the master bathroom and took a bottle of hydrocodone Jacob still had from when his wisdom teeth were removed. I knew where the needle and thread were and dreaded getting them, but I didn't have a choice.

My mother sewed. She loved making quilts for people. Especially babies. I stood at the closed door to my parents' room and took a deep breath. Right then wasn't the time to be a wimp. I opened the door and turned on the flashlight. The air smelled stale with a slight scent of Old Spice, my father's scent. I momentarily closed my eyes before walking through the room and to the sewing table. Taking what I needed, I hurried out of the room and closed the door. Seconds later, I was handing the supplies to Luke.

"Good girl." He looked at me for a second then said, "Do you have alcohol?"

"I just gave it to you a minute ago," I said, wondering if he'd lost his mind or if I had lost mine.

He chuckled, "I mean liquor. Do you have any hard liquor? Jack Daniels, Jim Beam?"

"Oh, yeah, one minute." I found an almost empty bottle of Jack and checked the boiling towel before going back to the living room and holding out the bottle for him.

"Can you open it for me, please?" he asked, his voice still calm and soothing.

I dutifully opened it and held it out again.

"Now, this is important." I leaned in, waiting for my next instructions. "Take a big swig and sit down."

I glared at him then thought maybe it wasn't a bad idea and tossed the bottle back and took a long pull. The liquid burned its way down my throat and warmed my belly. I set it down and took a seat on the floor next to my brother. "The towel is boiling."

Twenty minutes later, I was holding up a flashlight for Luke to see while he stitched Jacob and I did my best not to puke. Jacob woke, cursing up a storm when Luke disinfected the wound. I had to hold him down while Luke laid the boiled towel soaked in alcohol onto the wound. I knew Jacob was a strong man and even as weak as he was at the moment, I still had to use my entire strength to hold him down. Luckily, the pain medicine kicked in quickly and he fell into a deep sleep shortly after.

Once Luke was finished, he sat back, wiping sweat from his brow with his forearms. His hands were covered in blood, effectively causing my stomach to roll. "Do you mind holding the light for me so I can wash up?"

Nodding, I followed him to the kitchen sink and turned the water on for him. As he washed his hands, I asked, "What happened out there?"

Turning off the water, he turned around and leaned against the sink while drying his hands. "We were about an hour away and heading back when three thugs had a roadblock set up and we didn't have a choice but to stop. They wanted what we had and the truck, but Jacob refused. Fight broke out and one of the idiots shot him."

I had a feeling he was leaving a lot out, especially since he wasn't making eye contact. "And then they just let you guys go after that?"

He didn't answer.

"Are they going to come looking for you guys?" I asked, bile rising in my throat.

"They won't," he said, pushing himself from the sink, walking back into the living room and falling onto the recliner.

I followed behind, standing over him. "How do you know for sure? They had a car, right? Maybe they followed you two all the way here and are out there getting more of their buddies to come kill us all?"

"Because they're all dead." His voice was low and hard.

Stunned, I swallowed against the lump as big as a boulder that formed in my throat. I walked to the loveseat and sank down, resting my head on the arm, my body feeling heavy all of a sudden. I stared at my brother, watching his chest rise and fall. I hated the thought of my brother having to kill someone. He was such a kindhearted boy—always the one bringing home stray animals and nursing them back to health. It wasn't a surprise to any of us when Jacob decided to apply for medical school. I closed my eyes, wishing he could have had the life he deserved. Before I knew it, I had fallen asleep.

****

"Damn it," I heard in my head before my eyes had even opened. Blinking, I realized it was morning and Jacob was trying to sit up.

Tossing off a throw blanket I didn't remember putting over me, I jumped up. Luke was nowhere to be seen. Maybe he left in the middle of the night? I wasn't sure why, but my heart skipped a beat.

"Jacob, what the hell are you trying to do?" I came to stand next to him as he struggled into a sitting position.

"I need to piss," he said through gritted teeth. "This thing hurts like a son of a bitch."

"First, take a pain pill and then I'll help you up." I ran to the kitchen and brought him back a glass of apple juice and handed him a pill. I took inventory of him as he swallowed the pill. He looked better this morning. His coloring was starting to come back. That had to be a good sign.

I helped him up the best I could and walked with him to the bathroom door. "Do you need me to wait here until you're done?"

"Dear Lord, *no!* I can manage on my own. Where's Luke?"

"I don't know," I said running a hand through my hair. "He was here last night when I fell asleep. Maybe he left."

I was just going to ignore what the thought of him really being gone did to my chest.

Jacob paused as if he was going to say something then closed the door instead. I went to the kitchen to start some water to make Jacob oatmeal when the door in the kitchen came open. Picking up a knife from the counter, I whipped around to see Luke walking in carrying a basket. His smile was almost shy and uncertain.

"I got the eggs from the coop. I thought you could use more sleep." He set the basket on the table and look toward the living room, ignoring the knife pointed in his direction. "Where's Jacob?"

"I'm right here," Jacob said staggering out of the hallway bathroom, stumbling to a chair. Before I could move, Luke was already at Jacob's side, helping him to sit.

"You need to be lying down. You lost a lot of blood last night." Luke checked his wound. "It looks good, but you still want to be careful for infection. Let me help you to your room and we'll change your bandages."

"I'm not going to complain today," Jacob said, rising out of the chair with much needed assistance from Luke. "I'm starving."

"Go up and get settled in and I'll bring you breakfast," I said, rubbing a hand over his good shoulder.

They made the slow trek upstairs while I took the eggs from the basket and started preparing breakfast. I was shocked Luke was still there. That and the fact he thought enough to go out and get the eggs. Not to mention the fact he had taken great care of Jacob. The question was, why? Was he doing it because he was a genuinely good person or did he have ulterior motives?

My gut told me to trust him. He was a man on his own, just trying to find a safe place to live. *But, what was it he had to run from in the first place?* another voice in my head asked.

"Do you need any help?" Luke asked from behind me.

"*Shit!*" I yelled as I spun around. "You're like a cat, just popping out, scaring the shit out of people."

He gave a full smile this time, his arms crossed easily at his broad chest. I could swoon right then and there. The plain gray t-shirt he wore was Jacob's and though Jacob was physically in shape, the fit was a bit snug on Luke. It only made it look all the better. Luke wasn't overly large, but it was evident he took the time to keep his body in good condition.

"I'm sorry. I didn't mean to startle you." But the grin on his face said he enjoyed it all the same. "Do you want me to do anything?"

"Why don't you get the bowls out and portion out the oatmeal?" I pointed to the cabinet with the plates. "I can do the rest."

"Yes, Ma'am."

I eyed him with my peripheral vision as he scooped out the oatmeal. "So, Luke, what did you do before the end of the world?"

"I was an officer," he mumbled without looking up. "What did you do?"

Police officer? I guessed I could see that. He walked with clear authority and didn't panic like I had the night before. If only I could see him in one of those dark blue uniforms.

I sighed inwardly.

I could probably live the next five years just off that mental image alone.

"I could never be a cop. I was an accountant in Tulsa. We grew up here." I turned to the table and plated the eggs next to the oatmeal. Since he seemed to be answering questions, I was ready to start asking. "Do you have a wife, family?"

"Never been married, no kids."

"Me either," I sighed, unintentionally. I hoped he hadn't noticed. I went to the pantry and pulled out a jar of apple chutney. "Do you want some of this on your oatmeal? It's good."

"Sure, thank you." I put a dollop on top of all of our oatmeal before he took a small amount to taste. "That's really good. Did you make this, too?"

"I did." I pulled out a tray and set Jacob's bowl on it, then poured him a glass of juice. "I don't think there's anything that can be made with apples that I *haven't* made at one point in my life. To say we're sick of them wouldn't even *begin* to tell the truth."

"Considering being here has been the first time, in I don't know how long, I've had an actual meal instead of a can of something along the way, these apples taste like heaven on a plate." He sat at the table.

"I'm glad to help," I said, meeting his gaze before looking away. Every one of his stares were so intense, that I couldn't hold it for long. I felt like his gaze was going to catch my skin on fire and not necessarily in the bad way. "I'm going to run this up to Jacob and make sure he'll be okay for a while."

He remained silent as I picked up Jacob's tray and made my way up the stairs. Out of habit, I tapped on Jacob's door before pushing it open. He sat with two pillows behind him. Thankfully, he was awake so he could get something in his stomach. Pain pills had always made him queasy.

"Hey there," I came up next to him. "Time to get your lazy butt up and eat something."

He moaned as he pushed himself up higher. I set the tray on the nightstand and put another pillow behind him. "Easy, you're going to start bleeding and there's no way in hell I'm going to sit through watching him stitch you up again."

Once he was situated, I sat on the edge of the bed and rested the tray on top of his lap. "Do you need me to feed you?"

"No, I'm not a toddler," he said, picking up the spoon with his left hand. We sat in silence for a moment while I watched him eat.

"Don't ever scare me like that again." Tears filled my eyes before I realized they were coming and I fought them back with multiple blinks.

"I assure you, I never intend to get shot again as long as I live," he said between bites. He looked at my seriously. "I want you to be careful with Luke."

"I am, but why?"

He shook his head. "He saved my life, but he's hiding something. Just don't know what it is."

"I agree, but I don't think he's dangerous," I said, remembering him smiling just a few minutes ago.

Jacob chuckled before grimacing. "You didn't see him kill all three of those guys in a matter of seconds. He's dangerous, just hopefully not to us."

I sucked in a breath and my eyes widened. "He killed all *three* of them by *himself*?"

Jacob nodded solemnly.

I took a deep breath while rubbing my temples in contemplation. "You know I'm a good judge of character and I just don't feel malice from him. I was actually thinking we should ask him to stick around for a while to help out, but I don't know, maybe we should tell him to go?"

Jacob leaned his head against the wooden headboard and looked at the ceiling, something he always did when he was contemplating. "No, I think we should let him stay. He's strong and now that I'm down for a while, he can help get ready for winter."

I tapped my fingers on my upper lip.

"I want you to start keeping the handgun on you, at least for now." When I opened my mouth to protest, he stopped me. "Just until we get a better feel on him. And don't tell him where we keep the supplies."

Though I didn't like it, I nodded in agreement. The supplies were our lifelines and no one could know about them except us. Picking up his nearly empty bowl, I wondered if there was anything that could ruin his appetite. Doubtful. If there was, I hadn't found it yet. "Do you need anything before I go back down?"

"No, just put the pain pills close by please," he said already closing his eyes. I helped him lie down and pulled the curtains together to block the sunlight. Right before I closed his door he said my name. "I love you, Sissy."

A rogue tear fell down my cheek before I could stop it. He was everything to me. My next words to him were the truest I had ever spoken. "I love you, too."

When I reached the kitchen, Luke was still sitting at the table, not having touched his food. "Is something wrong?"

"No, I just didn't want you to have to eat alone. How's Jacob doing?"

I stood in amazement, staring at him and his manners. "Umm, he's doing okay. I guess as okay as you can get after being shot with no hospitals or doctors around."

I sat across from him and he picked up his spoon. "He said he had just started medical school when everything happened."

"Yep, he would have been one hell of a doctor, too." I was proud of him even if there was a possibility his dream wouldn't come true. I took a few bites, silently, before pulling up some nerve. "Jacob and I were talking and we wanted to ask if you wanted to stay for a while?"

The spoon stopped halfway to his mouth and he looked up at me. Those silver eyes studied me curiously. I cleared my throat and went on. I hadn't even thought that maybe he would refuse.

God, if he refused we were royally screwed.

"You'll have to work. I mean, we *all* have to work, but with Jacob down for a while and winter coming, we're going to need help. It would give you a place to stay and food to eat at least twice a day and relative safety. That has to be better than walking all day. I know we're annoying as hell, but we're better than nothing. Well, Jacob's annoying." I was in full word vomit, but I couldn't stop.

Leaning back in his chair, he took a long drink of his water, watching me. How did someone make taking a drink look sexy? Welp, this man did. Never having wanted to be a glass of water so bad in my life, I imagined the large hand he had wrapped around the glass wrapped around my thigh. Just the thought caused me to squirm in my seat.

"Where will I be sleeping?"

Did he mean what I thought he meant? I cleared my throat and could feel my face turning red. Was it really that clear that I wanted him in my bed?

Damn my lady parts.

He grinned, knowing full well what I had been thinking. "I meant, will I have to still sleep in the barn?"

I looked at my bowl, too embarrassed to look at him. "You'll have a room in the house. The winters are iffy here.

Sometimes we barely get any snow and sometimes we get a ton of snow, but either way, it gets very cold. You wouldn't make it long in the barn. That's if you *want* to sleep in the house. I mean, you can sleep wherever you want. House, barn, neighbor's place down the road. Wherever."

Shut up, Roni! Geez!

He drummed his thumbs against the table then stuck out the same hand I had just imagined touching me in so many inappropriate ways. "Sounds like a deal."

I took his hand and said a prayer that we hadn't just made the biggest mistake of our lives.

CHAPTER FOUR

It was easy to stay busy the rest of the day. I showed him where the generator was for the water and how to turn it on and off and how to refill the fuel. I showed him where we split the wood and where the sharping stone was for the axe. This was redundant as Jacob probably showed him the day before, but Luke didn't stop me. He actually seemed interested in everything I had said throughout the day and even asked questions. It was nice he wasn't patting me on the head and telling me to go back to the kitchen. After I did a walk-through of the rest of the land and discussed what we normally did throughout the day, it started raining. It was a bitter cold rain, but Luke didn't seem to notice. I was shivering and he hadn't even grimaced.

"Let's go inside, and if you don't mind, you can help me clean up the mess on the couch and then I'll show you to your room." I started toward the house with dread. The only room we had left was my parents' room. I had to let it go at some point and I doubted there would ever really be a good time. The only other option was for me to sleep in their room and give my room to him, but I wasn't ready for that. Jacob didn't have the same issues going into their room as I did. He was the one who had gone through everything to see what was usable and left everything else alone.

I gathered the things we needed to clean the couch, and surprisingly, we were able to get out the majority of the blood stains. It was odd that we worked well side by side without having to talk and still feel comfortable. At least I did. I wasn't a mind reader, but he didn't seem to mind the silence.

It wasn't until I was folding the throw blanket that I woke up with, did I realize that Luke had to have been the one to put it on me while I slept. I looked over to him and studied him with his back to me, picking up the remaining towels and setting them into a pile.

Who was this man?

"If you're ready, I'll show you to your room and I can check on Jacob." He picked up a small duffel bag behind the front door that I hadn't noticed before and came toward me. "Did you come with that?"

"Yeah," he said looking at the bag. "It was in the barn until this morning."

"Oh, well, remind me tomorrow and I'll show you where we wash our clothes." I took the stairs two at a time. "We'll need to find you more clothes for winter and probably a winter coat."

"You don't need to worry about anything for me. I'll get it all figured out."

I stopped in front of the door and turned around to face him. I clinched my hands to keep him from seeing them tremble. "Now, before you go in here, I just want to let you know . . . well, this was my parents' room." He straightened his back. "Please don't throw anything out. If there's anything you don't want to be in there, just tell me and either me or Jacob will get it taken care of."

"Really, I don't mind sleeping on the couch," he said with a tenderness in his tone that I felt to my toes and it warmed my core. Obviously, he picked up on the importance of the room to me.

"No, you're going to be here a while and believe me, when winter hits you're gonna want a place that you can get away from Jacob and me." I chuckled, trying to take the seriousness out of the air. "Even *I* get on my own nerves after a while."

He smiled. "I can't imagine that in a million years."

He took a step closer and I took a step back, my back pressed against the door. He noticed my hesitation and retreated. "I was just going to go into the bedroom. Veronica, one thing I can promise you is that you have absolutely nothing at all to be afraid of with me. I would *never* lay a hand on you."

He thought I was afraid he would hurt me *physically*? As ridiculous as it was, I wasn't afraid of him doing me bodily harm. No, I was afraid if he touched me I would attach myself to his leg like a dog in heat.

I took a deep breath and gave him a shy grin. "I know. I'm just not used to being around people anymore. It's been months since we've had a conversation with someone besides each other."

"I understand," he nodded and pointed his thumb behind him. "Why don't you check on Jacob and I'll come down in a few and make dinner?"

I perked up. "You can cook?"

"As long as you help me out this time and show me where everything is, I can. You don't need to be the only one cooking for all of us." He side stepped me and went into the bedroom, shutting it behind him.

"Maybe you could tell Jacob that, too!" I called through the closed door.

Grinning like an idiot, I opened the door to Jacob's room and watched him sleep with a frown on his face. I went to his side and laid a hand on his chest. He woke with a start, then groaned.

"Roni, what's wrong?" he said, his eyes wild.

"Oh, sorry. Didn't mean to freak you out. It's nothing. I just came to see if you needed anything." I pointed to the half empty pitcher of water I had brought him a few hours before. "Do you want something besides water?"

"No, what I *want* is to get out of this damn bed." He ran his good hand over his face. "How's everything going with Luke?"

"Real good. He's in Mom and Dad's room, settling in before dinner," I kept going when Jacob stilled. I didn't want to have a heart to heart on how I felt about it right then. "Get this, he wants to cook dinner. Imagine that, someone with a penis who's willing to do the woman work."

Jacob smiled, but it didn't reach his eyes. "Wait and see if it's even edible before you start dishing out hard times."

"Oh, but dear brother, I don't care if it tastes like shoe leather as long as I'm not the one cookin'!"

"Uh huh. I'm going to come down for dinner. I've had more rest in the last twenty-four hours than I've had in the last three years." He rubbed his eyes with the palm of his hand.

Knowing Jacob and his stubbornness, arguing with him would be useless. "Okay, if you think you can for a while. I'll come get you when dinner's finished."

Leaving the room, a slight clanking was coming from downstairs. I tried to feel bad about not going straight down and helping, but I just couldn't. I thought it would be best to give him some space and let him get acquainted with the kitchen while I cleaned up. Feeling so grimy since I hadn't taken a shower the night before, I figured it couldn't hurt for me to wash my face and brush my hair until I could get a bath after dinner.

I hurried in the bathroom. Once I felt mostly human again, I went downstairs to find Luke in full cook mode. I was both amused and impressed.

"Sure doesn't look like you need my help finding anything." He turned to me and gave a quick laugh. Seeing the joy in his eyes made my stomach do cartwheels, but I just couldn't quite figure out exactly what it was he was doing. "Do you need my help?"

"I hope you don't mind, but I used some of the flour we found yesterday."

"You found flour?" I asked, clapping my hands together in delight.

I could do so much with flour.

"We found a lot of things, including four five-pound bags of flour. I looked through the canned goods you have in there and found some whole tomatoes. I thought we could have spaghetti."

Spaghetti? That was definitely something we hadn't had in a long time. "Sounds great. I think we have some elbow noodles somewhere."

"No worries, I'm making the pasta from scratch."

My eyebrows shot up. "From scratch, you say? How do you know how to do that?" *I* didn't know how to do that and I didn't think my mother, queen of the kitchen, knew how to do that. I'd had it before in an Italian restaurant in Tulsa and loved it, but never thought about trying to make it myself. Having him there had already benefited us tremendously.

"My grandmother on my mom's side was Italian. I used to spend summers with her and she would have me help her cook while I was there," he explained without looking up. "Want to learn?"

He held up an apron for me to put on and looked me over. "Your hair looks pretty like that."

My hands when to my hair, having forgotten to take it out of its loose bun after I washed my face. I tried to keep my face from flushing, but was failing miserably. "Thanks. Sure, I'll try to learn."

"All pasta is, is eggs and flour." He moved me around to stand next to him at the table. The touch of his hands on my upper arms made me want to sink back into his chest. He moved next to me not noticing how he was making my insides melt. Making a small tower of flour in the center of the table, he used his fist to create a bowl. "All you have to do is mix."

I watched as he added the remaining eggs from that morning. Thankfully, they were being used instead of being thrown out. He started mixing the flour into the dough until it was the consistency of a pie crust. "I couldn't find the rolling pins."

"Pantry," I said, getting the rolling pin and handing it to him. I watched his concentration as he delicately dusted the table with flour once again and began to knead the dough. Just by watching him, I knew without a doubt he would be able to give killer massages.

My lady parts could use a deep massage.

"Now, your turn. Roll it out until it's thin and we can cut it. While you do that, I will start on the marinara."

He handed me the rolling pin. I got to work on the dough while he put a cutting board on the other side of the table. He took an onion and cut it almost perfectly. This was nice. It felt so *normal*, like the world hadn't crumbled outside and we were just regular people having a regular everyday dinner. He tossed the onion into a pan and stirred the pot full of whole tomatoes. Looking through the cabinets until he found the spices, he pulled out the garlic powder and oregano.

"You know, if you keep this up, I may refuse to cook from here on out," I said once I had the pasta ready to cut. I went to the drawer and pulled out a knife.

"I don't mind cooking, so how 'bout we split the duties?" He went to the utensil drawer and handed me a pizza cutter. "This works better."

He stood beside me, his arm brushing mine as he worked, sending tingles throughout my body. My libido was on overdrive if a mere brush of an arm could get me to want to rip his clothes off right there in the kitchen. He must have noticed I had stilled because he looked up at me. "Everything okay?"

"Uh huh." I bit on my bottom lip. "Everything's fine."

His body straightened as he considered me. His face only inches from mine, I swallowed hard, wishing he would just kiss me and praying he didn't. I felt his hand on my hip and his warm breath on my cheek before he took a quick step back, putting both hands on his head. The spot where he touched my hip felt bare and cold.

"Shit, I'm so sorry."

Why the hell did he stop? I thought and chuckled. "There's nothing to be sorry about. I'm a grown woman, you're a grown man. There's barely anyone left in the world so there's bound to be a little sexual tension."

Oh, shut the hell up, Roni, I thought.

My insides were all over the place and I hoped making light of the situation eased some of the tension and worry for him. What could a kiss hurt? *A whole hell of a lot*, I told myself. Two people in a three person living arrangement for at least five months could get really ugly if someone got their feelings hurt. That someone would end up being me.

"I'm starving." I refused to look up. Instead I went to the stovetop and tasted the sauce. It was fantastic. I closed

60

my eyes and fought back a moan. Damn him for being such a good cook, as well as sexy as hell. Why didn't he just serve up some Ramen noodles like most guys would and maybe I wouldn't have gotten all googly eyes at him?

Looking over my shoulder, I watched him stretch to reach the flour, causing his shirt to ride up, showing his fit abs, and I had to choke back an audible moan. Who was I kidding? He could have served mud pies and I probably would have thought he was just the sweetest thing while I ate them with a smile.

"How much longer 'til it's done?"

He took a quick glance in my direction before looking away, "Probably ten minutes."

"Oh, okay. I'm going to go get Jacob then. He wants to come downstairs for dinner." I dashed out of the kitchen like someone had lit a fire under my ass.

I helped Jacob out of bed and down the stairs. By the time we made it to the kitchen, Luke had the table cleaned and set, complete with candles in the center. It felt like we stepped into an Italian restaurant.

Damn him.

Jacob gingerly sat at the table. "You really outdid yourself with dinner, dude. Thanks."

Luke look almost looked embarrassed and nodded. He turned and I went to his side to help.

"Go sit down. You did all the cooking, I'll make the plates." I took the serving spoon out of his hand and nudged him with my hip. He quickly sat down. Probably to keep me from touching him again.

Dear Lord, what if I was the only one feeling the attraction? No, he had to feel it, too. There was no way this was one-sided. Not with the way he looked at me.

When I turned around, Jacob was watching me with his lips in a grim line. I shrugged my shoulders at him and he shook his head in disapproval. He always did that when he was annoyed with me. I just didn't know what he was annoyed about. After scooping the pasta on each of our plates, I ladled the marinara sauce on top. I went to the cabinet and pulled down the parmesan cheese and set it next to Jacob. He liked parmesan and though this was probably going to use up the last we had, this meal deserved all the bells and whistles we didn't normally get. I poured each of us a glass of water and sat down.

Jacob was the first to speak. "Maybe I should get shot more often if it'll get me fed like this."

I scoffed, "You ever get yourself in a situation like that again and I promise you're gonna get shot, probably by me." I narrowed my eyes. "Wait. Are you saying my meals aren't any good?"

He shook his head then winced from the pain. "No, Roni, you're the best cook on earth."

I glanced up to find Luke quietly watching the two of us interact with a slight smile. I wondered if he had any siblings and was afraid to ask. There wasn't a person on the planet who wasn't affected by the plague and tonight wasn't the night to dig up bad memories.

"Thank you for the fabulous dinner, Luke. It's truly the best pasta I've ever had," I insisted honestly.

"Not a problem. Thank you to you both for allowing me to stay and help out." He spun the pasta around his fork and took a bite.

"What part of Colorado did you say you're from?" Jacob asked. His tone was friendly, but I knew him like the back of my hand and he wasn't just making small talk. He was hunting for answers.

"Colorado Springs area." If I hadn't been paying attention, I probably would have missed the tightening of his jaw. "Have you ever been?"

"Can't say that I have, but Roni has been a few times." Jacob looked at me. He wanted me to quiz him and see if he was lying, but his driver's license clearly said Colorado so I wasn't sure what he was trying to get at.

"Oh really?" Luke looked me straight in the eyes for the first time since the almost kiss.

"Yeah, it was a long time ago." I brushed stray hairs from my forehead and moved them behind my ear. "I mostly stayed around the Denver—Boulder area."

"Is that where you went to school?"

"No. I just took a couple weekend trips." I moved my eyes to Jacob's and found his eyes were bulging. He wanted me to ask more, but I didn't know the first thing about interrogating someone and wasn't interested in learning. If he wasn't already hurt, I would have given him a good kick in the shin. As it was, I changed the subject. "Okay, there's a game Jacob and I sometimes play. We tell one useful thing or need and one outrageously frivolous thing we miss or want and one thing we don't miss from before. We call it our three things. Jacob, you start."

Jacob groaned and tried to give me his puppy dog eyes. "Roni!"

"Jacob Allen Williams, I made you breakfast *in bed* this morning! You start." I gave him my best big sister glare until he relented.

He let out an exasperated sigh. "Useful would be a hospital for very obvious reasons. Want would be a beer. Again, for obvious reasons. The thing I don't miss are student loans."

"Luke, your turn." I put the last bite of food in my mouth and watched him expectantly, but tried not to seem too eager. He seemed to be putting a lot of thought into it.

He cleared his throat. "Useful would be gas stations. Want would have to be bacon." This got a grunt of agreement from Jacob. "Don't miss would have to be taxes."

I could see by the blankness in his eyes that when he said gas stations he wasn't telling the truth. He wanted something else, but wasn't willing to let us in on it.

Tough nut to crack!

"Okay, my turn." I clapped, trying to keep the tension out of the air. "Useful would still have to be a fully working fridge and freezer. I miss sweet iced tea like nobody's business. Want would be a camera for photos. The one thing I don't miss right now is my cell phone."

"What the hell would you do with a camera?" Jacob asked incredulously.

"I would obviously take photos. I want to remember some of the happy times when I'm old and gray and hopefully drinking iced tea," I answered dreamily. Luke watched me with his usual quizzical brow. I wondered what he was thinking while he watched me. It was like he was trying to figure me out or something. It made me feel like I had something on my face or between my teeth and he was waiting to see how long it would take before I discovered it. "Anyways, we need to get you laid back down. Looks like you're going to fall face first on the table any minute."

"I would say I'll do the dishes, but being shot and all. . .," he smirked.

Luke and I stood and helped Jacob stand. "You better watch yourself. I don't think your sister is above taking out your knees."

I smiled. "Oh look, you already know me so well."

Adjusting himself under Jacob's good arm, Luke helped him up the stairs and back into bed. Letting him come downstairs for dinner may have been too much too quickly, he looked entirely drained of both energy and color. Luke left the room and I helped him take another pain pill, noticing we were running low on the pills. I washed him off with a wet washcloth the best I could before he grabbed the cloth from me. He made me admit I didn't have the handgun on me and promise I would from then on. I gave him a kiss on the cheek and brushed his hair from his forehead.

He was asleep within minutes.

I left the bedroom door cracked in case he needed me throughout the night. While cleaning the kitchen, I boiled water for a bath. After three buckets of boiling water in the bath, I still hadn't heard or seen Luke. I tip-toed to his door and listened. He was either already asleep and wasn't a snorer or he wasn't in the house. I walked to the top of the stairs and looked down into the pitch blackness. No way was he downstairs unless he had cat-eyes and could see in the dark. More than likely, he was outside, but what was he doing out there? Staring into the darkness a few moments longer, I shook my head and went to my bedroom.

I dug through my drawer until I found the ugliest pair of P.J.'s I owned, collected the handgun that sat on the nightstand, and crossed the hall to the bathroom. After a much needed bath, I did my usual routine and opened the bathroom door just as Luke was walking by, shirtless. I stifled a scream.

"Shit, man, I didn't mean to scare you," he said. "I thought you were already in bed. I was just about to take a quick shower."

I almost laughed seeing him hold the shirt he had removed over his chest. Was he worried I would see his nipples? "No problem. I'm about to go to bed."

Turning around, I gathered the towel and dirty clothes I had worn, tucking the gun in the mix. When I turned back around, Luke still stood in the hallway.

"Goodnight, Luke."

He held my eyes for a moment before nodding and passed me. "Goodnight, Veronica."

I quietly walked to the room and closed the door. I had to leave it open—a least a little—to be able to hear Jacob, but I wanted to wait a while first and make sure Luke was good and asleep. I wasn't sure why I was feeling weary. He hadn't given any reason to make me feel uncomfortable.

Heck. A few hours ago, I wanted to rip his clothes off.

Maybe it was because he was always so quiet. It felt like he contemplated every word he said before he said it. And the way he watched me. . . I would almost feel better if it were in a lusty way, at least then I would have an idea of what he was thinking. Could it be the cop training that made him that way? Always observing and assessing?

Waiting until I heard him get out of my parents' bathroom and settle in for the night, I crept to the door and left it ajar. Crawling into bed, I rested the handgun under the pillow next to me and prepared for what was going to be another long night without any sleep.

****

"Veronica." I was being shaken awake. Panic set in before my eyes were open. I slid my hand under the pillow, wrapped my fingers around the gun, and yanked it up and into Luke's stunned face. Before it fully registered that it was Luke and I could probably put the gun away, he stepped to the side, spun the gun from my grip and sat it down on the table. I blinked the sleep from my eyes.

Holy crap! Did he just pull some Matrix moves out on me?

"Why are you in my bedroom?" I tugged the blankets up to my chest. That's when I heard it. Jacob was moaning. I threw the blankets back and shoved Luke out of the way.

"Jacob has a fever," Luke said, following closely behind until I was next to my brother.

"Oh my God," I wailed. What I saw in the light of the kerosene lantern sent waves of heartache and panic rippling throughout me.

His eyes were red and sweat pebbled on the pale skin of his shaking body.

My brother had the plague.

CHAPTER FIVE

L uke tugged the blanket and sheet away from Jacob's sweat ridden body. Tears bubbled up and spilled from my eyes making my vision blurry.

"How could this happen?" I shook my head in disbelieving horror. "Did someone you fight out there have the plague?"

Luke halted his steps on his way to the door. He marched back to me and put a reassuring hand on my shoulder. I forcefully shrugged it off. Everything in the world that mattered to me was lying in that bed, dying. A hand wasn't going to stop that. No one could stop that.

"Veronica, look at me," Luke said, but I ignored him. "Roni, look at me *now*!"

I whipped my head around and spoke between gritted teeth, "You don't get to call me that."

He nodded, but didn't look offended. I really didn't give two shits if he was offended or not.

"He doesn't have the plague," Luke said in a low, steady voice. "He has an infection from the bullet wound."

It took a second for his words to penetrate through the misery in my mind.

Hope and uncertainty took turns beating inside my chest. "How do you know?"

"Look at his wound." Luke must have already unbandaged the wound before waking me. "It's infected and it's spidering out."

"So, he's not going to die?" I squeaked, my hand moving to my chest, pleading for the truth, but terrified of the answer.

Luke clinched his jaw, causing the muscles to jump. When he spoke, he kept his voice low and soft, like he was talking to a rabid animal that would pounce at any minute. "He's seriously ill. He needs massive amounts of antibiotics or I don't know if he will be able to recover."

I wiped my tears with the sleeve of my flannel pajamas. If there was a way, I would find it. "Okay, I have some antibiotics we can give him."

Without waiting to being told, I raced to the medicine cabinet and pulled out a bottle of antibiotics and ran back to the room with them. "I have these."

I opened the bottle and dumped four pills into the palm of my hand. My gut ached. I knew without asking, it wasn't going to be enough. Luke took the bottle from me and read the label. His lips formed a thin line.

"We need to give him these now and some Tylenol to fight the fever, but he's going to need much stronger antibiotics and he's going to need a lot of them." He placed

70

a hand on his hip and the other ran over his face and through his hair in aggravation. "Give him those and I'll be back in a minute."

My hand shook as I poured a glass of water from the jug by his bed. When I pulled him up, he moaned and more tears fell from me. His skin was unbelievably hot. It felt like it had once when we were kids. We had snuck out to play in the pond at the far back side of the property and Jacob didn't wear sun-screen and blistered his pale skin for days.

The image of him as a little boy was so clear it pained me to see it. He was such a joyous kid, always doing whatever I told him to do, just so he would have someone to play with. He never failed to have a smile that could brighten the worst days. Even now, he still had that ability.

I leaned in and whispered into his ear. "Jakey, I'm going to take care of you, I swear."

His eyes moved back and forth beneath his lids, but remained closed. With some coaxing, I managed to get him to take both the antibiotic and a fever reducer. He sputtered and coughed, but was able to keep them down. I had an urge to tuck him in tight, but it would only make the fever worse. What I wouldn't give for that damned hospital he wanted earlier.

God, please don't take him from me.

Luke came in carrying a bucket and set it down on the side of the bed. I peered into the bucket full of water with dish towels and wash cloths floating inside. He took a cloth, wrung it out, and laid it across Jacob's forehead. Without being told, I picked up another towel and did the same thing. Minutes passed and Jacob was covered in wet towels. By the time we managed to get all the towels on him, the one on his forehead was already warm.

I began the process of exchanging each towel for a cooler one from the bucket as Luke walked out of the room. He came back carrying two dining room chairs.

"It's going to be a long night." He moved the chair behind me and sat the second next to it. We made an assembly line. He would wring out the cloths, hand them to me, and I would hand him the cloth that was being removed.

I turned to him, wanting to thank him, but couldn't form the words. If I spoke, I would break and I couldn't break. Jacob needed me. Luke gave me a slight nod and reached out to squeeze my shoulder, letting me know he knew what I could not say.

"In the morning, I'll find him more antibiotics in town," Luke leaned back and ran a hand through his short hair. "Do you know of anyone who was sick a lot or had a serious illness like cancer? They'll probably have stronger antibiotics. I can try the pharmacy, but it's probably already wiped clean."

I leaned back in the chair, not taking my eyes from my sleeping brother. It was so hard to think clearly. "Um, maybe Mr. Reynolds' place. He had prostate cancer and his wife passed away from a stroke a few years before the plague. There's Taylor Decker's place. Mom said she had a bad case of mono that seemed to last forever."

He rested his arm on the back of my chair and lightly rubbed my upper back. This time I didn't shrug him away. "Do you have a map or could you draw out how to get to these places?"

"No map." Brushing the hair from my face, I knew what had to be done. "I'll get the antibiotics and you can stay with Jacob."

"No," Luke said with such intensity, I faced him full on for the first time since walking into the room.

"You can't tell me no." I bristled. "I know where these people lived and you would be wasting precious time and fuel trying to find them."

"I just did. No way are you going out there alone, Veronica." He leaned forward, resting both of his forearms on his thighs. "It's dangerous out there."

"So, you're telling me it's okay for everyone else to go out and put themselves in danger, but not me? Not when I could help?" I shook my head. "That's bullshit and you can't tell me what to do! I'm a grown-ass woman!"

I leaned back and crossed my arms over my chest, glaring at him, begging him to tell me no again. I would rip him a new one.

"It's not going to happen," Luke said, still shaking his head no. "You know Jacob would kick my ass if I let you go."

"Maybe you should be more worried about me whippin' your ass right now."

Luke chuckled, only pissing me off more. "It's not funny."

"I'm sorry. It's not funny." He entwined his fingers and looked at the floor, fighting a smile. "You're not going unless I'm going with you. Period. How long will it take to get to both houses and back?"

"An hour tops." I changed the towel on Jacob's head. He didn't seem as fretful as he had when we came in the room. His skin was still scorching, but he wasn't shaking anymore. The medicine seemed to be helping some. Not much, but some.

"Here's the deal. You can go, but I'm driving and you have to do exactly as I say if we run into any trouble." He looked at me, deadpanned. I could see there wasn't room for arguing. Plus, he was the one who killed the guys who shot Jacob. If I had to put my pride aside for Jacob's health, then I had no problem with that.

"Okay. Do we leave now?"

"No, it's too dangerous at night. Headlights would be a beacon just asking for trouble. We'll go as soon as the sun is up." He patted my back again.

"Roni, keep the cellar locked," Jacob said out of nowhere. My eyes widened and I stood next to Jacob. He stared up at me, his eyes looking frantic. "Don't tell anyone about the cellar."

I could feel Luke tense behind me. *Shit*, I thought. It was the one place no one on earth knew about but the two of us. Well, until now. I was hoping he would chalk it up to fevered hysterics.

"Don't worry, Jacob," I said, lifting a drink to his mouth, forcing him to take a small sip. "I love you."

Jacob gave a small smile. "Tell Dad he left the door open on the truck and the battery died again."

My heart skipped beats; I felt like I had been punched in the gut. He thought our parents were still alive? "Okay, just go back to sleep. I'll take care of everything."

I wiped tears away with my shoulders and sat down once Jacob fell back to sleep. Covering my face with my hands, I tried to regain my composer. Luke pulled me to his shoulder and held me while I cried. I buried my face into his chest as he wrapped a comforting arm around me and ran his hand over the hair that covered my back. I couldn't make out what he was whispering, but his tone was calming. Once I managed to stop crying, I pulled away and wiped my eyes.

"Sorry. I don't normally cry like a baby."

"There's nothing to be sorry about," he said, still holding my shoulder. "Tell me about your parents."

I smiled, thinking about them. "They were such good people."

He nodded. "They had to have been to have you two as their children."

"They would have loved to hear that." I leaned my head on his shoulder and sighed. "This farm was my momma's family farm. She grew up on this land. She was always smiling and laughing. My daddy was from a town a few hours south and came to work for her dad when he was on summer break for college. They fell madly in love. Daddy said he had to arm wrestle all the single men in town to win her."

Luke laughed and asked, "Do you look like your mom?"

I thought about it for a second. "Yeah, I guess. I'm taller than she was, but we have the same coloring and features. I have my daddy's height."

"Well then, I probably would have had to arm wrestle the entire state."

My stomach fluttered at the compliment. He was obviously trying to make me feel better, and it was working. I hadn't talked about my parents in so long. It hurt so much to think about their lives and how wonderful they were without getting angry they were no longer around. Thinking about them dredged up memories and feelings I would rather keep buried deep inside.

"What about your family?" I felt him momentarily stiffen under me, but slowly relax.

"My father died when I was twelve. I was the second oldest of four children."

I waited for him to say more, but when he didn't, I asked, "Is that why you spent summers with your grandmother?"

"One of the reasons. We always went before, just for a few weeks to visit, but after dad died, mom had to work a lot and took on extra jobs in the summer so she could make it on just one job the rest of the year." I watched his strong hands pick at a piece of loose thread on his jeans. I could sense that it was hard for him to talk about his family. This I understood all too well. "My father was French Canadian and I don't really remember seeing any of his side of the family growing up. I just remember cards with ten dollars in them on birthdays and holidays."

I guessed his flawless creamy skin tone came from his French heritage. "I remember getting those cards from aunts and uncles. Does any child actually read the card? I know I never did. I just went for the money and asked for a trip to Wal-Mart."

He laughed. "My oldest sister was the kind of kid that read them. She always acted like an adult, even when we were little. It used to drive my mother insane."

"I used to drive my parents insane, but for a whole other reason." I sat up and changed the towels on Jacob's head once again before sitting back, this time where I could see his face. "What were your siblings' names?"

"Rebecca was a year older than me. She ended up married with two beautiful little girls," he swallowed hard before continuing. "Then Mary was two years younger than me and," he paused again, "Adam is six years younger."

Did I catch that correctly? Did he say is, not was? "Adam is still….alive?"

His chin fell to his chest and he ran a hand through his hair, making it stick up in places. "I have to believe he is, but don't know anymore."

With that, he left me sitting stunned on the chair as he left the room.

****

Two hours later, I woke Jacob enough to give him the last two antibiotics and more fever reducer. The sun was almost on the horizon, so I went to my room and put on a pair of jeans, running shoes, and a hoodie naming my alma mater across the chest. I quickly brushed my teeth and threw my hair into a ponytail and headed downstairs, surprised to find Luke in the kitchen, scooping oatmeal into two bowls.

"You ready?" I asked, standing in the entrance between the living room and kitchen.

"Let's eat first," he said, sitting down and spooning food into his mouth.

"I'm not hungry. I'll get the guns ready." I turned to leave, but he stopped me.

"Eat. We don't know what can happen out there and you need your energy in case you need to run." He had a no nonsense attitude about him. He was clearly still on edge from our earlier conversation. "I already loaded all the guns, including your 9mm, and they're in the truck. Now sit down and eat."

Begrudgingly, I did as I was told. The quicker I ate, the quicker we could leave. I hadn't even realized I was hungry until I started to eat. If he was going to wait until I ate, then I was going to wolf it down. I shoveled the oats into my mouth, barely tasting them before I swallowed. Once my bowl was empty I went to the sink and set it at the bottom.

"I'll meet you outside," I said, bypassing him and rushing to the door. Cold air hit my face with a shock. Thanksgiving was only a week away and that meant winter was right at our doorstep. I couldn't think about how far behind we were yet. My only concern was for Jacob. Once he was healthy, we would get back on track. I would just have to work harder.

I climbed in the passenger side of the truck, noting that Luke must have cleaned it up before letting me ride in it. He always seemed to be thinking three steps ahead and until the last few days, I had always been the same way. Everything felt turned upside down. Jacob and I did well before. We had a routine and order and now everything was chaotic. We had a purpose. Without Jacob, I would no longer have a purpose. I wouldn't *want* a purpose.

I wouldn't even want to breathe.

Luke got in the truck and we took off. "Let's get this over with."

He tore down the driveway and turned at the road without stopping. It wasn't like there was going to be traffic to worry about. I glanced at him from time to time. His jaw was rigid and the muscles in his forearms bulged from gripping the wheel. I was starting to get nervous from all the tension he emanated. It had been months since I had been out—close to a year since I had been to the actual town. I wondered how much things had changed since then. Last time I had been in town it was scary and I was lucky to make it out alive.

Two men in their forties trapped me in the back of the grocery store. I didn't want to think what could have happened if my brother hadn't come along and beat them both with a baseball bat. That was the last time Jacob had let me go into Jasper.

I watched patches of overgrown fields and forest pass by, remembering the tractors that once worked those fields and the people who rode them.

The world felt sad and broken. Right then, so did I.

"You're gonna need to turn left at the next stop sign," I said.

"But Jasper is straight," he said, still looking ahead and not slowing down.

"Right, but Mr. Reynolds' place is left," I yelled before he blew through the stop sign. "What did you do that for?"

He glanced at me. "We need to get to Jasper as early as possible."

I waited for more of a reason, but he didn't divulge. This man was driving me insane. "And *why* exactly do we need to get to town so early?"

He didn't try to hide his annoyance. His tension had rubbed off on me. "Because more than likely, if there are people, especially people we want to avoid, in or around town, they're still going to be asleep. We may have a chance of getting in and out before anyone notices."

"Well, that makes sense, but why couldn't you just tell me that instead of making me ask you?" Frustration radiated throughout my body and I crossed my arms over my chest. "Sometimes talking to you is like pulling teeth."

He gave a quick laugh which pissed me off more. "I'm serious. You need to let me in on what's going on in that head of yours."

He waited a beat. "You're right. I should have given you more details. I'm not used to sharing information, so forgive me if I'm not as forthcoming as you need me to be. I will do everything in my power to get us both back to the farm safely."

He sounds like a cop, I thought. Exactly like what a cop would say to try to calm nerves in a serious situation. I wanted to punch him for it. He didn't need to be condescending.

"Can you not talk to me like I'm a weak woman?"

He gave me a sideways glance and momentarily closed his eyes. "I wasn't aware that I was. I apologize."

"Thank you," I said. "Maybe I'm being a little overly sensitive. I'm on edge and I'm sorry."

"Nothing to be sorry about." He reached out and squeezed my hand and quickly released it to switch gears. "We're going to park about a half mile outside town and hide the truck so we don't sound like a parade barreling through town." He nodded toward my feet. "Good choice of shoes."

"I figured if I was possibly going to be dodging bullets, these would be easier to move in than my heels," I said, raising my shoulders and blinking my eyes rapidly in a fake flirtatious way. It was clear he was making light conversation for my benefit more than his. I appreciated his efforts so I reciprocated.

We pulled into a rundown barn. It was small enough that we had to go in slow or hit the sides with the mirrors on the truck. It was so decrepit, I worried it would fall down on us if I accidentally poked it with a finger. We gathered our supplies and left the truck, being extra careful with the doors.

"How far is it to the first house?" he asked as he tugged on the backpack when we left the barn.

I crinkled my nose and tried to gauge the distance. "It's only two blocks once we get into town."

"Okay," he said scanning the area around us. He was on full alert. "We need to stay as quiet as possible once we start going so if you need to talk, whisper."

I walked past him and set a quick pace on the cracked pavement, "Let's get this over with so we can get back to Jacob."

It didn't take long to make it just inside of the town proper. The streets were littered with trash. Home after home fell victim to human destruction. Windows were knocked out, vulgar words were spray painted on siding. A few homes were reduced to charred remnants of what used to be someone's home. I bet I knew the people these homes had belonged to. It was heartbreaking to see the fragments of the looting and pandemonium of the survivors. This was Jasper. We weren't supposed to treat each other like this.

I hadn't realized I had stopped walking until Luke put his hand on the small of my back to get me walking again. Leaning in, he spoke in my ear, "We need to hurry."

I nodded. I put my cold hands into the pocket of the hoodie, feeling the cold metal of the gun against my palm. Once we made it to the block we needed, I pointed left. Luke jogged a few feet ahead and surveyed the street. He crooked a finger for me to come to him.

"Can you jog the rest of the way there?" he asked, still looking in the distance on full alert.

"Yeah," I confirmed, wondering if I had put the safety on the gun.

We jogged the rest of the way. My chest burned from sucking in all the cold air and my ears felt like they were ice cubes. I was glad the house was still standing when we reached Taylor's house. The majority of the windows were still intact and I was going to take that as a good sign.

"This is the house," I pointed to my right.

He did a sweep of the area with his eyes before grabbing my hand and leading me to the back of the house. "Stay here and let me clear the house first."

Rolling my eyes, I nodded. He stared at me a moment longer, not saying anything, but clearly wanted to say more before he shook his head and walked into the back of the house, gun drawn. I pulled my own gun out and double-checked to make sure the safety was in fact on. I wasn't entirely comfortable with guns. Especially handguns. I had used a .22 rifle, shooting cans off the fence most of my childhood, but I didn't feel that same control with a handgun.

Luke peeked his head out of the door and waved me in. I followed, plugging my nose with a finger and thumb.

"What is that smell?" It was putrid. My eyes went wide as saucers. Were their bodies still in the house? I held back a gag.

"It's rotting food in the freezer. Just try not to breathe through your nose. You'll get used to it in a few minutes."

"I seriously doubt that." I crinkled my nose. I was afraid to breathe at all. It was horrid. I rushed out of the kitchen and went to the master bathroom first. Searching the cabinets, I found antibiotics, pain reliever, and rubbing alcohol. I ignored any photos on the walls or dressers. I already felt like a common thief even though no one was left of this family. Making my way to the main bathroom, I hit the jackpot.

"Luke," I said in a normal voice. He stepped into the bathroom before I was finished saying his name. I jumped. "Shit. You scared me."

He smiled. "What do you need?"

"The backpack. Look at all of this," I said pulling out a bin from under the sink. "There's all kinds of antibiotics."

He lifted one of the bottles from me and examined it, then handed it back. "I think this will work. How many bottles are in there?"

"Five that I can see," I said, digging out all of the bottles. "Looks like someone decided they didn't need to finish their antibiotics."

"Lucky for us," he shifted his weight from one foot to the other. "Throw those in the pack and let's get going."

Using two hands, I tossed the bottles in and stood. I tapped his shoulder to stop him. "What size jeans do you wear?"

"We don't have time for that," annoyance dripped from his tone.

"It won't take more than a few seconds to check. Taylor's husband was a big guy like you. He might have something that doesn't look like you went through a growth spurt overnight."

With a frustrated sigh, he told me his size.

I went to the bedroom and found three nice pair of jeans that were the same size in the waist. I opened the closet and took a few shirts. We would need to make another trip if he ended up needing more clothes.

"See, I'm ready to go." I walked past him and plugged my nose as we went through the kitchen and out the backdoor.

Immediately, I heard a noise I couldn't decipher. It wasn't close, but not too far away, and it made a rhythmic clanking noise—almost like a sledge hammer hitting concrete. Luke put his hand on my upper arm and leaned in only inches from my face.

"Sounds like it's coming from the way we came, so we need to go around." His hand trailed my arm until he was holding my right hand with his left. I was too scared to let it go. Instead, I gripped his hand tightly and followed his lead. Later, I could analyze about how perfectly my hand fit into his and how gently he rubbed his thumb on my palm to keep me calm.

We were halfway across the street when someone carrying what could possibly be a club or bat came around the corner a block away. I froze before Luke yanked my hand and we took off in a full run.

"Yeah, stop!" the guy yelled then started running toward us.

We didn't stop, even though every breath I took burned my throat and lungs and I was starting to get a stitch in the side. After we made it around to the next block, Luke slowed to a jog while looking around. Just when I thought I had enough time to catch my breath, he took off again, pulling me behind him. This time he led us off the street and in between houses. He stopped behind an old shed. I bent over, hands on my knees, trying to suck in deep breaths. Luke raised me up and pushed me against the wall, his body flush with mine. Both of his hands were cupping my cheeks, his fingers in my hair, and his thumbs brushing my cheeks. He tilted my head back so I would look at him.

"Close your mouth and breathe in through your nose and out your mouth," he whispered and demonstrated what he wanted me to do. I did as I was told, but thought I was going to pass out from lack of oxygen. I reached up and gripped both of his forearms. When my breathing began to return to normal, he let go of my face and put a hand on my chest while he looked around the side of the shed. Switching hands, he looked around the other side, then back to me. "Can you make it?"

I nodded. He examined my face looking more concerned than annoyed. He took my face in both of his hands again and whispered. "I won't let anything happen to you. Do you believe me?"

I did. I believed him so I nodded.

Satisfied with my answer, he said, "Stay strong."

He held my hand again. It amazed me that a gesture as small as holding my hand would make me feel so safe. He wouldn't let anything happen to me. Just as we were beginning to jog again, the man who had been chasing us came around a corner of the house, not ten feet in front of us. Luke immediately released my hand and slid me protectively behind him. Slowly, he removed the backpack from his back and set it on the ground next to his feet.

"Lookie here, you two running off for no reason," the man said, turning his head left and spitting on the grass. His unwashed hair fell forward and he lifted a dirty hand to push it back in place. The thing that worried me was the aluminum baseball bat he held over his shoulder. His eyes looked eager for trouble. He leaned over, trying to look around Luke at me. "I's just wanting to talk to ya."

"We don't want any trouble. We're leaving town now," Luke said in a sturdy voice.

"You don't sound like you're from around here," he said. "Where you from?"

Luke didn't answer. The man tried to peer around him again to look at me and I could feel Luke's body go ridged against me.

"Aren't you Allen Williams' little girl?" he asked with a sly smile. I froze. "Yeah, that's you. You sure have grown up since I saw you last."

The way he said it made me want to vomit right there where we stood. Luke growled. *Growled.* It was frightening.

"Well, since neither one of ya wanna have a conversation, how 'bout I see what you got in that bag?" He took the bat off his shoulder and tapped the end into his free palm.

"How about you go about your business and leave us alone before you regret it?" Luke's voice went deep and menacing. If he ever talked to me in that tone, I would pee my pants.

The man cackled, then without warning swung the bat. In a split second, Luke pushed me back, causing me to land hard on my butt and ducked the swing. I crab crawled out of the way and watched in horror as the man reared the bat once again.

The man tried swinging for Luke's gut, but Luke managed to bow his stomach in just enough to prevent a hit. As the man pulled the bat back to get momentum for his next swing, Luke made his move. He took two quick steps forward, grabbing the top of the bat and yanking it out of his hands, then twisted the man's arm back before letting go. He tossed the bat to me and I threw it somewhere toward the backyard and out of reach. The man charged him and punched Luke in the chin. Luke smiled and swept the man's legs out from under him. He crawled on top of the man and punched him twice in the face before pulling out his gun from the waistband in the back of his jeans and sticking it to the man's head.

I jumped to my feet. "No! Luke no! Don't kill him, please."

Luke glanced at me then back to the guy. One of the man's eyes was already almost swelled shut and he was no longer fighting. "He knows who you are."

"I know, but you can't just kill him. He's not armed now," I said, trying not to get too loud, but still panicked. I walked to Luke's shoulder and looked down at the man. "You aren't going to be going around scaring people and trying to steal anymore are you?"

"No, no, I swear, man," he said, tears streaming from his battered eyes.

I pulled on Luke's shoulder until he stood and took a step back, still pointing the gun. The man stood and held both hands up. Luke handed the gun to me and punched him in the cheek hard enough the man was knocked out before he hit the ground. I used my free hand to punch Luke as hard as I could in the shoulder.

"What did you do that for?" I asked. My slug hadn't affected him in the least.

Luke scooped up the backpack and slung it over his shoulders. "Did you think he was just going to sit here until we made it out safely?" He started to walk, but stopped when he realized I wasn't following. His jaw clinched as he walked back to me. "Veronica, he's fine. I just knocked him out. He'll be up in a few seconds so we need to hurry.

We've wasted enough time as it is. We need to get back to the farm."

I glared at him knowing, he was right. We needed to get back to Jacob. The thing that bothered me the most was if I wouldn't have been there, he would have killed him. I had no doubt about that. The man was a creep and obviously up to no good, but he was just like everyone else, just trying to survive.

This time, when Luke held out his hand, I didn't take it.

"Let's go," I said as I walked by.

CHAPTER SIX

We reached Mr. Reynolds' property without any more incidents. I was grateful Luke hadn't tried to discuss what had happened with the guy on our way to the next stop. He only spoke when it was needed, I only answered when it was needed. We were lucky to find the mother load of antibiotics at Mr. Reynolds house and went home. Once we reached the house, I jumped out of the truck, grabbed the backpack, and ran inside and up to Jacob's room without a backward glance.

Entering his room, Jacob's body was visibly trembling. My heart skipped. As scary as it was to see him like that, it also meant he was still alive. That meant there was still a chance. Walking in, I set the backpack on the chair next to his bed and dug through until I found the strongest of the antibiotics. I was glad to see the water jug I had filled before we left was nearly empty, which meant he had been drinking. I took the jug and turned around to find Luke walking into the room.

"Will you refill this, please?" I held the jug out to him and avoided making eye contact. He took the few steps forward and took the jug from me and walked out. Going back to Jacob's side, I pulled a cloth out of the bucket and rested it on his head. His eyes flew open from the shock.

"Roni?" he struggled to say my name.

"I'm here, Jacob. We got you antibiotics and you're going to be just fine." I held his hand and used the other to slowly rub my hand over the top of his hand.

"I woke up and..." he shook with the effort it was taking to speak. I shushed him.

"I know and I'm so sorry," I said, using my shoulder to wipe the tears from my eyes. "I promise, I won't leave you again."

He nodded and closed his eyes. Luke came into the room, walked to the other side of the bed and handed me the glass of water. I thanked him and asked for help to raise Jacob into a sitting position. After we got him situated the best we could, I took out a pill.

"Maybe you should go ahead and give him two just to kick start it?" Luke suggested, putting his thumbs in the front pockets of his jeans.

I contemplated what to do. I didn't know if it would hurt him to have too many antibiotics, but knew he could be hurt having too *few* antibiotics. I said a silent prayer that we were doing the right thing and took two antibiotics out of the bottle. Jacob took them without much trouble, then gladly took a pain pill when I told him what it was.

Just as I was about to pull another towel out of the bucket to put on Jacob's head, Luke called my name. I turned my head to him and bit my bottom lip at the grim set of his mouth. That wasn't a look that was going to give good news.

"I'm going to have to disinfect his wound again and I think we should let it air out for a few hours. It's not going to be easy for him." His eyes went soft when he saw the look on my face.

I agreed, knowing how badly it was going to hurt Jacob. I choked back tears as I listened to my little brother's moans as we pulled the bandages away. Holding Jacob's hand, I watched as Luke took his time cleaning the area on both sides with alcohol. By the grip Jacob had on my hand, he still had his strength and he was going to need every bit of it to get him through this. I managed to get Jacob to drink a half a glass of water before he was exhausted and fell asleep. At least the pain pills we found where strong enough to actually control most of the pain.

I moved the backpack from the chair and sat, fitting my hand into Jacob's once more. I would give anything to make him better. But I didn't have anything else to give. Everything, besides him, was already gone.

"I'm going to take care of things outside," Luke said.

"Thank you, Luke." I briefly looked him in the eyes. Although I may not have agreed with what he was capable of doing, if it wasn't for him, my brother would never have made it as far as he had. I was truly thankful he was there. However, I would take Jacob's advice and be just a little more cautious around Luke.

His lips went to a straight line and he tapped his thumb on his thigh before he nodded and walked away. I listened to the front door close before picking up a book Jacob must have been reading before being shot. *Where the Red Fern*

Grows. I smiled. Jacob always loved the movie made from this book. I remembered, as a kid, teasing him relentlessly about crying during the movie. He always told me I just didn't understand and maybe I didn't. My daddy used to say there was a special bond between a boy and a dog. If our mother hadn't been so allergic to dog dander, I imagined my dad and brother would have had a houseful of puppies.

Opening the book to the first page, I started reading it out loud. At that moment, I determined that one day, I would find Jacob a puppy of his own.

****

Hours later, I woke hearing Luke turning on the shower in his bathroom. I raised my head and looked to Jacob. He seemed to be resting peacefully. Standing, I stretched my limbs, trying to relieve some of the soreness. I exchanged the cloth on his head and felt the skin of his cheek with the back of my hand. He still ran a fever, but it didn't feel as high as it had before. Picking the book off the floor where it must have fallen when I fell asleep, I found the last page I remembered reading, folded down the corner of the page, and set it on the nightstand.

I heard the sound of the shower turning off and listened to Luke's footsteps. Even though I told myself not to, I imagined him with a towel wrapped low on his hips as he picked out his clothes. *I didn't willingly imagine it*, I reminded myself. Thinking back to the times he held my face in his hands and how good it felt to have him touch me, I was reminded that for such a large man, he had a very gentle touch.

I shook my head, realizing I needed to be thinking about what mattered and not about a naked Luke running his large, strong hands over my body. Giving myself a mental shake, I stood.

I moved to the window and looked out, wondering what time it was. The sun was still out, but not quite as bright as it was when I fell asleep. The closer we came to winter the earlier darkness came. That was another thought I didn't want to have.

Luke leaned against the door jamb. "Hey, I'm about to start dinner. Do you want me to make anything in particular?"

I gave a weak smile, thankful yet again, for him being there. I hadn't even thought about food, but my stomach growled. "Anything is good as long as I'm not the one cooking."

He smiled back. "Okay, then. When I'm done, we'll give Jacob some more medicine. Do you have any canned soups in there he could eat?"

I thought for a second. "There's probably a can of chicken noodle soup in the pantry."

Luke went downstairs making a racket with the pots and pans, while I swiftly ran across the hall and used the bathroom. I changed into a pair of multi-colored knee high socks and flannel pajama bottoms and a dark blue, tank top. Hefting my much more comfortable wingback chair into Jacob's room, I bundled up my pillow and a crochet throw blanket and settled in.

The chill of the evening air began seeping into the house. It was going to be cold when the sun went all the way down. Before *too* many more nights, we were going to be

94

forced to use the fireplace to keep us warm at night. I sighed. That meant we were going to start using our limited supply of cut wood and we were falling further and further behind every day we weren't out there working. Not to mention it had been two days since I had worked the garden and I needed to get to canning as soon as the food was ready.

I leaned against the back of the chair and laid my feet on the edge of Jacob's bed, fingering the end of my braid as I looked around the dim room. Jacob's football trophies filled the top of a bookshelf on the wall. Prom and graduation photos lined the shelf below that. He never played baseball, but had a stack of baseball hats piled on top of the dresser below a poster of a beautiful woman wearing nothing but a bikini while biting her index finger. I rolled my eyes. I still couldn't believe Mom let him put and keep that poster on his wall. When I asked him to take it down, he refused, saying it may be the only hot woman he would ever get to see for the rest of his life.

My way of thinking was that men were forever overgrown hormonal boys.

The sun was almost entirely gone and since I would be eating with Jacob, I lit three candles and set them throughout the room. I closed his thick, plaid curtains, hoping it would help keep out some of the cool air, not to mention blocking the candle light so it wouldn't be a beacon for someone if they happened to be passing through.

Luke came into the room carrying a tray holding a bowl of steaming soup and a glass of apple juice. "I thought we should try to get him to eat before we do."

I took the tray from him, smiling my thanks. Luke moved to the other side of Jacob's bed and bandaged his wound. Jacob woke, but without chills from the fever, which I took as another good sign. Once we moved him into position, I sat on the side of the bed and spooned him the soup. After about half the small bowl, he refused any more. I set it to the side and lifted the juice to his mouth.

"You need to drink this," I said, but he shook his head no. He was so damned stubborn. I took the pills Luke had ready for me and put one to Jacob's lips. "You have to take your pills so drink this."

He grimaced and closed his eyes, taking all three pills before quickly falling back to sleep. My heart ached for him. He was falling asleep awful fast. I hoped that didn't mean we were giving him too many meds.

"His fever seems to be down a lot and sleep is good for him," Luke said, as if reading my mind. He picked up the tray. "I'll be right back with dinner."

I sat down, laying the throw blanket across my legs. I wondered what he had made. It smelled delicious, that was for sure, but I couldn't pick out any smells except garlic and onion. When he came back, he carried two plates, handing one to me before sitting in the chair next to mine. I looked at the plate in amazement. There was a bed of rice covered with onions, carrots, and . . .it couldn't be. Meat? Actual *fresh* meat? I couldn't remember the last time we had meat. The closest we got to it was a can of tuna early this summer. It wasn't that good, either. Tuna without mayo didn't belong on Earth.

He mixed the bed of rice with the stew resting atop before taking a bite and noticing I wasn't eating, only glancing between him and the bowl. His chewing slowed down as he watched me watching him. "What's wrong? Please don't tell me you're a vegetarian."

"Lord no, I love meat." I laughed then swallowed hard. "Hmm, what kind of meat is it?"

"Rabbit," he stated like it was an everyday thing.

I did love meat, but rabbit? I couldn't say I had ever had it before, but having a chance to eat meat after so long was worth the try. Plus, he had obviously put a lot of effort into the dish and I didn't want to hurt his feelings by not eating. Telling myself not to think about Thumper as I took a bite, I closed my eyes while I chewed. I couldn't believe it, but it was flipping delicious. It had a game flavor to it, but the meat was tender and juicy.

I opened my eyes to find Luke watching me with a grin. "Like it?"

My eyes widened. "Uh, love it! It's freaking fantastic."

"Thanks," he said between bites. "I took a few of the carrots from your garden. Hope you don't mind."

"Seriously? Mind?" I furrowed my brows at him in surprise. "I don't mind at all. If you keep cooking like this, I'm going on strike and you'll be doing *all* the cooking."

He chuckled. "Thanks."

"I would have never thought to eat rabbit. Seriously, this is amazing," I said, shoveling spoonful's into my mouth like a starved animal. It wasn't attractive, but if Luke's smile was any indication, he didn't seem to mind my lack of manners.

We ate in silence (other than my slurping) until both of our plates were empty. He removed our plates and came back with two glasses of juice. I took the glass with thanks and rested my feet on the bed again. He took off his boots and placed them at the foot of the bed, leaned into the chair, laid his head back, and shut his eyes.

I took the opportunity to really look at him.

He was simply gorgeous in a very complex way. His lips were full without being feminine, his jaw strong, but not overly so, and looked sexy as hell with a five o'clock shadow. His eyebrows were dark and full without being brutish, and I knew those silver eyes under his closed lids could make my heart skip a beat with a mere glance.

I watched his muscled chest rise and fall with his breaths, knowing that under his shirt was a firm body that wasn't overly muscled, but toned enough that I would bet a dollars he had a resting six pack. My eyes moved lower, quickly scanning past his fun parts. All I needed him to do was open his eyes and catch me staring at his zipper. I swallowed.

I bet everything under that zipper was just as large and perfect as the rest of him seemed to be.

He was wearing the new jeans from Taylor's house and they fit him perfectly. He shifted and I looked at the walls straight ahead. Hell would freeze over before I let him catch me ogling him.

"Thanks again for dinner," I said, picking up the glass and taking a sip, "I'm in awe that you can cook so well with so little."

"I grew up figuring out what to make with nothing so it's not much different now." He entwined his fingers

98

behind his head and peeked at me with his eyes half closed. "I'm glad you liked it."

"What's it like out there?" I asked, watching his eyes open and face me. "I mean, what's it like in other places? Is it the same everywhere?"

"It's mostly not good," he said, sitting up, resting his forearms on his thighs. "There were a few places along the way where they are beginning to restructure communities and markets."

That surprised me, but then again, it didn't. The majority of the people left didn't have the luxury of being on a functioning orchard with years of training in gardening and preserving foods. A thought hit me. What if I could trade some of the things I had to replenish things we needed? Like fuel or bacon! "Is there anything like that close to here?"

"Not that I found," he said, shaking his head. "Word will eventually spread and townships and markets will start showing up all over the place."

At least the thought gave me some hope. We had been alone for so long, I wouldn't know how to act in a crowd of people. I looked to my brother, watching the rise and fall of his chest and knowing it was still moving too rapidly. He would do great in a crowd of people. He always had. "Let's hope it's sooner rather than later."

"Do you have any cards or something?" Luke asked, changing the subject.

"Hmm, yeah. Actually, we do." His question caught me off guard. I stood and walked past him, my thigh brushing against his knee, making my whole body react in tingles.

It's a sad day when joints are a turn on, I thought as I went to the hallway closet and pulled out a deck of cards. I walked back and tossed them into his lap and turned to replace the damp cloth on Jacob's head, smiling when I felt his cheeks. The fever was coming down. The pills were working. Jacob was going to be okay. Life was good again.

"He feels cooler than he did an hour ago," I said looking over my shoulder at Luke and catching him watching my ass. I smiled as he quickly looked away, his face turning red. He cleared his throat and I sat back down. "What are we going to play?"

"What would you like to play?" he asked, opening the cards and keeping his gaze to his hands. Seeing him embarrassed was, well, cute. I would think a big, sexy man like Luke wouldn't get embarrassed about anything.

I positioned myself cross-legged in the chair facing him. It might have been cruel, but I was ready to have a little fun with him. "Well, I think it may get awkward playing strip poker if my brother woke up and you were butt naked, so let's stick with Rummy."

His hands stilled and he looked up at me then laughed. A real, full, heart-tugging laugh. My heart skipped then jumped in my chest. To see his eyes shine and his lips thin across his straight white teeth was almost like looking at the sun—it was beautiful, but hurt to watch because it can't be touched without being burned. I wanted to make him laugh more. Like every day for the rest of my life, to start.

"Rummy, it is." He moved to the nightstand on the other side of the bed, cleared it off, and carried it in between us.

He shuffled the cards once more and dealt them out. We played for a few minutes in silence before Luke asked, "What are your three things tonight?"

I looked at him quizzically before realizing what he was asking. Well, wasn't he just full of surprises? "Oh," I tapped my finger on my bottom lip, thinking. "A doctor for Jacob would be really useful right now. I would love to have a glass of milk, and don't miss reality TV one bit. You?"

"A glass of milk?" he asked, picking up a pile of cards and laying sets out on the table then discarding before looking at me with his eyebrows scrunched together in mock horror.

"No judging," I said, eying the cards on the table. "I like milk."

"I could use a hot shower. I *want….*" his tone dropped to an almost growl. I looked up into his eyes, seeing very clearly in them everything he needed but wouldn't say, "to watch football."

I hoped the disappointment I felt didn't show on my face.

"And I don't miss wearing a uniform every day."

I thought it was ironic that seeing him in a uniform could easily be one of my wants. "Were you always a police officer?"

Had I not been looking at him, I more than likely wouldn't have noticed his moment of hesitation before he picked up a card. He pretended to be concentrating on his cards, but he was debating on what to say. What did he have to hide?

"No," he said with a forced light tone. "I was in the Army."

"The Army?" I sat back, holding the cards in my hand by my chest. "That's interesting. Is that what made you want to be a cop?"

He ran a hand through his hair and glowered at me. "I was never a cop, Veronica. I was in the Army when the shit went down."

Stunned at the news, I tilted my head slightly, trying to understand. "But . . . why did you say you were a cop?"

"I said I was an officer," he said, his voice getting irritated.

He knew that I knew I had clearly said I couldn't be a cop during that conversation so he purposely didn't correct me and I wanted to know why. "Why didn't you correct me?"

"Because, it's complicated," his voice got harder. When I glared at him, he relented. "I didn't know I was going to be staying here more than the one night and didn't think I would have to tell you anything. Then I knew you would feel safer thinking I was a cop while your brother was hurt. I would never do anything to harm you or Jacob. I hope you know that."

Okay. That made sense. Kind of. I mean, I could understand him not thinking he would have a reason to set me straight, so he didn't. Still...

It also explained a lot, but left more questions than answers. My gut reaction was to trust him at his word, but I still knew there was more he was hiding and knew he wasn't going to let me in on what it was. I had so many questions, but didn't know which to ask that I felt I would get an honest answer.

"Are you really from Colorado?" I heard the hurt in my own voice and it pissed me off to no end.

"Yes," he nodded. "I grew up there and was stationed at Fort Carson when the plague went airborne."

"And everything about your family is the truth?" I asked, praying that was the truth.

"Yes."

I studied him. His eyes never left mine. I didn't understand. What was I supposed to do with that?

"Why are you telling me this now?"

"I should have told you both before. I *really* didn't think I would be staying after the first night and you asked me straight out." He sighed and his eyes stared intently into mine. The candlelight danced off his intense silver eyes, making my insides melt. "You're a good person, Veronica. I don't *want* to lie to you."

Then why are you still lying? I thought. I believed he was telling the truth about the Army, but he was holding back. About what? I just didn't know. There was no doubt in my mind he would do everything he could to help keep us safe while he was with us. He had proven that multiple times in the week he had been at the house. And I trusted my gut when it told me I was safe with him. What could be so bad that he couldn't tell? Did he run away from the Army or something?

We all had secrets. Jacob and I weren't going to let Luke in on everything either so maybe it was none of my business? Perhaps his secrets were all he had left in the world.

"I don't want you to lie to me, either," I told him just above a whisper. He reached out and brushed a strand of fallen hair behind my ear and let his hand linger on my cheek. I lifted my hand to cover his and slightly leaned my face into his hand before letting go. "Would you have killed the guy in town today if I hadn't stopped you?"

His hand fell to his lap, his eyes never wavering from mine. "Yes."

My heart sank and I shook my head. "But, why?"

"Because he recognized you." He tossed the cards in his hand down to the table. It was obvious we weren't going to finish the game. Fire burned behind his beautiful eyes. "He's probably out there right now planning on coming out here and killing me and taking you."

"No, he was just an idiot and trying to survive like we all are. Yeah, he wasn't a good guy, but he didn't need to die," I said, my voice rising. "Plus, it's almost a twenty minute drive out here from town. *Drive!* Not many people drive anymore, and I doubt he would know how to get here even if he did."

Luke leaned in, his face no more than a foot away from mine. "You would be surprised at what a man is capable of doing when someone else has what he wants."

CHAPTER SEVEN

Roni?" Jacob's unexpected voice caused me to jump. I leaned away from Luke before standing up and taking Jacob's hand and pulling it to my chest.

"Hi there. Do you need something?" I kept my voice calm and soothing.

"I need you two to shut up so I can sleep," he said, his voice hoarse, but there was a half grin on his face. I smiled wide and glanced back to Luke. Luke was running a hand over his face and probably wondering how much of our conversation Jacob heard, just like I was.

"Since he's awake, we should go ahead and give him more water. He needs to stay hydrated." Luke stood and handed me a glass of water before moving to the other side of the bed.

Jacob didn't argue as I helped him with the water. Luke pulled the bandage back on the gunshot wound. He looked up at me and grinned, then put the bandage back down.

"It doesn't look nearly as red as earlier." He walked to the chair and sat down.

"It's cold," Jacob said, tugging on the thin sheet resting on top of him. I felt his head and couldn't believe how much the fever had gone down. My heart leaped for joy. He was going to make it. I reached for the blankets I had folded at the bottom of the bed and pulled them over him. He was back asleep before the blankets reached his chin.

Jacob was going to be okay.

I whipped my body around and bounced in place with happiness before taking the two steps to where Luke sat in the chair and wrapped my arms around him. His body tensed beneath me, but I wasn't letting go.

Not yet.

I needed to hold him for just a minute longer.

"Thank you," I said, tears running down my face. "Thank you so much."

His body relaxed and he pulled me into his lap and wrapped his arms around me, letting my cheek rest on his strong shoulder. He slowly rubbed my back as I cried. My baby brother was going to be okay. That was because of Luke and everything he did to save him. I squeezed my eyes closed. I needed to remember everything this man had done for us when many others would have walked away or killed us both for our supplies the next time I questioned his integrity.

"I'm sorry I talked to you like that. I know you were just protecting me." I raised up to face him and saw sadness and hurt behind his eyes. Hurt that he tried so hard to keep locked away.

Leaning in, I never took my eyes from his until our lips touched. Immediately, my body went soft against his. His full lips were warm and painstakingly timid. I wanted more. I *needed* more. Touching the tip of my tongue to his top lip, I coaxed his mouth open. He gave a low groan as his hands gripped each side of my top, causing me to smile against his lips.

I had him.

Finally, he gave in and kissed me back. My nipples went hard and my world spun. His hand went to the back of my head, and the other wrapped around my waist, pulling me closer as he worked his tongue around mine. I had been so lonely for so long and could easily live off this one kiss for the rest of my life. The way he held me told me it meant just as much to him as it did me.

Moments later, he pulled back. I rested my forehead against his. His breaths were labored from the effort he was making to keep himself under control. And that was from just a kiss. I couldn't remember a time I ever had that effect on someone.

I didn't think anyone could ever make my entire body tingle from just a kiss. I couldn't imagine what the rest of him could make my body feel.

"You're a good man, Luke." I kissed his forehead and stood.

I went to my bathroom and quietly shut the door and leaned against it. My heart just about pounded out of my chest. I raised my fingers to my swollen lips and smiled. Luke was a mystery, but there was no doubt beneath it all he had a kind and beautiful heart. Kissing him might have been dangerous, but it felt right. I was determined not to second-guess myself or regret anything anymore.

I would do what my gut told me and live with the consequences. I just hoped I wouldn't be paying with my heart.

****

Four days later, I looked out the front window, watching snow flurries swirl in the mid-morning air. I sipped a cup of hot apple cider while listening to Jacob and Luke argue about who was the better Denver Broncos quarterback. We were behind on preparing for the winter that refused to wait any longer, but hearing them banter made me feel like everything was going to be fine. We would get everything that needed to be done, done. I wasn't sure why, but I wasn't worried.

The past four days went by in a blur. There wasn't awkwardness between Luke and me. We gave each other what we needed with the kiss and let it go. That's not to say I didn't fantasize about his mouth and I didn't still catch him watching me, because both were true. We worked harmoniously on the farm as if we had been working together for years.

The day before, Jacob refused to stay in bed any longer and after much badgering from me, wore a sling and stayed in the living room resting. He would probably be okay to do whatever he felt comfortable doing, but until the wound was completely healed, I wasn't going to let him risk it.

Finishing the cider, I took the mug to the kitchen and set it on the counter before I put on my coat. I slid my feet into work boots and opened the front door. "I'll be back in a few."

"Where you going?" Jacob asked. Both men eyed me protectively.

"Gosh. . . I'm just going to make sure the chickens' water isn't frozen and pull the tarp over the fencing on their cage," I said. I hurried and closed the door behind me so I wouldn't have to argue with them about going out alone.

The frigid air whipped around my face, causing my hair to fly around in mini tornadoes around my head. Cursing, I pulled the hood of my coat over my head and stuffed my hair inside.

I walked to the chicken coop and checked their water. Sure enough, the top layer was frozen over. Picking up a small stick, I broke through the ice and set it inside the chicken house. The hens greeted me with wails, knowing they were about to get a treat. I reached behind me and pulled a handful of chicken feed from the bin and scattered it across the floor. While they were busy eating, I hurried and added more hay to their beds and took the eggs from their nests, sliding them gingerly into my pockets.

Last year, Jacob did a great job of filling in the cracks of the pen and insulating it enough for them to make it through the winter. I pat my favorite hen, Georgia, on her back before stepping back out into the cold. Luke was standing there holding the tarp.

"Thought you might like some help." He handed me one end of the tarp, walking backward so it would unfold between us.

"You didn't have to. I could have gotten it myself," I grumbled. I had been enjoying my few minutes alone in the quiet morning.

"I know you could have," he said, going still. "I came out here to ask if you knew what day it was."

My eyebrows drew together trying to calculate the days, but coming up short. "I'm not sure."

He smiled, making me miss those lips on mine. "Actually, it's Thanksgiving."

"Seriously?" I asked as we tossed the tarp across the side of the pen and fastened it. I counted the days it had been since Jacob had been shot. He was probably right.

It was Thanks-freakin'-giving!

"Yes, I'm serious," he said, brushing his hands off on his jeans. "I was thinking, maybe I could go hunt up some meat and we could have a Thanksgiving feast tonight. I've been waiting for your famous apple pie."

Excitement filled me. Thanksgiving had always been my favorite holiday and this year I had a lot to be thankful for. "Absolutely!"

I ran up to him and gave him a quick hug and a kiss on the cheek before pulling back, afraid I was going to smash the eggs still tucked in my pockets. "Go get us some rabbit!"

He chuckled and shook his head. Reaching into the pocket of his coat, he pulled out a beanie and put it on his head. "Get inside. I'll be back in an hour or two."

I started toward the house before turning around. I bit my lip before saying. "Luke." He eyed me waiting. "Please be careful."

"Always," he said before turning back around and walking away.

I burst through the door, smiling as I stripped off my coat and boots. Taking the eggs out of my pockets I hurried to the kitchen and gently set them in a bowl.

"What are you doing?" Jacob asked. "Where's Luke?"

"It's Thanksgiving!" I yelled. Hearing Jacob struggle to get up, I went to the living room to see if he needed assistance. He didn't. "Luke is catching rabbit and I'm getting everything ready for dinner. Want to sit in the kitchen with me while I work?"

Jacob put his weight on one hip and the hand from his good arm on his other hip. He looked at me incredulously. "Luke is catching rabbits?"

Letting my head fall back, I laughed before I pulled a kitchen table chair out for him to sit. I patted the back of the chair until he sat down. "Yes, rabbit, and you're going to love it."

His nose crinkled. "I'm not so sure about that."

"Trust me," I said, while getting the ingredients I needed for dinner out of the cabinets and setting them on the counter. "He made this rabbit stew stuff while you were out and it was delicious. Seriously."

He huffed, "A lot of *stuff* seemed to happen while I was out." The way he said the word *stuff*, left no question to his meaning.

I slowly turned, hands balled into fists on my hips and glared at him. "Jacob Allen Williams, what exactly are you trying to say?"

His lips formed a thin line. "You know exactly what I'm saying Veronica Jolene Williams. You can't be in a room without him looking at you every five seconds and I see the way your eyes get all girly when he's talking. It's gross and you two need to stay away from each other before it goes too far, if it hasn't already."

Seriously?

If I wasn't so mad at him, I would have smiled at the thought of Luke looking at me every few seconds. But, unfortunately for Jacob, I *was* mad. My blood boiled under my skin and I pointed a finger at him while leaning on the table with my other hand to get closer to his face.

"You listen here. What Luke and I *do* or *don't* do would be none of your damn business." He started to talk and I hushed him by holding up my hand. "I'm a grown-ass woman, Jacob. And he's a grown man."

"You're my sister, so like it or not, it *is* my business." He had enough sense to look away, embarrassed, but he wasn't ready to give in just yet. "And you don't even know him, Roni."

I chuckled and shook my head. "You can believe this or not, but I know him better than I've *ever* known a man. I've done more with men I barely knew than I have with Luke and what I *have* done with him was *me* initiating it." Jacob squirmed in his chair and I went on. "Oh no, *you* started this, so you're gonna listen. I know he saved your life more than once, and he saved mine, too. I know that he has a kind heart and a great sense of humor, but half the time he's on guard and afraid to show it. He's a great cook and loved his family and makes sure that I'm safe when I'm with him. I know him just fine, Jacob."

Jacob cleared his throat, having just been thoroughly put in his place. "Well, just be careful."

I stood up straight. "I am. Now, I need to get this pie started."

We sat in silence while I set to the task of making the pie crust. Making a pie in the makeshift oven wasn't easy and I wanted it to taste perfect for Luke. I toyed with the idea of not letting Jacob get a piece just because of his attitude, but had to let it pass. He may have overstepped his bounds, but he was only trying to protect me.

That seemed to be going on a lot lately.

When would they learn that I could protect myself?

It was more irritating that they both thought I needed protecting. I wasn't weak and incapable, having made it on my own for years without a man to take care of me.

Since I had returned to the farm, I did just as much around here as Jacob.

"Why do you still have that pissed off look on your face?" Jacob asked tossing a pecan in his mouth.

I raised the rolling pin I was using for the pie crust and pointed it at him. "I think by the tie dinner rolls around tonight, you should be thankful I haven't knocked you out yet."

Jacob laughed as he stood and walked to me. As he smiled down at me playfully, I tried to push him away without hurting him. He looked at me with those same eyes as he did when he was a kid and wanted just one more piece of my candy bar after he ate all of his. "Oh, Sissy, you know I love you."

I huffed, knowing I couldn't stay mad at him no matter how much I wanted to. "I love you too Asshole. Go do something useful."

"Yes, ma'am." He turned and walked away, laughing as he went.

Without interruption, I managed to get the pie ready and the oven preheated. We had been only lighting one fire per day to save wood for when we would have no choice but to use it and the heat from the oven felt good on my skin. It hadn't taken long before I had to pull off my sweater or start sweating.

While I was in the pantry digging through the cans to find anything that would resemble a Thanksgiving feast, I heard the front door open and Luke's voice. I grinned like an idiot. He was home. He was safe. I listened to Luke and Jacob talking to one another, but couldn't make out what was being said. As I walked out of the pantry with my hands full as they were walking out the front door, both of them smiling like little boys.

Curious, I sat the cans and jars on the table and went to the front window, managing to pull the curtains back just in time to see Luke holding up four dead rabbits. I released the curtain, grossed out. My body gave an involuntary shake. I was fine eating meat, but didn't want any part of getting it on my plate.

I heard more mumbled talking and laughter. At least they were getting along. It was good for both of them to have a guy around. They had someone who wouldn't chastise them for burping and scratching. Sometimes I wanted a girlfriend just so I could have someone to talk to about my hair or the damage my nails and skin were taking every day. I couldn't even say the word *cramps* without Jacob going pale and walking away.

I made my way back to the kitchen, remembering the countless Thanksgivings I spent helping my mom make dinner for all our family and friends. I smiled. My mom would have liked Luke. I thought my dad would, too, if he got to know him. He, like Jacob, didn't liked to think of his little girl with any man. My mom would be able to see the real Luke, like I did. He had a softness in him that he tried to hide, but it was clear as day to me. I had seen it in his eyes the first night.

I opened a can of yams and poured them into a small baking dish, sprinkling brown sugar on top before moving on to the green beans. I wondered if we would have met before the plague, if we would have even noticed each other.

I sighed. I had no doubts I would have noticed him, but would he have noticed me? Maybe, maybe not. I was average in looks and admittedly had bad taste where work clothes were involved, doing my best not to be flashy so I could be taken seriously. I was different then—so focused on my career that I really didn't see much else. Yeah, I would have seen an attractive man like Luke walk by, but I would have put my head back down to my phone reading work emails as soon as he was out of view.

I had been fresh out of college and working my way up the ladder with goals of being CFO of a major corporation. There was no uncertainty in my mind that one day I would have gotten the job, too. I had lost focus on what was *really* important.

Family.

Before the plague, it had been over six months since I had visited them. Six months of barely any calls. Six of the final months of my parents' lives. Today I had to be thankful I made it home in time to be with them in the end and was able to tell them how much I loved them.

Today I was thankful for *finally* being the person they raised me to be.

CHAPTER EIGHT

I have a surprise for you guys," I sing-songed after we were all seated in the formal dining room. The guys didn't looked pleased. The table was filled with food and I was making them wait to make their plates. I picked up two bottles of wine I had placed under the table. "Found these a few months ago and was waiting for the right time to open them."

Jacob whistled and took a bottle from my hand. "Momma had wine?"

I laughed. "Seems so. They probably kept it for a dinner party or something."

I stood and got a corkscrew from the kitchen and handed it to Luke. He winked at me and took it. "You look beautiful."

I felt my face turn red and Jacob groaned. I had put on a red dress with thin straps, a tight bodice, and a slight flare from the waist down. It was one of my high school dresses, and thankfully, it still fit. I even put on full makeup and did my best to fix my hair. Although, I hated to admit it, I did it all for Luke. I wanted him to see I could look like a woman and appreciated him taking notice.

"Thank you."

I moved to my seat with a little more pep in my step and sat down as Jacob held up a glass with his good hand. "Fill me up."

Luke stood and filled Jacob's then walked to where I sat at the head of the table. "Want some?"

Wow! *That* was a loaded question.

"Fill me up!" *Please!* I really hoped the dim light from the candles on the table hid my certain blush.

Watching Luke on my left and Jacob on my right as we made our plates, my heart swelled. I wasn't sure when it happened, but I cared for Luke. *Really* cared for him. It was dangerous, and one day he was going to walk out the door and never come back, but I couldn't stop the ever growing feelings I had for him. It felt like he belonged with us.

He fit.

"What do you think of the rabbit?" Luke asked Jacob.

Jacob nodded, his mouth full, then he smiled. "I hate to admit it, but it's freaking awesome."

"Told you," I said, triumphantly.

We kept our conversations light and fun during dinner. Once the plates were empty Luke helped me clear off the table and set dessert plates out. I carried the apple pie to the table, nervous about how it was going to taste. Luke refilled everyone's glasses of wine as I cut the pieces and handed them out. It only took minutes before the guys wanted more. I gladly dished out seconds.

I took a sip of wine as I watched them shovel the pie in their mouths. I was on my second full glass and felt warm and fuzzy all over. "I think it's time to say what we're thankful for."

"Do you care if I go first?" Luke asked, surprising me. I was happy to see him feeling comfortable enough to take the lead. Jacob and I nodded at him.

"I'm thankful for you two for letting me stay here when most people would have turned me away." He halted before turning his beautiful, silver eyes on me and saying, "I'm especially thankful to you, Veronica, for making the best apple pie I've ever tasted."

"You're very welcome," I said, and he winked at me. My belly gave a jump and I turned to my brother. "Jacob, you go next."

"I'm thankful for rabbits and wine and pain killers." We all laughed and then his face turned serious. "Really, I'm thankful to be alive and for both of you for making that happen."

I reached out and patted the top of Jacob's hand. "I'm thankful for you Jacob. I can't imagine a life without you in it." I turned to Luke. "I'm also thankful for you. You didn't have to do all that you did to save Jacob, but you did it anyway."

He nodded and picked up his dessert plate and disappeared into the kitchen. I followed his lead and cleared the rest of the table before we all met in the living room. Luke was filling his glass of wine again, not looking up at me when I walked into the room. Instead, he stared into the glass of wine in his hand. I wasn't sure what was going on in his head, but he was closing off again.

Jacob walked in carrying a Monopoly board game and dropped it on the coffee table. "Who is ready to get their butts kicked by a one armed man?"

We played for hours, Luke relaxing as time passed by and eventually laughing right along with Jacob. I stopped drinking right at the point of drunk, afraid I was going to make myself sick. We had all had so little alcohol to drink for so long it didn't take much before we were tipsy. Thankfully, two bottles of wine didn't go far between three people. Jacob's eyes were barely open when he finally made his way to his bedroom and closed the door.

I took a deep breath.

I was alone... with Luke. He was lying back on the other side of the couch, his eyes closed, but I knew he wasn't asleep. Picking up the pieces of the game, I set them to the side. I reached over and nudged his leg with my hand.

"Luke, it's time for bed."

His eyes opened, but he didn't move. Instead, he held out a hand and waved me toward him. Not sure what he wanted, I stood and walked the two steps in front of him and grabbed his hand to pull him up. He grinned, his eyes a bit glassy, and pulled me down next to him. Wrapping his arm around my shoulders, he tucked me in against his chest. I sat, motionless, not sure what to do. I wasn't sure what he was doing. I was scared that if I spoke or moved, he would stop and I *so* didn't want him to stop.

He began moving his fingers up and down my bare arm, giving me chills. Thoughts began to creep into my mind about how it would feel to have his fingers touching me in

120

other places. I wanted to know and this could be my only chance.

Feeling brave, I moved my hand to the hem of his shirt and slid my hand under, feeling his warm abs beneath my palm. He sucked in a breath. I looked up at him to gauge if he wanted me to stop. The fire burning behind his eyes told me what would happen if I didn't stop.

I didn't.

"Roni," he groaned a warning as my hand worked its way up his chest.

"Luke," I said in a whisper. "Please."

He watched me for a moment before moving a strand of hair from my face. I took that as an invitation and leaned away from him, tugging his shirt up until it was over his head and on the floor. I pulled my leg over his until I was firmly straddling him. I may have just been crazy, but I wasn't the least bit nervous or scared. Maybe it was the alcohol or the fact that even though I hadn't known him for two weeks, I felt more in tune with him than I had with any other man before.

My skirt rode high on my thighs, his hands not moving further than what was showing, but I felt how much he wanted me pressed against my panties. Gripping his hands, I moved them up, around to my ass. With that, any hesitation he may have had, vanished. He gripped me, pushing me down on his hardness as he arched his hips up. I traced his face with my hand and leaned in and kissed him. The kiss wasn't timid this time. Not at all. He plunged his tongue into my mouth, then working his lips down my neck and to my chest. I leaned my head back and moaned, giving him better assess to my neck. My body trembled with a tremendous amount of both want and need. Never in my life had I wanted something so bad.

He moved my hair to the side, reaching around my back and unzipping my dress, pulling it from my shoulders as he peered into my eyes. His silver eyes were dark and heated and his voice came out gravelly. "You're so fucking beautiful."

I swallowed, not sure what to say. Boys had called me pretty and even sexy before, but never had a man told me I was beautiful. The way he looked at me, made me believe it. Even if I was only beautiful to him, that was all that mattered to me.

How the hell did he come to matter so much, so quickly?

Because he was sweet, protective, and sexy as all hell, that's how.

Using his index finger, he took his time tracing the strap of my bra before gently pulling it down my shoulder, releasing my left breast. He sucked in a breath before covering my hard nipple with his mouth. I held the back of his head, his hair between my fingers, while taking his other hand and moving it between my legs, to my wet panties.

"Don't stop touching me," I whimpered.

"I didn't plan on it," he mumbled as he yanked my panties to the side.

A loud thud hit the side of the house and laughter came from somewhere outside, making us both still and look toward the kitchen. Before I had time to wonder if I had really heard anything, Luke cursed and lifted me up and sat me on the couch in one swift movement. "Blow out all the candles and get your brother."

Stunned because I could still feel the moisture of Luke's lips on my nipple I sat dumbfounded staring up at him. "Who is it?" I pulled the top of my dress up to cover myself as I leaned over and blew the first candle out. He didn't answer, so I said, "What are you going to do?"

He ignored me as he moved to the living room door and locked it. He picked up the shotgun resting behind the door and started for the kitchen before turning back. "Roni, go get your brother and tell him to meet me in the kitchen, then hide in your room with your gun and don't come out no matter what."

There wasn't time for me to sit and argue with him about the ridiculousness of me hiding while the men did everything, so I stood. He must have blown out the last candle because the room went pitch black. There was more than one voice out there. At least two men were talking and laughing. They couldn't be too close because their words were still faint.

Fear moved me. I crawled to the stairwell and made my way up to Jacob's room. I opened the door to his dark room, but made out his shadow as he stood at his window, holding the curtain open just enough to see outside.

He turned to me. "Help me with my boots."

I rushed to his side as he sat on the bed.

"Could you see how many there were?" I asked, out of breath.

"Three or four, couldn't see that well." Once his boots were on, he stood and removed the sling and opened the nightstand, pulling out two handguns. He turned to me, his face stern and serious without a hint of the laid back brother I knew. No, this was a full grown man in front of me. "Go hide, and if something happens, get to the cellar and don't come out until you know for sure they're gone."

I glared but wasn't going to tell him there was no way in hell I was leaving them. I tugged at my dress as it began to fall again. Jacob glared at the state of undress and rolled his eyes. "Get some damn clothes on first."

"Go!" I waved. "Luke is in the kitchen waiting on you."

Running to my room, I yanked the dress off and tossed it to the ground. Grabbing the first pair of jeans I could find and a hoodie, I threw them on, not bothering with a shirt. I crammed my feet into running shoes, just in case I needed to run. Taking the handgun, and making sure the safety was on, I put it in the pocket of the hoodie before going to the closet and digging out my shotgun and bullets. I sat on the floor, putting two bullets in the chamber and the rest of the bullets in the pocket with the handgun. Standing, I moved to my window, but I couldn't see anyone—the sounds were coming from the other side of house.

I made my way to Jacob's window and peeked out. I could see four men standing in a row, starting toward the porch. One of them lazily held a shotgun pointed toward the ground. The others were carrying weapons but I couldn't identify what they were. I bit my bottom lip.

Did the guys go outside to confront them?

Fear kept me moving forward and I went to my parents' door and slowly opened it. Taking a deep breath, I could still smell my daddy's cologne, but now it was mixed with Luke's smell. I walked through the room and pulled the curtain back on the balcony door.

I peered out, seeing the men perfectly, but they wouldn't be able to see me since a tree blocked the moonlight. Jacob and Luke were going to be royally pissed, but I had to do something. Resting the shotgun against the wall, I examined the door. Knowing it had always scratched across the floor when opened, I gripped the handle and pulled up before twisting and slowly pulling toward me. I took my time, even though the sounds of the men were clear and more agitated. I opened it just enough that I would fit through comfortably and be able to get back in quick if needed. Lifting the shotgun, I crept out to the balcony, keeping low.

"Just tell that sweet little thing to come on out here and we'll just spend a little time with her and be on our way," one of the men yelled toward the house before they all started laughing.

My stomach knotted. It was definitely the man I had stopped Luke from killing in town. Did those idiots really come all the way out here with the sole purpose of gang raping me? I had no doubts they probably would, but that wasn't their only reason for being there.

This man's pride was wounded and he wanted Luke to hurt. Luke was right—people would do crazy things when they wanted something.

I felt like a moron for saving his life.

There was no reply to their ridiculous demand. With no idea where Luke and Jacob were, I found a good spot, went to my knees, and sat on the heels of my feet, leaning my left shoulder on the railing for stability. When that rapidly became uncomfortable, I pulled one foot forward until my knee was raised and I rested my elbow on it, holding the gun stable. I could tell by the way the men were shuffling around and the one tapping the gun on his hands, they were getting antsy. If the boys didn't do something soon, it wasn't going to end well.

I heard the screen door open and slam shut. My body went rigid. The men stood straighter and the gun was pointed to the porch. My heart began to race with trepidation. I hated that I couldn't see what was going on, but didn't have to wait long because seconds later Luke stepped into view, raising his arms from the elbows up.

"We don't want any trouble, so why don't you guys crawl back under the rock you came out from under?" Luke's tone was cocky and sounded more annoyed than angry.

My mouth went slack. *Why in the hell is he antagonizing them?* Luke stood straight and strong, not showing an ounce of fear. I wasn't sure if he actually felt any fear. If he did, I was yet to witness it. He was always the pillar of calm.

I wished I could've absorbed some of his calm right then.

"Boy, you ain't in no position to be talkin' to no one with so much disrespect," the man from town said. His voice sent chills down my spine. I gripped my fingers around the barrel of the gun and moved my finger to the trigger. I hoped Luke shut the hell up. I didn't want to have to shoot anyone, but if it meant saving Luke or Jacob, I would in a second.

"Then why don't we settle this like men, or are you afraid you'll get your ass whipped again?" Luke said, his voice dripping with cockiness. I pinched my lips together and blinked a snow flurry away from my eye. The idiot was going to get himself killed.

The man with the gun took a step forward, stopping about ten feet in front of Luke. "Get over here," the man said, motioning to the ground with the gun.

Luke sauntered the few steps, towering over the man, and went to his knees, his hands still up. My stomach clinched. If they hurt one hair on his head, I would rip all their throats out with my bare hands. The man from town stepped forward and punched him on the side of the face, knocking Luke over, but he managed to catch himself with a hand before he fell down.

Yep, their throats were coming out.

Luke righted himself and grinned. Why was he goading them? Where was Jacob?

When panic began to fill my body, I breathed through my nose the way Luke had taught me to do when we were running from one of these creeps.

"Come on out here, honey, and we won't hurt him anymore," one of the men said then leaned in and whispered in another one's ear and they cackled. Did they really think I was stupid enough to actually believe them? The men obviously had the combined intelligence of a slug, so yeah, they probably did.

Heavy footsteps fell almost directly beneath me. I went stalk-still, afraid to even breathe. If I was spotted, I was as good as dead, plain and simple.

If the men didn't kill me, Jacob and Luke definitely would.

"Let's just go in and get her," the man who was just directly underneath me said, as he walked toward the group of men.

They looked in my direction, but not up. Not yet. My body started to shake. *Please don't look up! Please don't look up!* Luke looked in the direction of the new voice before momentarily closing his eyes. He hadn't expected another man either. Then, Luke's eyes darted directly to where I was perched. Did he see me? He swiftly looked away from the balcony and to the ground, his fists clinched.

Yep, he saw me.

One of the men who had been silent before walked up to Luke and punched him in the face before bending his upper body, resting his hands on his knees. "Where's your whore?"

When Luke didn't say anything, the man punched him across the face again.

"I didn't walk all this way to not get a piece of some sweet ass." The newcomer grabbed his crotch and rubbed grotesquely.

"Where's your fucking whore?" yelled the man who punched him.

"Call her a whore one more time and you'll never fucking talk again." Luke's fists were still balled at his sides.

128

Did he have a death wish? Five against one wasn't good odds. Sure, I loved that he was sticking up for me, but at what cost? I could handle being called a whore. He was on his knees getting the shit beat out of him for me! This was all my fault and I had to do something.

The man with the gun stuck the rifle to the back of Luke's head before yelling. "Listen here, you stupid bitch. I'm going to count down from five and if you aren't out here, I'm going to blow his brains out."

It was freezing outside, yet my body went warm and still. All the fear racing through my body turned to white hot anger. I wasn't going to let these pathetic pricks come out here and hurt the man who had saved our lives – the only man who made my insides melt just by a look. He had gone above and beyond proving that he was willing to die for me, but I could not, and sure as shit *would* not, let that happen.

Not on my damn watch.

The countdown began. "Five, four…" when he reached *three* a shot rang out from the other side of the house and a bullet struck the man with the gun. The gun dropped from his hands as he went down. Luke was swinging at each guy as they scrambled to reach him. The man who was shot, laid on his back, but reached for the rifle. Luke's back was to the man as he fought off two of the others. The man on the ground raised the barrel; I had no choice and no time to think. I fired hitting the man in the chest.

He went still.

The prick who had called me a whore growled as he dove for Luke. Luke caught the man by the neck and squeezed before spinning him around and with a quick twist of the neck, the man went limp and fell to the ground next to the other dead man. My eyes went wide. Luke looked up at the balcony like a man possessed.

"Veronica! Hide!" he yelled, before looking around for the remaining men.

I had lost sight of the other three men. The front door slammed and I heard Jacob yelling for them to stop before a shot rang out. I jumped from my position and ran back to the room. Tossing the shotgun on the bed, I pulled the handgun out of my hoodie, holding it with both hands, and made my way into the hallway. The front door opened and slammed again.

Everything went quiet and still.

The only thing I had on my side was it was pitch black inside the house and I knew my way around it like the back of my hand. Staying close to the wall, I made my way to the top of the stairs when I heard one of the boards creak. That was the third step from the bottom; it was the step my brother and I knew to avoid when we were sneaking in or out as teenagers.

I backed up and took two steps through the opened door to my bedroom before a hand covered my mouth, and something sharp and cold touched my neck. Trying to keep from passing out, I took slow, deep breaths nearly gagging from the stench of the man behind me. Letting go of my mouth, he grabbed the gun and replaced the knife at my neck with the gun.

"Found you," the man whispered in my ear before licking my earlobe, his rank breath filling my nostrils. I cringed. He walked us to the entrance of my bedroom and leaned out just a hair and yelled, "I got her, Ricky! I got her and we're coming out. If you give me any trouble, she'll be dead before she hits the ground."

He started walking, using his body to force me to follow his lead. When we reached the bottom of the stairs, he picked up a flashlight from the coffee table. The light was blinding as he swung it around the room, landing on Jacob standing against the far wall, blood dripping from his top lip and his right arm was slack. I looked to his shoulder, but didn't see blood coming from his previous gunshot wound.

"Lookie what we found," he said into my ear.

I tried to push against him, but he only pulled me closer.

The glare from Jacob's eyes was thunderous. He probably wanted to kill me himself. "Ricky, get in here." He pushed the gun harder against my neck and pointed to Jacob. "You light that candle, then sit your ass down."

"I'm sorry, Roni." Jacob took slow steps to the candle and lit it. He stood, backed up to one of the recliners, and sat down, never taking his eyes from the man holding me. I wanted to hug him and tell him this wasn't his fault. Without moving my head, I looked for Luke but didn't see him anywhere. Someone, I guessed Ricky, came from the kitchen and gave a satisfied laugh. When he came into view, there was no doubt he was the man I had ignorantly stopped Luke from killing in town. The bruises on his face were a yellowish green now with even more dirt than before. *Okay,* I thought, *two of the three men who are still alive, are in the same room as me.*

Where was the other man?

He pushed me down onto the couch and stood next to me, the gun at my head. At least his revolting body wasn't pushed up against mine anymore. I tried to get Jacob's attention without the men noticing, but he didn't look my way. His eyes were fixed on the two men. I had never seen him look so murderous.

It was scary.

"Call your boy in here," the man pushed the gun harder into the side of my head forcing me to lean to the right. When I clamped my mouth shut, he backhanded me, causing flashes of light behind my eyes. I had been hit once before and it hurt like hell, but that one pissed me off even more. "Now!"

I looked at Jacob through tear-filled eyes. His hands were gripped on the chair, ready to pounce. I had to protect my brother before he did something stupid. "Luke!"

Both men straightened when Luke opened the front door, his frame taking up most of the entrance. When he took me in, his hands went into fists. I mouthed *I'm sorry.* Almost unperceptively, he shook his head no.

"Where's Keith?" Ricky asked to the room.

Luke gave a demonic grin. "He's not going to be able to make it."

Ricky raised the gun and took two steps toward him. "I should shoot you now."

Luke didn't respond, only stared, daring the man to step into his territory, but Ricky seemed to have learned his lesson from the last two times they met and kept his distance.

"Guys," I said, without thinking. I just needed to try to defuse the situation. "Can't we work this out so no one else gets hurt?"

Ricky turned to look at me with bloodshot eyes and leaned his head back and laughed. "See," he waved a dirty hand toward me. "This woman wants to work something out."

"Sit down over there," he told Luke, using the gun to indicate the seat next to Jacob. Luke quietly obeyed, glancing down at me as he walked by.

Ricky lit the kerosene lamp on the coffee table, filling the room with light. "You sure do have a lovely place here. Don't you think, Gary?"

"Real nice," Gary said, running his disgusting fingers through my hair. I had to fight the instinct to push his hand away.

"We can leave and give you the place," I said, hoping it would work. "There's food. You'll be set. Just let us go."

Ricky eyed me, making me feel like bugs were crawling all over my skin. "Okay, maybe we *can* work something out."

"You name it," I said, eager to get us out of there. All we had to do was make it to the cellar and we could at least get away from the farm alive.

"Roni," Jacob warned. I turned to him and both men were like granite. They would both die to protect me and I didn't care what they wanted, I would gladly give it to them if it meant all three of us got to walk away.

Ricky crouched down in front of me and ran a finger across my knee. "We'll let you three go, but first, we're gonna have some fun with you."

"Hell fucking no!" Jacob roared, as he tried to stand. Ricky was on his feet in seconds and pointing a gun to his forehead. Gary pushed a gun he had on my head again.

"Sit your ass down, boy," Ricky yelled. "Unless you would all rather die right now and we can go ahead and start with her."

Ricky's head swung to me and Jacob sat back down.

"Jacob," I gave him a weak smile that shook at the corners, "it's okay."

"Okay," I said, looking at Ricky. "I'll do it, but you have to promise you'll let all three of us go afterward."

I could feel Gary's excitement pushed next to me and Ricky smiled, showing the few teeth he had left.

"Darlin', I give you my word."

CHAPTER NINE

If I wasn't so completely terrified and disgusted at what I was about to do, I would have laughed at him giving his word. Like it meant anything to me. I just had to pray that somehow, if I did what they wanted, we would get out alive. I would just have to close my eyes and get it over with as quickly as I could.

"Ricky, I want to go first this time." Gary was so excited, he was bouncing up and down.

This time? I looked up at Gary, seeing him clearly for the first time. He barely looked twenty years old. How could these men *want* to do this?

Ricky patted Gary on the shoulder and laughed. "Settle down, boy, or you'll be done before you get your dick wet."

I heard Jacob curse under his breath and Luke growl. I couldn't look at them. If Jacob saw the fear in my eyes, he would end up getting killed. I stood and turned to Gary and Ricky, holding my chin up high and hoping I didn't tremble. "We can go upstairs to my room."

Ricky shook his head slowly before smiling. "No, ma'am. We're gonna do it right here." He looked around, then walked to the kitchen and pulled the kitchen table until it was halfway in between the rooms and patted the top of the table.

Using his hips, Gary pushed me toward the table. "Take your clothes off."

I swallowed and took off the hoodie. I wished I would have taken the time to put on a shirt when I changed. Gary wooted and Ricky moaned, but I ignored them. I glanced up at Jacob. Tears ran freely down his red face, reminding me why I was doing this. This was hurting him more than it was hurting me, but he would be alive when it was over.

"Close your eyes," I said calmly and tried to give him a reassuring smile, but couldn't. "Jacob, please." He blinked twice and closed his eyes. I looked at Luke as he rested a hand on my brother's arm. Luke had done a lot for us over the past two weeks but this was the sweetest thing I had ever seen anyone do, ever. And he did it for me. He knew what it would mean to me. It pained me to see the storms brewing in his eyes and his jaw was so tense he was liable to have broken teeth. "Close your eyes."

He shook his head no. Gary couldn't wait any longer and set his gun down on the table behind me. He eagerly reached up and roughly grabbed my breast. I couldn't prevent my body's recoil at his touch, though he didn't seem to notice or care. Ricky stood by, his gun pointed to my head as he watched Gary fondle me. Gary pulled his pants down and put his hand in his underwear while he touched my breast. I looked straight ahead so I could block out as much as possible.

136

"This is all for you," he said, rubbing his erection before he turned me around and pushed my upper body down on the table. At least I wouldn't have to look at them while they raped me. Gary pulled on my pants until they were halfway down my ass when I realized the gun was right next to my face and Ricky was too busy watching Gary and keeping an eye on the guys to pay attention to what I was doing with my hands. I ignored Gary as much as I could and inched my hand to the handle of the gun. As soon as I wrapped my hands around it, I twisted to my side and pulled the trigger twice, hitting Ricky both times. I turned to see Jacob on top of Gary, his hands wrapped around Gary's throat. Luke swept me from the table and carried me two steps at a time to my room.

"*No*, I have to help Jacob," I said, trying to break free from his grasp. He let my feet touch the floor, but held me tightly to his chest.

He kissed the top of my head and stroked my hair. "Sweetheart, let him do what he has to do."

That's when I broke, my body caving into him. I was grateful for the darkness in the room so he couldn't see my face. Wrapping my hands around his waist, I gripped handfuls of his shirt, crying hard into his chest. I didn't know how long I stood holding him before pulling away and drawing up my pants.

"I'm so sorry I couldn't stop it sooner," Luke said just above a whisper. "I swear to God, I'll never let anyone that close to you again. On my life, I swear it."

"This is all *my* fault!" I yelled.

Luke took off his t-shirt and put it on me, tenderly brushing my hair from my face. "No, baby, this is not your fault."

I shook my head. "If you had killed him in town, then none of this would have happened."

Luke sighed and tugged me to him again, the warmth of his skin seeping straight into my soul. "If I would have killed him in town you would have never forgiven me. I had a choice in town. We didn't have a choice here."

Realization of the truth of his words hit me. He was right. I would have thought of him as an animal. With that, I acknowledged I had killed two men and worse, I would do it again.

The smell of the men who held me lingered in the air and saturated my nostrils. The thought of what almost happened downstairs made my skin crawl and at that moment I wanted to strip off all of my clothes and burn them.

"Go be with Jacob, please." I pushed away from him.

"I don't want to leave you by yourself."

"No, please. I just want to get in the bath. Jacob doesn't need to be alone. I'll be fine."

He studied my face, then nodded. "I'll get you some hot water."

It was clear he didn't want to leave me alone and I appreciated it, but wanted to be alone more than anything right then. Jacob was the one who didn't need to be alone and he wouldn't want it to be me with him. Not yet. Not in the state I was in right then.

When I was alone, I yanked my clothes off, not leaving a stitch of clothing on me. I grabbed an afghan from the foot of my bed, wrapped it around my naked body, and went to the bathroom and sat on the floor against the towel closet. Luke came in twice, carrying buckets of steaming water, but didn't talk to me. After the third bucket, he lit a candle and closed the door behind him, letting me know he wouldn't be back in until I needed him. Finally standing, I let the afghan fall to the floor. I walked past the mirror, averting my eyes. I didn't want to look at myself. I didn't want to see the mark left on my face where I could feel swelling settling in.

I sat stiffly in the bath and scrubbed myself until my skin burned, washing my hair twice before letting the water out. I didn't move. I laid back in the empty tub and listened to Jacob and Luke's voices from downstairs. The front door opened and closed multiple times. I didn't want to think about why, but knew that when I went down the next morning, there wouldn't be any trace of what happened on this night.

We were all alive and that was all that mattered. Somehow we had managed to make it through.

Avoiding the mirror when I got out, I extinguished the candle and wrapped a clean towel around me. I walked to my room and put on clean clothes. Gathering the clothes I had been wearing, I threw them in the hallway. The sound of the truck's engine roared through the windows, filling the quiet house. I crawled into bed, listening to the sound of the front door opening and closing a few more times before the house went silent.

I stared at the ceiling for I don't know how long, before two different showers turned on and off within minutes and

139

Jacob's bedroom door closed. My stomach hurt. I wanted to be there for him, but it wasn't the right time.

Luke's tall figure filled the doorway, leaning against the wall just outside of my room. His chest was bare, but it looked like he was wearing a pair of flannel pajama pants. I raised my head to get a better view.

"Do you need anything?" Luke asked in a gentle voice.

Holding a hand out to him I asked, "Will you sleep with me tonight?"

Even through the darkness in the room, I saw his shoulders relax as he walked to me. I moved to the far side of the bed and raised the blankets to let him crawl in next to me. He lay on his back and wrapped an arm around my shoulder, pulling me to his warm chest. Kissing the top of my head, he used his other hand to rub his thumb on the back of my hand.

"Go to sleep, sweetheart. I'll be right here," he said in a whisper.

I fell asleep feeling safe for the first time in two years.

****

The next morning, I woke to Luke brushing hair from my face with the tips of his fingers. I laid on my stomach, my head facing him. I opened one eye to find him watching me intently. There was anger in his eyes, but he was trying to hide it from me.

"What's wrong?" I asked, rolling to my side. "Is Jacob okay?"

"Nothing's wrong," he said.

140

I winced when I tried to give a small smile. My left cheek hurt and felt swollen. That must have been what was making Luke angry.

"Do I look like Rocky Balboa?"

He grinned as he ran his hand up my arm and rested it in my hair at the back of my neck, his body half over mine. "No, Sweetheart. You're beautiful. Absolutely beautiful."

With both hands, I cupped his face, feeling the stubble of his unshaven jaw in the palms of my hands. *Now, this is beautiful*, I thought, looking into his steely, silver eyes. There was so much emotion behind those eyes. They held all the words he kept inside and I wanted to know them all. I raised my head and kissed him lightly before resting my head on the pillow.

"Tell me what you're thinking," I said.

He started to move away, but I held his forearm in place. I waited patiently for him to let me in. "I was thinking the man who ends up waking up next to you every morning will be the luckiest man alive."

I held my breath and closed my eyes, trying to live in those words for as long as I could. I didn't know what to say to something like that, so I kissed him instead. How could I tell him I wanted *him* to be the luckiest man in the world? How could I when one day he would walk out the door and I would never see him again?

The front door opened and closed, so I released Luke and sat up.

"I need to go talk to Jacob," I said, moving to the edge of the bed. Luke put a hand on my shoulder.

"This is none of my business, but I talked to Jacob last night and right now he needs some time." Luke raised to a sitting position next to me.

"Time for what?" I asked confused by what he was saying.

"To be able to look at you." I went rigid, so he put a calming hand on my thigh. "He's a proud man, Veronica. Last night, he didn't feel like a man. He felt like a failure."

"But, that's not true," I interrupted. He squeezed my thigh gently.

"No, it's not true. No matter what, I wasn't going to let them rape you and it killed me to know they laid even a finger on you. I was waiting for the right time so none of us ended up hurt in the process, but you beat me to it." Luke tilted his head to mine and grinned with what I could only decipher as pride mixed with hurt. "Jacob didn't know what to do that wouldn't get you hurt worse or killed. He felt helpless and he felt like a failure to the one person in the world who matters to him. Trust me, not being able to protect the ones you love is the worst feeling imaginable."

From the pain that pooled in his eyes, he had to have felt the same way with the people he loved. My chest ached for the hurt the two men that I loved had to feel this way. I would do anything to take that pain from them and show them just how amazing they both were. My mind paused.

Holy Hell. Did I love him? Like, *really* love him?

I looked at his strong hand on my thigh and traced a small white scar across his knuckles and thought of all the things he had done for me and my brother, how he made me feel, and how I would do just about anything to see his smile and hear his deep laugh. It was only a matter of time and I

142

would be head over heels for him and there wouldn't be any going back.

I didn't want to go back.

Yeah, I freaking loved him.

I stood and kept my eyes from his face before I did something stupid, like tell him. "Do you mind talking to Jacob? Make sure he's okay?"

"Of course, but he probably doesn't want to talk to me either." Luke stood, his flannel pants hanging low on his hips.

I moved in front of him and wrapped my hands around his warm waist, laying my head against his chest. "Thank you for everything."

He pulled me back enough to look into my eyes, "Please don't thank me. I'm the one who should be thanking you."

"What on earth for?" I asked, quizzically.

He smiled and gently ran a finger over the bruise on my face. "You and Jacob have given normalcy back to me. I haven't felt that in years. Watching you two laugh and love each other so much . . ." he shook his head, "there's not a lot of that in the world anymore, but you don't give up or in. Neither of you had to let me stay, but you did, even though you really shouldn't have."

He grinned, showing his perfect, white teeth. "Plus, there's you. Every day I look forward to seeing you smile. You've given me something beautiful to look at in a very ugly world."

Heat rose to my face. I poked him in the stomach. "Have you been taking peeks at Jacob's poster?"

143

He put a finger under my chin and studied me, his face hard and serious. His eyes looked haunted by the memories of the past and I wanted to kiss all his hurt away. I went to the tips of my toes to kiss him, but he pulled back and closed his eyes.

"I don't want to hurt you, Veronica."

I watched the internal struggles he was having. Could he hurt me? Yes. Most definitely yes! He could. One day he could walk out the door. He had the power to break me into pieces - so tiny it would be like sand—but maybe he wouldn't. Maybe he would choose to stay.

Either way, if there was a chance to feel love after the end of the world, I wasn't going to let it pass me by. Not when at any moment life could be over.

"Don't worry about me," I whispered.

"That's impossible," he said with a shake of his head. He ran his hand over his face.

"Well, how about you trust me then?"

He stiffened, his eyes going bitterly cold. He took a side step away from me and headed for the door. "Damn it. I trust *you*, but you shouldn't put your trust in *me*."

****

I spent the majority of the day inside. Just as I predicted, there wasn't anything remaining downstairs to remind me that last night had ever happened. I doubted it would ever really go away for any of us, though. No amount of cleaning would wipe away our memories.

I wasn't as freaked out as I probably should have been. Maybe I was in some sort of shock over the entire thing, but

I didn't feel like I was in shock. All the men were gone. They weren't going to come back and hurt us and even in the light of day, I still didn't regret pulling the trigger each time I had been forced to. I wasn't going to let them take away my happiness. If anything, the night before made me appreciate life more.

I waited as long as I could stand before heading outside. The sky was as gray as our moods. The snow had finally stopped and only a thin layer was left on the ground. Both men were off in the distance cutting firewood, but close enough that if I needed them they would be there in less than a minute.

I wondered if I would ever be left alone again. This house had always been the place I felt safest and I still did. After what happened, I doubted Jacob felt the same way.

I strolled through the garden, picking the few vegetables that were ready and took them inside. Boredom had me walking around the house aimlessly until I found a basket of yarn nestled under a side table by the couch. My mother always crocheted while my parents watched evening television. Mom taught me when I was around eight, and every now and then I would pick it up and make something quick. Decision made, I dug out the basket, took it to the porch and sat on the porch swing. It had been years since I had tried to crochet, but with nothing else to do around the house and not pushing myself on either of the guys, I had nothing better to do.

After a few tries, I managed to get a chain going and thought about what I would make. I could make a granny square blanket, but doubted my attention span would last long enough. Instead, I decided on a beanie. Beanies didn't take long and I could make both of the men one. I twisted the red thread around the fingers of my left hand, held the hook in my right hand, and got to work. The rhythmic motions were surprisingly relaxing and I soon settled into a comfortable pace.

With my hands dutifully working the yarn, it gave my mind time to think. I glanced up between stitches. Luke chopped wood while Jacob stacked it in the back of the truck. Jacob's shoulder seemed to be getting better every day, but I hoped he wasn't out there wearing himself out. Every now and then, I would hear a laugh or a curse coming from one of them. The sounds echoing in the air pleased me.

Luke had an easiness with Jacob he didn't have with me. An easiness I wasn't sure how to go about having with him. He was a bit of an enigma—a full-on mystery I wanted to solve. He joked with Jacob and they teased each other but when it came to me, he was mostly serious and moody. I didn't want him to feel like he had to be in protective mode every time he was near me.

Could he feel some sort of connection with Jacob because he reminded him of the brother who could still be alive? And what did that mean? What was the story there? He said he trusted me earlier, but would he trust me enough to tell me what happened with his little brother? He either felt guilty or responsible for whatever it was that left him not knowing if his brother was alive or not. I could see it clear as day in his eyes when he talked about his family. Whatever guilt he was holding on to had to be the reason he told me not to trust him.

There were too many questions and I wanted the answers.

Yeah, okay, and I also wanted Luke in my bed. Before everything went crazy last night. I knew with absolute certainty that Luke would have taken me right there on the couch. *Now though*, I sighed, *he was going to be hard to get.* That overbearing protectiveness would no doubt rear its ugly head and he would feel honor bound to refuse to touch me. I rolled my eyes as I worked the yarn. Yes, I was disgusted by what the men had done to me – to us all – but I wasn't going to let what happened take away from what Luke had made me feel.

The image of Luke's deadpan look this morning as he walked out of my room flashed through my mind. He was the type of man that once he had something in his head, it would be hell trying to get him to change his mind. I smiled.

Challenge accepted.

It would be entertaining to watch him fight his needs for a while, but he would give in. I felt how much he wanted me as he pushed between my legs on the couch and I would just have to make him remember it without being overly blatant about it. In the end, he would think it was his idea to begin with.

The truck's engine roared to life. I looked up to find the men coming back toward the house with Luke behind the wheel. They pulled to the side of the house and without paying me any attention, began unloading the wood and stacking it against the house. Jacob stood on the ground while Luke handed him log after log. I held the crochet hook and the almost finished beanie in my lap and watched them work.

I eyed the bulging muscles wrapped around Luke's arms. It was freezing outside, but he only wore a t-shirt and a pair of work gloves on his upper body. The shirt had sweat marks on the chest of his shirt, making a wet V down the front. I swallowed hard. A few years ago, this look wouldn't have been my type. I mean, Luke was hot no matter what he did or didn't wear, but I probably would have crinkled my nose at the sweat. I had always been attracted to a man in a business suit – someone who looked like he had himself together. Seeing Luke right then was by far the sexiest thing I had ever seen.

Luke looked directly at me as if he could feel my eyes devouring him. His back was bent forward and his head tilted my way with his eye brows raised. I almost turned away, embarrassed that I had been caught before I remembered my devious plans. I let my bottom lip drop from the top, hoping it gave me a sexy pout instead of a fish out of water look. Taking my index finger, I traced the inside neckline of my shirt in slow movements. Just to add a kick, I bit the right side of my bottom lip. He raised an eyebrow, so I raised an eyebrow right back at him as he slowly moved his body into a standing position while looking bewildered.

"Dude?" Jacob said with his hands on his hips, waiting for Luke to hand him another piece of wood. Luke snapped his gaze away from me and looked at Jacob. Jacob raised his hands, palms up. "Do you need a break or something?"

"Um, no. I'm good." He cleared his throat and began working again.

I returned to the almost completed beanie, pretending to be in deep concentration and fought back a smile. I had never tried the role of a seductress, but damn, I was pretty sure I was going to enjoy it. I barely had to do anything and caused him to stop in his tracks. Oh, what fun things I could do to him – the things I was *going* to do to him.

The world had too much seriousness and sadness in it. I was ready to have some fun.

They emptied the truck and went around the corner. After speaking to each other for a moment, Luke climbed into the driver's side of the truck without looking my way and drove down the driveway. Jacob walked toward me, his eyes aimed at the ground as he took off his work gloves and shoved them into his coat pocket. The truck was now out of view.

"Where's Luke going?" I asked, afraid I had scared him off.

Jacob stopped on the stairs, his left foot resting on the top step. Using the back of his thumb, he scratched his temple. "He is running to town to look for a few things."

My chest squeezed and I sat up straight. "Alone?"

"Yeah, he'll be fine Roni." Jacob started walking again and motioned for me to move over and let him sit next to me. My heart skipped a beat. I scooted over and watched as he sat down. He skimmed my lap and looked straight ahead. "What are you making?"

Rubbing the yarn between my thumb and fingers, I watched Jacob's profile. His bottom lip was scabbed where he had been hurt the night before. "It's a hat for you."

He smiled and looked back at the beanie. "Oh yeah? That's sweet. Can't wait to wear it."

I smiled at his sarcasm. Now, *this* was the Jacob I knew and loved. I mustered up fake excitement. "I bet I could make you a matching scarf to go along with it. Maybe even some mittens!"

"Wouldn't that be something?" His head bent and shook in a laugh. Bent forward, his shoulders hunched over and his head dipped a fraction lower. "Roni, last night…."

"We don't need to talk about it," I interrupted, wrapping my hand over the top of his.

"*I* need to talk. *You* need to listen," he insisted. He let out one quick breath and leaned against the back of the swing not entirely ready for what he had to say. "I'm sorry about last night."

"Jacob," I said, shaking my head, "you don't…"

"Roni, shut up and let me talk!" His voice rose as he looked at me with exasperation. He stared at me until I mimicked a zipper closing my mouth. "Last night, Luke and I had a plan and I screwed it up. I was supposed to shoot two of the men with the guns and Luke said he could handle the rest. Once I got the first shot off, my freaking shoulder felt like someone ripped it off. By the time I was able to breathe again, and lift my left hand, everything went to shit."

I wanted to tell him how none of what he told me was his fault, but knew better than to try to speak. He needed to get it out, and when he was finished, I would tell him how ridiculous he was being.

"If I had been able to do my part they wouldn't have made it into the house and they wouldn't have found you." He exhaled hard and ran his left hand over his face. "Seeing him come down the stairs with the gun on you and then what they did after . . . I've never felt so helpless in all my life."

His last words came out in a pained whisper.

"I can understand that. I felt the same way about you." I kept my voice low and my tone even. The last thing he needed was for me to lose it.

A single tear made its way down his face, landing on his hand. "The last thing Daddy said to me was to take care of you. I failed him."

I felt as if someone had dug their fist into my chest, wrapped their hand around my heart, and squeezed. He had never told me that before. Our dad was a great man – the best man I had ever known – but he shouldn't have put that burden on Jacob.

"No, Jacob, you haven't failed him." I shook my head vigorously. "Daddy would be so proud of you."

Jacob let out a sad chuckle. "He wouldn't have been if he had been here last night. Those guys would have raped you if you hadn't stopped them and there wasn't a damn thing I could do about it."

"If he would have been here last night he wouldn't have been able to do anything, either. I got out of that by sheer luck. If you would have tried to do anything they would have killed me." I wasn't about to tell him that Luke told me he had been waiting for the right time to attack the men. He already carried enough guilt around and I wasn't going to compound it.

"I killed that guy last night," he said calmly.

"I know," I replied. "I killed a man last night, too."

He turned his head in my direction without actually looking at me. I thought of the boy who always brought home stray animals and helped the kids at school who were getting picked on. The man who wanted to be a doctor to *save* lives and this world had forced him to *take* them instead. It wasn't fair.

"He wasn't armed when I killed him and I would do it again." I got it then. He felt guilty for *not* feeling guilty. I didn't know how to fix this. How could I make him understand that he had been pushed to do it and he was still a good man? He was the most kindhearted man I had ever known. Possibly the most kindhearted man left alive.

"Jacob, listen to me," my voice was stern. "That man was evil. If you would have let him up, he would have taken the first opportunity to kill us all. He could have gone back to whatever hole he crawled out of and got another group of men to come back out here and do exactly what they failed to do this time. I'm *glad* you killed him, Jacob. *Glad*. Now I can sleep at night just knowing they aren't coming back.

"Don't ever blame yourself for what you did. *They* made the choice to come out here. *They* decided their fate when they thought they could rape me and take what was ours and you and I both know they were probably going to kill us all, anyway."

Fury pulsed through my veins. I meant every word I said, and had I had the chance, I would have killed every last one of them myself. Jacob twisted his upper body, and with his good arm, pulled me to him. I wrapped myself in his big chest trying to stay clear of his still tender shoulder. Once he let me go, we both leaned back again, taking deep, cleansing breaths.

"So, what's going on with you and Luke?" Jacob asked, changing the subject. I wiggled in the seat. This conversation could very well be harder than our last.

"What do you mean?" I bit my bottom lip, trying to decide how I was going to answer. How did I explain that I truly had no freaking clue what was going on between us, but I couldn't wait to find out?

"You know exactly what I mean." He rolled his eyes at me. "I'm not blind. I see the looks between you two and how he stares at your ass all the damn time."

My face felt hot and I couldn't look at him. Instead, I watched the driveway, wishing I could magically summon Luke back. "I care about him and I'm pretty sure he cares about me. Before you say it, I *do* know him. Or at least I know the important stuff and that he's a good person."

Jacob hummed low in his throat. "Yeah, he cares about you, but he's hiding something Roni. And I don't want you hurt when we find out what that is or when he decides it's time to move on, and he *will* move on."

I knew this, but hearing it still felt like a knife in the chest. Sure, in the back of my mind I imagined I could to woo him into staying, but more than likely it wouldn't work. I couldn't tell Jacob that it was already too late and if he left right then it would break my heart.

"I know what I'm doing. Don't worry about me."

"That's impossible," he said, mirroring the same words Luke had said that morning.

CHAPTER TEN

The sun went down and we had been fed. I sat on the couch reading a romance novel by the light of the fireplace to pass the time. Luke had come back from town a couple of hours earlier with a few supplies and even fewer words. He wasn't out-right avoiding me, but he was clearly keeping his distance.

"Roni, could you cut my hair?" Jacob asked, walking in wearing shorts, no shirt, and a towel hung over his shoulders. He stood by the fire and pulled his hair down over his eyes.

He was so adorable sometimes, reminding me of a puppy that just found its tail. "Sure. Bring a chair in here, though, there's more light."

He got a chair and set it close to the fireplace while I grabbed a pair of scissors from the kitchen junk drawer. "Did you bring a comb down?"

"No, I forgot."

"I'll run up and get one." I lifted a lantern, and just before I started up the stairs, I turned back to him. "Get a cup of water for me to dip the comb in. Your hair is going to dry quick so close to the fire."

He nodded and I went upstairs. Luke was coming out of his room when I reached the top of the stairs. My breath caught in my throat at the sight of him. He wore plaid flannel pajama bottoms and a long sleeve thermal shirt that was pulled halfway up his forearms. Crossing his arms over his chest, he leaned against the door frame of the room.

"What's going on?" he asked, eyeing the scissors I had a death grip on in my hand.

I forcibly closed my mouth and licked my dry lips. The limited lighting made his face golden and mostly shadowed, which only made him look sexier. He looked down at the floor and I could have sworn he had a hint of a smile. Finally, I remembered how to form words. "I'm, um, giving Jacob a haircut. Do you want one?"

"Do you know what you're doing?" he asked, running a hand through his hair.

The muscles in his arms tensed with the movement and I had the urge to squeeze my legs together.

Damn right I knew what I was doing and I was more than ready to show him.

"Yes," I said with as much calm as I could muster, but it came out sounding like I was going for sultry. *Kill me now!* He was unintentionally seducing *me* and it pissed me off. He didn't even have to put forth any effort and I was ready to jump his bones, yet I was actually trying and he wasn't jumping.

"Okay," he said, walking past me, but making sure his body went sideways to keep from any physical contact as he passed. My eyes turned to slits.

Oh, I would get my revenge. And soon.

After retrieving a comb, I made my way downstairs and started cutting Jacob's hair. It normally didn't take so long, but Luke sat in the recliner and watched my every move. I pushed Jacob's head down for the third time in thirty seconds.

"Be still. I'm going to mess up and you'll end up looking like you backed into a weed-whacker."

Jacob kept his chin close to his chest, but his head still moved when he spoke to Luke. "Did you play any high school football?"

Men and their obsession with football, I thought. I *did* want to know the answer, though. I always felt awkward and intrusive asking about his past since he had shared with me about his family. I didn't want to bring up bad memories for him. Lord knew we all had plenty of those to dwell on without bringing more to the forefront.

"No, I didn't," he answered easily with a bit of a sigh. He seemed more at ease than he had earlier in the day and it made the entire house feel less confined.

"Seriously? With your size?" Jacob's voice rose a good three octaves.

"I was a freaking beanpole in high school, for one." He leaned back and folded both hands behind his head. "Two, I went to work as soon as I was old enough so there wasn't time for football."

I didn't look up, not wanting him to see any emotion on my face. I may not know much about him, but I knew he wouldn't want my sympathy. He had to go to work to help

156

take care of his family. I was sure of it, because that's the type of guy he was.

"I played. I happened to be the best receiver Jasper High ever had," Jacob boasted, even though he wasn't asked.

Oh no, here we go again. At least this time there was actually someone in the room who hadn't heard this a million times before.

"Yeah, he was," I agreed while moving to the top of Jacob's head and pulling his hair through the comb before clipping it. "Every guy wanted to be his friend, every girl *was* his girlfriend at one time or another."

"The guys only liked me until I dated their girlfriends." He laughed. "Let's say I was a loner by the end of my senior year."

"What about you, Veronica? What did you do in high school?"

I shrugged my shoulders. "Nothing, really. Made plans to get out of here."

"You could find Ms. Williams prepping for ACT's and SAT's instead of enjoying her teens like normal people."

My face felt hot and I shrugged again. "That's true, but my college years were a different story all together."

"Yeah?" Luke asked with a half grin and a gleam in his eyes.

He probably wouldn't believe I had it in me to be the bad girl. Wild was how I would have described myself in college. It was my first experience in a city and away from anyone who knew me and my parents wouldn't be getting a call from someone in town asking if they knew what their little girl was up to.

I had studied when I needed to and never missed classes, but also never missed a party. I drank so much, I was surprised I *still* didn't have a hangover.

Jacob snorted. "What did you do? Skip a class or make a C on a test?"

I lightly smacked the top of his head with the comb and pushed him away. "None of your business. You're done. Move."

I nodded my head to Luke to tell him it was his turn. He sat in the chair, his arms tight in his lap, with his fingers laced together between his knees. I took a clean towel and wrapped it around his shoulders, my fingers brushing against the sides of his thick neck as I pulled it tight. Keeping his head still, his eyes looked at me. With him so close, it reminded me of how soft his lips felt around my nipples. I hoped the padding in my bra would be enough that no one would be able to see my nipples harden. I dipped the comb into the water and ran it through his thick hair.

"How do you want it?" My voice came out a little more breathless than I would have liked. Of course, I had purposely put in the suggestion, but didn't want my brother to hear me sounding like a harlot. I tried to recover.

"It's not really all that long. Maybe just a trim?" I suggested.

"Sounds good," Luke said. He looked physically pained to be sitting there. His jaw was taut, his lips in a thin line, and his hands were clasped together in a firm grip on his lap. I was afraid that at any minute he was going to take off running for the hills.

I walked around the back of him so he couldn't see my devilish smile. I started trimming his hair.

Yep, he was going to cave.

"Did you join the Army straight out of high school?" Jacob asked from his seat at the far end of the couch.

"Pretty much," he answered, but didn't elaborate.

"You been overseas?" Jacob asked.

Luke chuckled. "Yep. I've been overseas a lot."

"Oh really?" I asked, intrigued. "Like where? I've always wanted to go overseas."

"You wouldn't want to go where I went." His tone was a more serious. "I've been everywhere, really. Nowhere I would ever go back to by choice."

"Doubt we'll ever have to worry about that now," I said, mourning all the trips I would never get to make.

Behind me, a log rolled around in the fireplace, followed by a pop right before I felt a burn on the back of my bare leg. I jumped and brushed the back of my leg, knocking the ember off. My calve already started to sting from the burn.

"Dang it, that hurt." And it did. Bad.

"You okay?" Luke asked, turning in his seat to look at me.

I could see Jacob's eyes go wide and cover his mouth with his hand. I raised my brows to Jacob, but spoke to Luke. "I'm fine."

"Jacob, what are you doing?" I asked when his face turned almost beet red.

Luke looked back at Jacob and that's when I saw for myself what it was. My heart raced and my eyes went so wide, I feared they were going to pop right out of their sockets. A big chunk of hair was now missing from the crown of Luke's head. Jacob started laughing with his whole body. I began to panic.

"What!" Luke yelled, before looking back to me. He wasn't mad, but more annoyed that he didn't know what was going on around him.

Seeing the dismay on my face, he reached up and touched his head and moaned before letting loose a string of curse words. He stood and took two full steps away from me.

"Oh shit, this is priceless!" Jacob squealed between breaths.

"Oh my gosh! Luke, I'm so sorry." As if someone held Medusa's ugly head in front of me, I was frozen like a statue, the scissors and comb raised at the elbow by one hand while the other covered my mouth in horror.

I was so dead.

He paced back and forth, one hand on his hip, the other repeatedly touching the back of his head like he was convinced I had played a sick joke on him. He kicked at Jacob's laughing body, only making Jacob laugh hard enough to double over on the couch, wrapping his arms around his stomach. Luke turned to me. I swallowed, awaiting my eventual death sentence.

"Sorry," I squeaked, as I gave my best, *please don't strangle me* smile.

He dropped his hands to his sides and stared at me. His face giving no indication of his thoughts. I had to do something. I dropped my head in shame and my shoulders slumped when the basket of yarn came into view. I crouched down and grabbed the beanie I had made for Jacob.

"You can wear this!" I raised it high above my head, like I was offering the Holy Grail.

His lips parted in exasperation and his brows furrowed together.

"Hey, that's mine," Jacob said, sitting back up, his laughter finally dying down.

"Shut up," I growled under my breath then turned a smile to Luke. "It's getting colder outside anyway, so you'll want something to cover your head."

When he still didn't move, I walked to him, pulled the beanie over his head, and tugged it down.

"See," I waved a hand, "can't tell at all."

He turned to look at Jacob. Jacob fell into another fit of laughter. I pursed my lips and glared at my asshole brother. Through it all, Luke hadn't said a word. He looked almost in shock. I felt sick. He had such beautiful hair. Well, until me and my Edward Scissorhands got a hold of it.

This had to have set me back a full week in the seduction area.

He turned to his right, where a mirror hung on the wall. Walking toward it, he looked between his reflection and my face. Bending over, he put both hands on his knees and began laughing. Full, body shaking laughter.

Biting my bottom lip, I watched him wearily. Had he finally flipped his lid? After all that calm he exuded, would my screwing up his hair be the straw that broke the camel's back?

Should I run?

Maybe I should run!

Luke stood, tears in his eyes, and crooked his finger at me. "Come here."

He was smiling, but it was wicked, and I didn't believe he was calling me over for a kiss. I shook my head no. He lowered his head just an inch, his eyes now looking slightly up at me.

"Come here, Roni," he called again. His voice was calm, his tone gentle. His grin was a mix of humor and eagerness. It was the eagerness that worried me.

Maybe he planned to cut my hair off as payback? Instinctively, I reached for my hair. His wicked smile widened.

"No way," I said, shaking my head determinedly.

"Sweetheart, I just want to check your leg." He took a step closer, his hands raised like he was approaching a wild animal. "I promise, retaliations will wait until later, when you're least expecting it."

As if on cue, the back of my leg burned. "Okay… but if you do anything to me, I'll poison your breakfast."

"First you assault my hair, then you threaten to poison me?" He smiled wide and laughed. "Get over here."

He sat on the couch and I slowly walked in front of him. I turned so my back was facing him and my rear had to be almost in his face. This was so embarrassing. Jacob moved over closer to Luke as they inspected my throbbing leg.

"What do you think?" Luke asked Jacob.

"It's a good blister. Looks like second degree burn, probably," Jacob said, poking around the edge of the burn. "I think all it needs is triple antibiotic ointment and gauze and it should be fine."

"Does it hurt much?" Luke asked me, resting his large hand on the side of my leg. And this was the reason I still took the time to shave my legs.

I bent my head down and debated if I should pretend it hurt ten times worse than it did, so maybe he would forgive me for the hair debacle or if I should just tell the truth. It *did* hurt. The burning was constant, but it was manageable.

"Kinda, but I'll be fine." I never was good at the damsel in distress role, anyway. Not to mention, Jacob had always been able to read me like a book and he would rat me out.

Jacob stood. "I'll grab the Tylenol since I need to take my antibiotic again, anyway. Luke, you got the other stuff?"

"On it," Luke said, smacking me on the rear. It wasn't sexual at all. *Damn it.* It was more like a locker room smack.

I didn't move out of the way fast enough and he brushed up against me as he stood.

"Don't worry about it. I can get it." Our bodies were only inches apart. The hair on my arms stood straight. Even *they* were reaching for him.

"Let us take care of you, Sweetheart," he said, brushing my hair behind my ear. He stared at me for a moment, his eyes going soft before leaning down and kissing me lightly then walking into the darkness of the house.

I closed my eyes. My leg no longer burned. My lungs could no longer breathe. My heart forgot to beat. I couldn't feel anything except tingling in my lips where he had touched them.

I reached up and touched my lips and smiled triumphantly.

My Luke was back.

****

"Take two of these and call me in the morning," Jacob said, handing me Tylenol and a glass of juice.

I tossed the pills in my mouth and chugged the juice until both pills were down my throat. Trying to get him out of my bedroom before Luke made it up the stairs, I thrust the empty glass in Jacob's hand.

"Will you take this to the kitchen when you go down to turn the generator off?" I was close to pushing him out, but the instant Jacob realized what I was doing, he would refuse to leave.

"You okay?" he asked, watching me between squinted eyes.

"Yeah, why?" I asked, trying to do the nonchalant shoulder shrug.

"Because you've been wringing your hands together since I got up here."

I looked down at my white knuckled hands and immediately let them fall to my sides. Just then, Luke walked through the door. He had removed the beanie, but he was so tall I couldn't see the bald spot. I made a point to keep my eyes away from Luke and picked up something from my nightstand and examined it like a relic. If asked, there was no way I would have been able to explain exactly what I found so fascinating about a blank notepad. I inwardly rolled my eyes at myself and hoped neither of them had noticed.

I tossed the pad back down on the nightstand and looked up to find Jacob shaking his head at me with his mouth hanging open in an over-exaggerated O. Luke was thankfully oblivious to both of us while he arranged the supplies for my burn.

"Don't you have something you need to do?" I asked Jacob, wide-eyed and head tilted toward the door.

"No, not really," Jacob said with an evil grin. "Luke, you need any help?"

Making sure I was behind Luke's back when he turned to Jacob, I raised my hand to Jacob and gave him the bird. Jacob smirked and it pissed me off even more.

"Do you think it needs cleaned first?" Luke asked.

"Nah, you don't want the blister to burst. The antibiotic ointment should keep it cleaned."

I raised both hands and mimicked choking him. Jacob broke out into a full grin. Luke stilled with packets of gauze half opened in his hands and turned back to me. I quickly pulled my hands down and smiled innocently at him.

Jacob laughed. "I'm out. Goodnight."

"Night," Luke said, more as a question than a statement.

"Goodnight," I said with a smile and gritted teeth.

CHAPTER ELEVEN

I t'll probably be easiest if you lie down on your stomach," Luke said, avoiding eye contact while moving the supplies from the top of the quilt to my nightstand.

Oh, how I would have loved to hear those words in a different context. Instead of answering, I pulled the top of my oversized night shorts up and crawled onto the bed in slow motions, trying for a lioness-like pose before lying flat. Unfortunately, I probably looked more like a cat with tape on the bottom of its feet.

Lying on the unbruised side of my face, I could see Luke's burning eyes focusing firmly on my ass. His hands clenched the ointment and I wondered if at any minute the gooey gel would spring from the top. Guess my lioness crawl wasn't all that bad.

My gaze moved lower to just beneath the waistband of his jeans and to the bulge behind his zipper. I noticed the jeans visibly pulling tighter as his hard-on grew. It was everything I could do not to reach over and pull him on top of me.

"I'm ready," I said, not being able to stop myself.

With a slow shake of the head and a smile, he took two steps forward and began working on my leg. Though he kept his touches to a minimum, every time his fingertips brushed my skin, it felt like a direct line to between my legs. I squeezed my thighs together to try to relieve some of the pressure building.

"Damn it, Roni," he said gruffly. "You're fucking killing me. Be still!"

I raised to my elbows and bent my head down to watch him. He was leaning over, his hands hovering over my legs with his eyes squinted closed. Those lips that were chiseled after a Greek God were in a tight, angry line. Knowing the kind of effect I was having on a man that looked as good as him, turned me on even more. I was afraid if I pushed too far, he would end up saying forget it and walk away.

The only thing I wanted him to do was *me*, so I settled back down.

I needed to talk, to keep my mind from thinking of all the dirty things I wanted him to do to me.

"Where did you go today?"

He took a few seconds to answer. "I wanted to make sure no one was looking for the assholes that came out here."

Surprised, my upper body rotated slightly so I could see him better. I hadn't really even thought of that possibility, but it scared me.

"And?" I prodded.

He turned his silver eyes on me. "No one is coming."

That really didn't answer if he had found someone looking, but if he said no one was coming, I trusted in that. Well, as much as I would ever trust that men weren't going to show up at our house in the middle of the night again. We had seen more traffic through our area in the last few weeks than I had seen in the last two years.

I lay flat on my stomach again and bit on my thumb nail. Luke finished doctoring my leg and wrapped it in gauze, and to my surprise, he sat on the end of the bed. Reaching over, he gently rubbed my lower back.

"You don't need to be scared, Sweetheart."

"I'm not," I said, but my voice cracked, proving me a liar.

He leaned forward, holding his body up with his elbow while using the other hand to brush the hair from my face. *How could I not fall for him when he did things like this?* Even after going crazy on his hair, he still wanted to make sure I felt safe.

I rolled to my side, unwanted tears welling up in my eyes. "Can you stay with me tonight?"

His hand stilled and he closed his eyes.

"I'm not asking you to have sex with me, Luke. I just don't want to be alone." And that was the truth. I had been trying to get him in my bed for completely *other* reasons, but right then, I wouldn't feel right without him there next to me.

I needed him. My soul needed him close.

He stood and my heart felt like it was in a vise grip. He was leaving me alone. Turning, he left the room and I covered my face with my hands, hiding my mortification. I felt like a complete and total moron. Like the biggest loser ever known to man.

If that wasn't an *I don't want to be with you*, then I didn't know what was. I wanted to run to the cellar for supplies, jump in the truck, and run far away, never to be seen again so I wouldn't have to face the humiliation I felt with him ever again.

Just as I was sitting up to blow out the candles, Luke walked back into the room carrying a pillow. I tried to wipe the tears from my eyes without him noticing, but failed.

"Oh, Sweetheart, don't cry," he said, moving to the bed. He tucked his arm under my leg and wrapped a hand around my back and lifted me. Sitting on the bed, he placed me in his lap. "I swear on my life, I will never let anyone or anything hurt you again while I'm here."

While I'm here, I heard over and over in my head causing me to cry even harder. My only reprieve was he thought I was crying solely because I was scared of more people showing up at my home. That was scary, but not nearly as terrifying as the thought of Luke walking away one day and never seeing him again.

That was *real* fear.

"I'm sorry. I don't mean to be a big baby," I said, wiping under my eyes with the backs of my hands and sitting up to see him.

"You are not a big baby. You're one of the strongest people I've ever met, actually."

He thought I was strong? I put a palm on the side of his face and watched the color of his eyes grow darker before his jaw clenched and his eyes closed. He was so beautiful.

Anyone could look at him and see his physical attributes were almost unreal gorgeous, but his heart, that was something I had a feeling he didn't show many people and I was lucky enough to see it was even more beautiful than his face.

I love this man.

Everything about him. Even that he was trying to be good and honorable and do the right thing, because as much as it ripped out my heart, I knew he would leave one day. He wouldn't be fighting being with me so hard if he didn't have his heart and mind set on it. Although I knew he would probably never tell me, he was looking for his brother and he would never stop looking. Even for me.

That was the kind of man he was.

That's what made it okay to love him.

The words were on the tip of my tongue and that was the last thing I wanted to say. Instead, I ran my thumbs on his stubbled cheeks between both of my palms, and with tears falling down my face, I leaned in and kissed him. At first, he felt like a rock next to me, but I continued pressing soft, gentle kisses on his lips until he relaxed and wrapped his arms around me and kissed me back. It wasn't rushed or sexual. It was beautiful, like him.

He pulled back, stood with me still in his arms, and laid me on my side of the bed before climbing in next to me. We moved under the covers. He laid on his back and tucked me into his chest, kissing the top of my head as he rubbed the top of my arm.

"I don't want to hurt you, Roni," he said low, his voice cracked with pain.

He had saved Jacob's life. He had done so much for us, for me. Maybe he would never know it, but he let me love. I never thought I would be able to love someone after the end of the world. He gave me that. So, I had to live with the fact that he couldn't love me back. I didn't fault him for that. I *couldn't* fault him for that. He had warned me enough. I wanted to love him. Even one sided. I wanted to give him the one thing I knew he wanted.

Me.

"Luke, you don't have to be honorable with me. You don't have to worry about hurting me. I know you have to leave one day and I understand that. I will be okay." I wouldn't, but this would be the only way I would be able to have him and to give him a fraction back of what he had given me in the two longest weeks of my life.

I sat up and leaned over him, blowing out the candles on the nightstand. Still above him, I looked down at him. The light from the moon shone through the sheer curtains of the window and streaked across his face. I swallowed hard and found the set of balls I wasn't born with and moved my leg over him until I straddled him.

His hands instinctively went to my outer thighs. Grabbing the hem of my shirt, I raised it over my head and tossed it on the floor. I felt his hands grip into my thighs and watched his mouth open slightly at the sight of me in my white lace bra.

"Roni," he whispered. I reached down and put my finger over his lips, my hair falling from my shoulder to his chest.

"Don't talk, Luke. Just feel me," I said, moving his hands from my thighs to my waist.

172

His hands started moving slowly at first, kneading my hips. I could feel him grow beneath me. His hardness a clear indication he wanted me as badly as I wanted him. Warmth spread between my thighs into my core. I moved my hips and grinded myself down on him. A low growl came from somewhere deep in his chest, vibrating on the palm of my hand. I ran my hands over his chest, feeling every muscle under his skin beneath my fingers.

Leaning down, I started just above his navel and used my lips and tongue to make my way up to his neck. At the base of his neck, I could feel his pulse pounding against my lips and tasted the slight saltiness of his skin. I scraped my teeth against his shoulder and felt him shudder under me. It felt good to have that kind of power, to make a man like Luke shudder.

He pushed me back and I thought he was going to try and make me stop, but he reached behind me and unsnapped my bra. Using the tips of his callused fingers, he moved the straps of the bra from my shoulders.

I held my breath, waiting for his reaction. My breasts weren't perfect. They weren't small or large, really, they were more of a normal, average size. I never wanted approval before, but now, I wanted to be everything he could ever have dreamed of.

"God, Roni. You're so damn beautiful."

He sat up and wrapped an arm around my waist. In an instant, I was on my back and he was between my legs, hovering above me. My chest rose and fell with my deep hard breaths. I had never wanted anything as bad in my life as I wanted him that very second.

"Luke," I said between breaths and reached for him.

He didn't hesitate. His lips came down on me hard, with purpose. My heart leaped. He was done fighting. He was mine. At least for tonight. I would take what I could get. I wouldn't feel self-conscious like I had in the past. I wouldn't hold back. This could be the first and last time I got to make love to the man I loved and I would leave this room in the morning with no regrets.

I wrapped my arms around his back and moved my hands down his spine to the waistband of his night pants. I slid my hand under the elastic to his firm ass and pulled him to me harder. Knowing what I wanted, he pushed his hardness against my center, giving just enough pressure on my sensitive nub to feel it throughout my body. I broke the contact with his mouth and arched my back, trying to get as close to him as I could. I wanted him inside me right then.

"Luke, please," I begged. He hadn't even touched me yet and I was ready to have the best orgasm of my life.

The grey glow from the window showed his sexy half grin. He knew the affect he was having on me and he was enjoying it.

"No, Sweetheart. We have all night and I plan on making use of it all." He lifted up to his knees and grabbed the waist of my shorts in his fingers and slowly pulled them off of me, leaving me in just my panties. "I've thought about this from the first time I saw your sweet face. I'm going to take my damn time and enjoy every inch of you."

"*Oh God*," I said, feeling like I would explode at any second.

He chuckled and moved back another few feet before he leaned in and took my nipple into his mouth, expertly sucking and nipping. I knew feeling his lips on me was going to be amazing, but had no idea it was going to be like this. Slowly, he worked his hands down my body to my panties and rubbed me from the outside, sliding his finger up and down the folds of me.

I was soaked in seconds.

"Holy shit, Luke. I can't take it. I need you in me."

"I'll be in you, Sweetheart. Eventually. Until then, just let go and let me have my fun." He moved to the band of my panties and worked them down my legs.

He sat back, gazing down at my naked body, and rubbed a hand over his face.

"Fucking beautiful."

I was panting so violently, I literally had a fear of hyperventilating. He kissed down my stomach, sweat starting to cling to my skin from the heat between the two of us. I gripped the quilts beneath me as he kissed my hip bones and finally, his mouth found its way to me. Unconsciously, my heels dug into the bed and my hips arched up to his mouth. His tongue licked my clit.

"You're so wet for me. That's so hot, Sweetheart." He moved a finger just outside of my core. "You're going to come for me now baby."

He thrust his finger deep in me while his mouth and tongue worked my clit, until I reached down and put my hands in his hair and fell into hard spasms against his hand. A gush of air left my lungs in a moan. Once the convulsions left my body, I let my arm fall to my side like a noodle. Luke looked up at me, the wetness glistening on his lips as he smiled.

My heart dropped from my chest to my back. If only I could feel this with him every night. I closed my eyes and pushed thoughts of the future from my mind and concentrated on the now. On the man who was hard as a rock and between my legs.

"Is it my turn?" I asked.

He chuckled again. "Next time. I don't think I can wait to be inside you any longer."

Just like that, I was up and ready. Anticipation for what was coming had my nipples hard and my body tense once again. Never before in my sex life had I ever felt like this and he hadn't even entered me yet. I felt like a house of cards and at any second the slightest breeze would have me crashing down.

He moved from the bed and pulled his flannel pants and underwear down. I started at his face and made my way down. I noticed a darkened spot on his left peck that had to be a tattoo, but I couldn't make out what it was in the low light. I let my gaze dip down to his well-formed abs and to his hardness standing straight out. My eyes widened and my mouth went dry.

I wasn't sure I could take that.

He was large. *Very* large.

I heard him curse and run a hand through his hair.

"What's wrong?" I asked, coming up to my elbows.

"I don't have any condoms."

I closed my eyes and cursed. "I promise I don't have anything and unless you were a whore after the plague, the military would have done regular testing on you, right?"

He climbed back to the bed and sat next to me. "I haven't been a whore. I haven't been with anyone in almost four years, Roni."

I was glad his body cast a shadow on me because my eyebrows nearly shot off my face. *Four* years? It had been about three for me, but I was a girl. Did men really *willingly* wait that long? With his body and looks, there was no way there weren't women throwing themselves at him left and right.

"I think we're good then."

He cleared his throat. "What about pregnancy?"

I mentally calculated the days since my last period and didn't know what the hell any of that meant so I shrugged. "Why don't you pull out when you're getting close and I'll take care of the rest?"

He groaned. I wasn't sure if it was from the way I said I would take care of the rest or because it wasn't something he was willing to do. Hell, as much as I hated the thought, if I had to go knock on my brother's bedroom door and ask for condoms, I would. That was only if I didn't have any other choice.

"Are you sure, Sweetheart? I don't want you to do anything you're going to regret later." His hand ran along my face and cupped the back of my neck.

I shook my head. "I won't have any regrets."

"I'll pull out."

He tugged me to him until my lips met his, the kiss deeper and more fevered than before. His body shook next to me with need and I knew he was doing everything in his power to stay in control of himself. After four years without this, I didn't know how he had been as patient as he already had.

I had gone three years without sex, but my entire life without something like this, and if I had to wait even one more minute, I was going to have a major tantrum.

"Luke, I'm begging you, please!"

He moved to a crouching position between my legs and held himself above me on his elbows. "You're so fucking perfect, Veronica. Thank you for this."

When I felt like everything inside me was going to crumble into little pieces, he kissed me, and in one motion, pushed himself deep inside of me. I dug my fingers into his back and his mouth muffled my cries as his hips stayed still inside me, letting me adjust to his size.

His body trembled with self-control.

Once the tightness around him felt comfortable and my body adjusted, I moved my hips against him and wrapped my arm around his neck.

"Let go," I whispered in his ear.

His body reacted immediately to my command. He pulled his hips back and thrust them forward, over and over, until my body coiled tightly and released around his full, hard dick. He groaned when my body clamped around him, fueling his body.

"Fuck, Sweetheart."

Feeling this, him inside me, was absolutely beautiful.

His took his time making love to all of me, touching all of me, even though I had already come. It wasn't until I came the second time, did his thrusts get harder and quicker. I said his name over and over, until with one final push, his chest and head rose high from my body, his hips pushing hard into mine, and I felt his release inside of me.

"Fuck," he said, pulling out. "Fuck!"

It wasn't until he sat back on his thighs that I realized why he was so upset. He came inside me.

Inside of me.

Oh shit!

I flew up and ran to the bathroom and cleaned myself up. Sitting naked at the edge of the bathtub, I thought about what had just happened as I tapped nervous fingers on the side of the bathtub.

Okay, so he didn't pull out like planned. Worst case scenario, I was right then carrying Luke's child. My heart gave an unexpected jump. I didn't know if that was a good idea or bad. Either way, there wasn't anything I or he could do about it now. What I could do is go back out there and calm the nerves of the man I loved.

Even if he would never know that I loved him.

Or if I happened to be pregnant with his child.

I groaned as I picked myself up and walked across the hall to my room. I quietly opened the door and closed it behind me. Luke sat at the edge of the bed, his night pants back on, with his hands on his lowered head. Not caring that I didn't have a stitch of clothing on, I walked to him and lifted his head to my stomach until I was between his legs and his arms were wrapped around my waist.

"I'm so sorry Roni," he said, sorrow in his voice.

I ran a hand through his hair for a few moments, then pulled back and tugged on his hand until we both lay in bed facing each other.

"Please, don't be sorry. You didn't do anything wrong."

I couldn't see his face anymore, his back was to the light at the window, but I knew he could see mine and I had to be brave for both of us.

"Really, I should be fine. I thought about the last time I had my period and we should be okay. Plus, you didn't do anything I didn't want you to do and I have no regrets." I pulled him to me, his face inches from mine. Maybe I said it because I was in shock or trusted him not to think I was crazy, but I shared, anyway. "I've never felt like that in my life, Luke. Never."

He wrapped his arm around me and pulled me close, making me feel so small against his large frame.

"Neither have I."

Those three words slayed me. It wasn't just me. He had felt what I had. Probably, more than likely, he didn't love me, but he felt the same connection I felt when we were together.

No, no matter what came of it. I had no regrets.

"Do you really think you're schedule is okay, so you won't get pregnant?"

The fear and uncertainty in his voice broke me, but outwardly, I stayed strong. For him. Guilt at what I pushed him to do ate at me. He didn't deserve to worry. None of this was his fault.

"I'm ninety-nine percent sure." I stroked his back with the tips of my fingers trying to memorize every inch of him before he was gone. "Can't help that I'm so enticing you couldn't control yourself."

I felt his laugh against my hip. "That is true."

"Now that we know what we like, imagine what next time will be like."

I felt his body stiffen at what I had said – the one thing he didn't want to hear. He didn't want a next time. He was spooked.

"Don't you even try to tell me we aren't going to have sex again, because we will. We'll just plan better. I *really* don't think we have anything to worry about now and you can make a supply run for condoms and we'll be good to go for weeks."

He moved me to my side and molded his body behind me.

"I don't think I could stop now if it was my only mission in life." He wrapped his arm around me and kissed the sensitive area where my neck met my shoulder.

If there was one thing in my life that I could be sure of, it was that very moment. Lying there next to the man I loved . . . it felt good and it felt right.

****

Just as light from the morning filled the room, I woke feeling warm with Luke's hands making their way across my belly to my bare breast. His hardness pushed against my hip.

"Good morning," I whispered.

"Shh," he replied.

He worked his way down my body until he touched the sensitive nub between my legs. I moaned and moved my legs apart to give him easier access. His motions were slow and exquisitely torturous. Every few strokes he would slide his thick finger inside of me.

I opened my eyes to find him up on his elbow, watching me. His eyes were more of a light blue than the silver I was used to seeing. Having never been watched while this happened, I wasn't sure what I was supposed to do, so I reached for him and pulled his lips to mine. He kissed me gently, all the while still working my clit, then leaned back and watched me again.

Tension coiled through my body, knotting inside my stomach.

"I want you inside me," I said, my words coming out breathless.

He shook his head no and flicked his finger over me faster. My back arched up, my head pushing into the pillow as the tension in my belly worked its way down my pelvis and to his hand. My body shook with the orgasm he gave me.

When my body relaxed, Luke moved his hand to my stomach and leaned in, kissing me on the top of the nose. I opened my eyes to see him smiling down at me.

"Good morning." His hardness still pushed against my leg. "I'm going on a supply run today."

I laughed, reached down into his night pants, and wrapped my hand around him, pulling him free. He sucked in a breath. He was so large and hard in my hand, it made me lick my lips before looking into his eyes.

"Until then, guess I'll have to find ways to return all the favors you have been giving me."

I moved to my knees, positioning myself over his thigh, while still stroking him slowly. The muscles in his abs were moving up and down with the fast rhythm of his breathing.

"Sweetheart, you don't have ..."

"Shh," I said, looking up at him and smiling. "It's my turn to say good morning."

I eyed the enormity of what I was about to put in my mouth. I had only done this a few times, but never on anything this large. I licked my lips again and heard him moan. I smiled as I moved down and placed him in my mouth.

I would figure it out.

****

I stood in his t-shirt, drinking a glass of water, looking down at his motionless body. Well, other than his heavy breathing. I started at his toes and worked my eyes up his thick legs, his exhausted manhood laying on his thigh. I smiled behind the glass. Keeping my eyes moving so I wouldn't climb on him again, I continued my viewing of his body. His hips were narrow and his abs were currently rock hard and pebbled with beads of sweat. His pecs were formed, but not like some built guys who were so large they looked like they needed a bra to control them. That's when I noticed the tattoo on his left breast.

I walked to the side of the bed and traced my finger along his tattoo.

"What is this?"

His eyes opened, looking at the ceiling, his jaw clenched then relaxed. It was like he just realized his tattoo was visible.

"It's my unit's insignia."

I nodded and raised my eyebrows, not knowing what the hell a unit was.

"I like the way you look in my shirt," he said, reaching over and running his hand up my thigh and under the shirt. I slapped at him and stepped back.

"What's a unit and what does De Oppresso Liber mean?"

Seeing that I wasn't going to give in, he sat up and pulled his pants on then sat back down on the edge of the bed.

"A unit is the group I was in in the Army. De Oppresso Liber is Latin for Free the Oppressed."

I bent and looked at the rather beautiful insignia. It had a banner at the bottom with the words, and above it were crisscrossing arrows and a knight's sword standing in the center. *Free the Oppressed*, I said in my head. That fit him.

"It's beautiful." I sat next to him. "Can I ask you a question?"

He nodded, brushing my hair over my shoulder and sliding an arm around my back. He made slow circles with his finger on my hip.

"Why do you look like you're sucking lemons every time your Army life is brought up?"

He pulled his arm from me and leaned his forearms on his thighs intertwining his muscular hands. I waited patiently while he contemplated what to say.

"I was in a Special Forces unit."

"Oh, so you were a major badass." I nodded my head and nudged him with my shoulder. "Is that where you get your ninja-like speed and agility?"

His head fell, his shoulders slacked, and he shook his head. I was afraid I said something wrong until he turned his head to me with a smile.

"You amaze me, Sweetheart."

"You're funny," I nudged him again.

"And you may be the *only* person on the planet who thinks I'm funny." He leaned back, resting his elbows on the bed. "You amaze me that even after everything you have gone through so far, you still get up and laugh."

"If we don't try to at least enjoy life, it wouldn't be worth living." I shrugged. "There's a reason we didn't get sick or killed and I don't want to waste the life that was ripped away from so many undeserving people just like us."

Reaching up, he grabbed my upper arm and tugged me down into the curve of his arm and chest. Right where I felt like I belonged.

"You remind me so much of Adam sometimes." With his arm wrapped around me, he used his fingers to run through my hair. "He always finds the best in any situation."

The fact that he used present tense again didn't get past me, but I elected to keep it to myself. There were so many things I wanted to know, but pelting Luke with a hail storm of questions would be the quickest way to shut him up. He was letting me in inch by tiny inch.

I needed the one thing we couldn't have together.

Time.

CHAPTER TWELVE

After taking quick, freezing cold showers, we made our way downstairs and to the kitchen. What I witnessed when I turned the corner made my chin almost drop to the floor. Jacob had his back to us at the stove, scrambling eggs. Jacob was cooking.

"Has the end of the world come twice?" I asked, teasing, and kissed Jacob on the cheek.

He kept his face concentrated on the pan with his lips in a thin line. Uh oh, Jacob wasn't in a good mood. More than likely, he knew what had gone on in my bedroom last night and wasn't all that thrilled about it. I glanced at Luke who was stuffing his feet into work boots and slipping on a coat.

"Jacob, do you mind if I use the truck today?"

"Sure." Again, Jacob didn't turn around.

"Want me to go with you?" I asked, raising my eyebrows up and down at Luke. We could maybe pull over somewhere and have a little vehicle action on the way home. Luke smiled that knowing smile, but before he could say anything, Jacob whipped around.

"No, you're staying here." He pointed a spatula at me.

My hands went to my hips and I narrowed my eyes. "*Excuse* me?"

"You don't have a hearing problem."

"You are about to having a seeing problem when I knock your ass out."

"Hold on, hold on." Luke started toward us when we both turned to him.

"*Stay out of it*," we said in unison and he held his palms up and stood back.

Jacob turned and put the eggs on the plate and not so gently tossed the plate onto the table. My mouth hung open at his behavior. Why was he so mad? I had already spoken to him about my feelings toward Luke he surely wasn't upset about that? What the hell was going on with him? I wasn't sure if he needed punched or hugged.

Hands on my hips, I spoke to Luke through gritted teeth while glaring a hole through Jacob's forehead. "Luke, why don't you go ahead? Jacob and I need to talk."

When I didn't hear his feet move, I looked up with raised eyebrows at him. He looked a little stunned so I mustered a weak smile to let him know there wouldn't be any bloodshed and waved for him to go.

He took a step toward me, possibly for a goodbye kiss, but thought better of it and turned toward the door. Just before walking out the door, he looked back to me.

"I'll be right back."

Once the door was closed, I yanked a chair from the table and sat myself down across from him.

"What's going on?"

"Nothing," Jacob said, taking a bite of his eggs.

"Bullshit, Jacob. What's wrong?"

He tossed his fork on the plate, making a loud clanking noise before sitting back and letting his hands rest on his lap. I drummed my fingers on table, waiting to find out what had Jacob's panties in a wad. If he didn't start talking, and soon, I was going to give him a noogie until he did.

Finally, I slapped the palm of my hand on the top of the table. *"Damn it*! Tell me what's crawled up your ass."

"Roni, I swear, you are the most annoying person left alive!" Jacob said, running the hand from his good arm over his face.

I couldn't help but smile. I prided myself in my ability to drive him insane. It was payback for how nuts he made me all the time. A perk of being an older sibling.

"I know you told me you have it handled with Luke, but I don't like it." Just as I was about to tell him to mind his own business, he held up a hand for me to stay silent. I thought I might bite my bottom lip off keeping my mouth shut, but Jacob had to say his piece before he could move forward. "You just don't know enough about him yet."

"I know what I need to know for now. I know things are weird and I'm sorry, but I like him." I sat back and crossed my arms over my chest. "It's a different world, Jacob. It's not like he can pick me up and take me to dinner or a movie and get to know each other and even then I still wouldn't be guaranteed he would be exactly who he said he was. Believe me, I've gone out with some pretty big losers who have told a lot of lies."

"Oh, I remember a few of your losers. I just don't want you getting so comfortable and trusting him, that you put yourself in danger." He pointed a finger at me. "And I would have said the same thing before, too. Okay?"

I sat back, looking at the man he had become. I was absolutely right the day before when I said Dad would be proud of him. He would. I was proud of him.

"Okay," I said and Jacob stood. "But can you try not telling me what to do and try to discuss things with me *first*?"

"I'll try, but only if I never have to wake up to the noise that I had to wake up to this morning." His face contorted into a sickened grimace.

My mouth hung open. *Oh my gosh, he heard us?* No wonder he had been in such a pissy mood this morning. I closed my eyes and covered my face with my hands in utter humiliation. I nodded and heard Jacob's chuckle fade away before the door opened and closed.

I was never *ever* going to be able to look my brother in the eyes again. *Ever!* I groaned loudly and banged my head against the table in horror.

I stayed with my forehead resting on the top of the table until I heard thumping against the side of the house. Jacob was stacking wood again. I needed to get up and do something productive, so I pulled my body out of the chair and yanked a sweater over my head and went outside. Turning in the opposite direction of Jacob – I just couldn't look at him yet – I went to the neglected garden and got to work.

I continued to work on the garden until I heard the truck coming down the driveway. I stood, my hands covered in dirt and holding a bunch of carrots as he pulled to a stop and climbed out of the truck wearing the red beanie I made him. He hadn't noticed me yet when he climbed out of the truck and called to Jacob. When Jacob came to the truck, Luke pointed to the bed of the truck and they both looked in and laughed. I wondered what was in there that had Jacob grinning from ear to ear, but my mind went to other places when Luke turned and caught my stare. His smile grew even wider, making him look younger and happy. It made my heart skip a beat.

I raised my eye brows in anticipation, and he wiggled his eyebrows, patted the pocket of his jacket, and gave a wink. I raised a dirty hand and gave him a thumbs up. A thumbs up? What the hell was that? I was such an idiot.

Luke leaned his head back and laughed with his whole body. I smiled because he was smiling, but I could feel the heat building in my face. Jacob turned from the bed of the truck and looked back and forth at us. Quickly looking away, I began fiddling with the carrots. I didn't pay attention to what I was doing, but I didn't look back at them.

"Roni," Jacob yelled, his voice filled with joy, "Luke found us some goodies!"

Wanting to discover what had both of them so happy, I couldn't keep from standing up and walking toward them. Luke rubbed his hands together and big puffs of steam filled the area in front of him. What had him so excited?

I headed toward the opposite side of the truck, deciding it would probably be less awkward than standing between the man I had sex with the night before and the brother who *heard* us having oral sex just that morning. Added to that, I couldn't help but feel like the condoms in Luke's pocket were waiting for the perfect moment to pop out of their confinement to embarrass me in front of Jacob all over again.

Watching their goofy smiles as they watched me move up to the bed of the truck, I couldn't deny I was getting a little anxious about what Luke had back there. Jacob was easy to make happy, but Luke wasn't as easily excitable.

Hopefully, later, I would find many *other* ways to get him excited.

I sighed. I had a full day to make it through before I would get to feel him inside me again. It was going to be a long day.

Coming to a stop at the bed of the truck, I purposefully kept my eyes up, watching the guys' growing irritation at my slowness. Placing my hands on the side of the truck, I tilted my head down and rolled my eyes, my mouth forming a smile.

"Beer? Seriously?" I shook my head at them. What was it with men and beer?

"It's more than just beer, Sweetheart. I also found canmed foods, books, toilet paper, and a box for you," Luke said, reaching into a box and pulling out a smaller box. He walked around the truck and stopped next to me.

Taking the shoebox from him, I looked inside. It was filled with soaps, lotions, and perfumes. I leaned back to be able to look at him. His hands were in his front pockets and he had a look of uncertainty.

"Thank you. This is so thoughtful," I said just above a whisper. Not caring if Jacob was watching or not, I reached up and wrapped my hand around the back of his neck and pulled his mouth to mine. His hands automatically wrapped around my waist and pulled me to his chest. I felt his happiness grow against my lower stomach and I pulled away.

We smiled at each other and Jacob made a gagging noise.

"Sorry," Luke said, looking at Jacob and letting me go.

"You're lucky you brought beer," Jacob said jokingly as he picked up a case out of the back and carried it inside.

Alone again, Luke wrapped a strong arm around my waist, turning me until my back was pushed against the door of the truck. He leaned down and kissed me, slow and measured. I used my free hand to grab a handful of his jacket. I groaned and my panties dampened just as he pulled back. He took both hands and cupped each side of my face.

"I want inside of you." His voice was low and guttural.

"As good as that sounds, we're going to have to wait." I pushed a hand against his chest until he groaned and moved back a few steps. "Jacob heard us this morning."

Luke's eyes first went wide then gleamed with humor. "So *that's* what had his panties in a wad this morning?"

"Yeah," I laughed. "He may be my little brother, but he's protective."

It was Luke's turn to laugh. "Trust me, I know. He's threatened my life more in the last two weeks than I've been threatened my whole life. He's very creative with his ways of killing me, too."

Shocked, my eyes widened. "No, really? I'm so sorry."

"Don't be sorry, Sweetheart. He loves you and wants you safe. He's doing exactly what a brother should do. If he didn't, I wouldn't like him so much." He walked around the truck and pulled out the box, carrying the supplies.

Shit, I was in love. Freaking *in* love!

I was so screwed.

How could I not be in love with him? He was as close to perfect as anyone I had ever met. He put up with and even *liked* my jackass brother. He did things for me all the time. Big things, like saving Jacob's life and protecting me and little things like bring me girly lotions and perfumes because he thought I would like them.

Following his lead, I picked up a case of beer and trailed behind him into the house. Though the house was chilly when I left earlier that morning, it felt much warmer after being outside. I set the beer down and rubbed my numbing fingers together.

"We should leave the beer outside tonight so it gets good and cold," I said, going to the sink and washing my hands in ice cold water. I cupped my hands near my mouth and blew warm air on them. Luke noticed and came to my side, tugging on my hand.

"Good idea," Jacob said, pulling items out of the box and setting them on the table.

Chills ran up my spine as Luke rubbed my fingers with both of his hands. Yep, I was all warmed up now. He took the other hand, doing the same thing and I ended up down right hot by the time he was done. My cheeks felt hot and my neck clammy.

"Feeling okay?" he asked, looking down at me with a wink.

"I feel fine," I said, pushing against him at the same time I stepped away from him. "I need to get the vegetables from the garden."

"Need help?" Jacob asked from the living room.

I walked past them both and to the door. "No, I got it. Do you mind starting a pot of water to boil, though?"

I had learned from the previous winters that it was always a good idea to have water boiling. It came in handy for household chores, cooking, and helped keep the much needed moisture in the air. My skin always turned to shit in the winter months. It dried out terribly and if I wasn't prudent, my skin would itch nonstop. If I wasn't careful, Luke would think he was crawling in bed with an elephant.

Thanks to Luke, I had a new box of lotions to help stave off the effects of winter.

I gathered the vegetables and took them into the house. After taking the shoebox of goodies upstairs, I went back to the kitchen. Surveying the contents of the box Jacob had laid out on the table, I was excited, picking through each item slowly. There were beans, rice, canned tuna and tomatoes, flour, and sugar. Every last item was like a pound of gold in the old world and I would treat them as such.

I went to the pantry, grabbed the inventory notebook, and began putting the items on the list. Once done, I put them away, leaving out the beans. I took a small piece of wood and put it in the bottom of the cast iron stove and got another pot filled with water and placed it on the stove. At the sounds of wood being stacked at the side of the house, I held my hands over the first pot of water to warm them. They had to be cold out there and after I took care of a few things, I was going to make them a hot mug of apple cider.

Sitting at the table, I poured just enough beans for the three of us and flattened them out on the table. If only we had a fridge, I would be able to make enough to keep leftovers and just heat them. Alas, I was forced to spend most of my time starting a meal from scratch. As annoying and time consuming it was, I was really thankful we had any food at all.

Picking through the beans, I tossed any broken pieces or rocks. It reminded me of helping my mom pick through the beans. She would always save the broken or half beans and make Jacob a country version of a hacky sack with socks that had lost their match to the dryer monster. *She was always doing something creative like that*, I thought as I washed the beans thoroughly before adding them to the boiling water.

I had always been more practical like my dad. He was a good-looking man – Jacob favored him a lot – and was quiet most of the time. When he laughed, his whole body laughed with him making his joy vibrate to everyone around. He did a great job teaching my brother, *and* me on how a woman should be treated. My mother never had to wonder if she was loved because he made sure in every way that she knew. Images of how my father would watch my mother while she cooked or worked on a project and how they would smile at each other when she would catch him staring flooded my mind. It was exactly the same way Luke watched me and smiled – a smile I knew was reserved only for me.

My heart skipped a beat and my head felt fuzzy. *Luke looked at me like my dad had always looked at my mom.* At the sink, I looked through the window at Luke. He was concentrated on his work. He must have felt my stare because he looked up and smiled sweetly. My chest ached and I smiled a shaky smile back.

Was he in love with me too?

I moved away from the window and sat, shaking, at the table. I loved him. I already knew that, so why the hell did the thought of him loving me back completely terrify me?

Clarity filled my mind. Any feelings he had for me weren't going to stop him from leaving to find Adam.

I would end up hurting him as much as he would hurt me.

CHAPTER THIRTEEN

H oly hell, this beer is good," Jacob said, tossing back another long swig of his can as we all sat in the living room playing a game of Yahtzee.

Both Jacob and Luke were on their fourth or fifth beer and happy as could be. I had refrained in partaking, too nervous about what would spill out of a drunken Veronica. It had been a little more than two weeks since Luke had brought the beer home. Two weeks since I first wondered if Luke was in love with me and in those two weeks it had changed from wondering to flat-out denial.

When I started my period two days ago, we were both relieved, and even though there was no chance I was going to have sex with him in that state, he still came to my bed each night and held me while I slept. I kept telling myself he was only coming back each night because he thought I was scared to be alone. I could be a good liar when I needed to be.

"It's your turn, Jackass," I said, pushing against Jacob's good shoulder.

"Why are you in such a big hurry to get your butt kicked?"

"Was Adam as annoying as Jacob?" I asked and wanted to punch myself in the face repeatedly. *Why the hell did I bring up Adam?*

"Maybe even more," Luke said with a smile, handing Jacob the dice. When Jacob's brows dipped, I knew I had made a big mistake.

"Who's Adam?"

I looked at Luke and mouthed *I'm sorry,* but the damage was done. He reached over from his seat on the other side of the coffee table and squeezed my knee in reassurance before answering.

"He's my little brother. How old are you?"

"I will be twenty-three in January. I didn't know you had a little brother." Jacob, though drunk, seemed to take the seriousness of what he was hearing. Luke had never spoken of his family to us before and only spoke of them freely the night Jacob had been running a fever. Maybe he was more intoxicated than I had assumed from his demeanor.

"Adam will be twenty-three in April. He's a great guy. Always looking on the bright side of everything." Luke stared at the wall behind me. He was somewhere else right then. His eyes burned with the pain of talking about his brother.

Jacob stared at Luke for a minute before the questions in his head came out his mouth. "You mean he's still alive?"

Luke rubbed a hand over his head and took another drink of beer. "As far as I know."

"Where the hell is he then?"

"Jacob!" I chastised him.

"It's okay," Luke said, holding a hand up to me. "I'm not sure where he is right now, but I will get him back."

"I gotta take a piss," Jacob announced before getting up and walking to out of the living room.

"I'm sorry," I said as soon as Jacob was out of the room.

Luke came to sit next to me and kissed my temple. "Why are you sorry?"

"It can't be easy for you to talk about Adam, knowing he's out there and you're here with us." *Shit, I probably just made it a hundred times worse.* I closed my eyes. "I mean…"

"Roni, being here has helped me in more ways than you could ever imagine." He gave me a quick kiss. "I know I don't tell you a lot about my past, but there's reasons I don't tell you. I want to keep you safe. I will do *anything* to keep you safe. One day, I'll get Adam and if I'm still welcome, I would like to bring him here."

"Really?" I asked in complete shock. "You would come back?"

He chuckled. "Why do you seem so surprised? You're amazing and beautiful. Having to leave you at all pisses me off, but I have to. Adam depends on me and I can't let him down."

I had so many questions, and I didn't know where to start. Jacob came back to the room and took his turn. What had Luke meant by "get him back"? Did that mean someone had him and if so, who? And he *wanted* to come back? Did he mean for good, or for a while, or to stop by on their way somewhere else? So many freaking questions, and if I were honest with myself, I would admit I was more than just a little afraid of the answers I would get.

"Let's do the three things," Jacob said. "I'll go first."

"Okay?" I asked, surprised. He never offered to play this game before, so I wondered what was up with him.

"My need would be a damn television. I bet there would be some awesome reality TV going on right now. Want would be Laura." His face went slack and his eyes far away. "I fucking miss the hell out of her. Hands down, I don't miss alarm clocks."

Okay? I thought. *Who the hell was Laura?* So I asked him. "Who's Laura?"

"A girl I used to know." He waved a hand dismissively. "Luke, your turn."

I glared at Jacob. He *would* tell me. Maybe not right that minute, but I *would* find out who Laura was and why the hell that was the first time I had heard of her. Why the hell was everyone keeping so many secrets? I was *really* beginning to get pissed off.

While Jacob wasn't paying attention, Luke quickly grabbed Jacob's beer can and hid it under the coffee table. Jacob was officially cut off for the night. Luke cleared his throat.

"My need right now?" he said, glancing at me and quirking an eyebrow. He was trying to lighten my mood and it was working. "My need would have to be a chainsaw. That axe is kicking my ass. All I need is a flannel shirt and you could call my ass Paul Bunyan."

Jacob laughed. "I'm almost well enough to start cutting."

"Take your time and let it heal properly." Luke winked at me. "Anyway, I think your sister likes to watch me cutting wood."

My lips broke out into a wide smile because he was wholly accurate. Watching him wielding an axe could quite possibly be the sexiest thing I had ever witnessed in my life. Though, I didn't think of Paul Bunyan at all. I thought more along the lines of Thor and with every strike, I felt lightning through my nipples. Oh wow, I really needed to lay off the romance novels.

"That's really gross. What's your want? And if you say my sister, I'm going to get some practice swinging that axe a lot sooner than we thought."

Luke and I both burst into laughter. Jacob glared at both of us.

"Yeah, it's all fun and games 'til I get pissed off!" Jacob said, only half joking.

"Okay, okay," Luke said, wiping the moisture from his eyes. "My want is music. I love good music."

"And what don't you miss?" I asked.

"Flying. Never liked it, never will."

"Seriously?" Jacob asked.

"Really?" I asked, at the same time.

"Yes. If I'm going to die, it should be with my feet on the ground the way God intended."

"Yet, you flew all over the world?" I asked.

"Face your fears and all that crap. It's been faced and I'm glad I don't have to do it again."

This time it was Jacob's and my turn to laugh. *Who would have thought Mr. Badass was afraid of planes?* I couldn't imagine him really afraid of anything; he always seemed so calm and in control of everything. Maybe that was the fear? If he were in a plane, he didn't have control?

"Looks like it's your turn, Sweetheart." Luke sat next to me and pulled me into his chest, wrapping an arm around my shoulders.

I had a hard time concentrating with the warmth of his body soaking into mine. Both of them had shocking lists tonight and I needed mine to be just as intriguing. I rattled around in my head, trying to come up with something, but I was basically a boring person.

"Any time now, Roni," Jacob said standing and heading for the kitchen.

"Drink water or you're going to have a hangover in the morning," I called after him.

Jacob came back and sat down sipping on a glass of water. I tapped my fingers on my chin still trying to come up with something good.

"My need is…" I was so blank and it was annoying as hell, "my need is another woman around the house to talk to when you guys start driving me nuts."

"We drive you nuts?" Luke asked, and if I didn't know better, I would have thought there was a bit of hurt behind his words.

"More estrogen in this house is not a need, Sis," Jacob said with mock horror.

I picked up a pillow and tossed it at his head, missing by a good two feet. I had always sucked at softball. Or *any* sport, for that matter.

"Yes, this house is brimming with testosterone and it would be nice to have someone else here so I could talk about my nails and hair." *Okay, now I was sounding ridiculous, but it was true.*

"Sweetheart, you can talk to me about your hair and nails anytime you want." His voice didn't hold even a hint of sarcasm. He leaned in and kissed the top of my head. "I'll even paint your toes if you want me to."

I laughed. "Paint my toes?"

"What? I had an older sister, and a younger sister. I can't tell you how many times they made me play dress-up and painted my nails when I was young." Jacob and I laughed at the thought. "Didn't you ever do that to Jacob?"

"Hell no!" Jacob laughed. "I would have cut all of her hair off in her sleep!"

I leaned away so I could get a good look at Luke. His perfect complexion was turning a bit pink. Luke Greslon was blushing. The wonders of the night just kept coming. Feeling bad, I gave him a kiss.

"I would love it if you painted my toenails." I bit my top lip to keep from laughing again as his face turned from pink to red.

"Shut up you two," Luke warned, but was smiling, too. "You have two more to do."

"Want is easy. I want a camera."

"Boring," Jacob said in a sing-song voice. I stuck my tongue out at him in a mature reply.

"I don't miss Harvey Baker."

"Who's Harvey Baker?" Luke asked.

"He's a dickhead ex-boyfriend," I said.

"Dickhead doesn't even *begin* to describe that son of a bitch," Jacob said, hands fisted.

Maybe bringing Harvey up wasn't a good idea. Harvey was one of the major reasons I focused on my career instead of dating.

"What did he do?" Luke asked, his voice going hard.

"He-," I started, but Jacob cut me off.

"He punched her. *That's* what the hell he did," Jacob said, his anger clear in his deep voice and red face.

I felt Luke's body go rigid beside me and his hand pull me closer to him. When he spoke, his voice was dark and cold. "He punched you?"

"Only once and I kicked him in the balls," I said with a shrug. I was proud of myself that night. I had been completely shocked that he punched me, but I wasn't about to put up with it. "He went down like a stack of cards."

"I should've kicked his ass when I had the chance," Jacob said before taking another drink of water.

"You were barely eighteen and he was, what, twenty-five by then?"

I remembered Jacob finding out like it was yesterday. He happened to come up to visit about two or three days after the incident and the mark and swelling on my cheek wasn't bad, but still visible without makeup to cover it. He didn't tell me he was coming so I didn't think anything of it when I opened the door straight out of bed.

Jacob had flipped his lid. He took my phone from me and called Harvey and threatened his life. Even at eighteen, Jacob was a big man and probably would have gone through with his threats if I hadn't pulled him down by his ear and talked him down. He had hugged me so tight, I thought I was going to break in two.

We had always been close, but since that day, we were best friends, too.

Jacob rolled his drunken eyes. "I would have beat his ass."

"Good thing the mother fucker is dead or I would kill him myself," Luke said, dark and menacing.

I believed him.

"On that note, I'm going to go turn off the pump and go to bed." I stood and Luke tugged me down onto his lap.

Wrapping one strong arm around my waist, he used the other to brush the hair from my face as he pulled me down and kissed me. His kiss was slow and gentle and safe. It was exactly what I needed. I pulled back to find an empty chair where Jacob had been sitting. I had been so focused on Luke's mouth on mine, I hadn't heard Jacob leave.

"I'll get the pump, you go pick a nail color and some lotion and I'll be up in a minute." He planted a quick kiss on the base of my neck before he lifted me up like I weighed nothing.

"You're seriously going to paint my toenails?" I stared at him with incredulity.

"Yes, Sweetheart. You deserve it." He patted my butt and headed to the door leaving me standing in awe.

Is this man for real?

"Only if you let me give you a back rub. I know your shoulders are killing you," I said, throwing out a trade of services. He did much more physical activities around the house than I did. When I tried, he always stopped me and took care of it himself.

He wiggled his eyebrows at me and gave a boyish grin. "You can rub anything on me you want."

I couldn't stop from giggling like a teenager as he walked out of the house. I turned just as Jacob was coming down the stairs. The water must have done some good because he looked steadier than he had an hour ago. He walked straight to me and wrapped me in a big hug.

"I love you, Sissy."

I held on to his shoulders and buried my head into his good shoulder, trying not to choke up. "I love you."

He released me and took a step back, still holding my shoulders. "You know he does too right?"

My eyes widened and I started to stammer. "I, uh, don't..."

"Oh, he does." Jacob chuckled and kissed my forehead. "Just haven't figured out if that's a good or bad thing yet."

"Me, either," I whispered, not meeting Jacob's eyes. If I did I would cry, so I stared into his chest instead.

"I'm here anytime you need me." He kissed my forehead again. "Goodnight."

"Night."

I stood in the middle of the room thinking about what Jacob said. So, I wasn't the only person who saw what I saw? Okay, so I wasn't bat shit crazy. Well, I probably was, but not about this. This, I was pretty damn sure of. At least now I knew he wanted to come back; I just didn't know for how long.

Forever wouldn't be long enough.

"Now," I said out loud to myself. "Just enjoy the now."

Now was more than anyone else I knew had.

Luke came in and tilted his head to the side. "What are you still doing down here?"

My eyes took their time examining him. He wore a pair of worn blue jeans and a dark blue knit sweater he found on his last supply run; it actually fit him quite well. The mass of his upper arms was still visible under the sleeves. He stood still and I could see him swallow when I reached his muscular neck. God, I loved that neck. I loved running my tongue over it and feeling his moan vibrate under my touch.

My gaze finally made it to his face and I smiled. He was so damned beautiful it made my chest ache.

"Keep looking at me like that and I'm not going to be able to paint your toenails."

I raised my eyebrows and grinned. "I'm on my period, remember?"

"Like I said, keep looking at me like that and it won't matter." He smiled, making my thighs tingle.

"Umm, well, okay then." I looked down and scratched the back of my head because I didn't know what else to do.

Luke sauntered up to me. "Wait here and let me turn off, I mean, blow out the lights."

I nodded and took a seat on the couch and watched him. He put another log on the fire and put the gate up to make sure nothing came out while we were asleep. Systematically walking around the space, he blew out the candles, making his way to me.

Just as he had his mouth ready to blow on the last candle, he glanced at me while he blew it out.

I swear I felt like my heart was going to beat right out of my chest.

I watched him come to me by the red glow of the fire. I could barely make out one side of his face and it held a sly grin. Oh, he *knew* what he was doing to me.

I freaking hate my period.

Fate, will you please stop being such an asshole to me?

Luke bent down in front of me and tucked one arm under my legs, the other around my back, and picked me up. Surprised, I wrapped my arm around his neck to steady myself.

We didn't speak as he carried me up the steps and into our room.

My room.

Okay, *our* room.

I helped him feel his way through the pitch black room until his shin hit the bed railing.

"Shit," he cursed with a groan, then a laugh.

He tossed me on the bed and lit a couple candles. While he checked his shin, I went to the bathroom and took care of business. When I got back to the room, his sweater and jeans were off and he was in a pair of flannel pajama bottoms.

Sexiest. Man. To. Ever. Live.

"You ready?" he asked.

I took a stuttered step on my way to him. "For what?"

He bent his head down–showing his marred hair–as his chest and shoulders shook.

"For me to pamper you."

I blushed and headed for my makeup stand. "What color do you like?"

"Red," he said so close behind me I jumped.

I slapped at his arm. "You *have* to stop doing that! You're going to give me a heart attack one day."

He pressed his chest to my back as he looked over my shoulder to the options. "This one."

It was an almost auburn red.

"You sure?" I asked.

My toes were probably going to end up looking like they had been run through a meat grinder. I was hoping he would pick pink so it wouldn't be so noticeable when he went outside the actual nail.

"Sure. Unless you want something else. I like you in red though."

210

"Red it is!" I picked it up and handed it to him.

"Where's that lotion that smells like flowers?" He waved a finger at the stack of lotions on top of the dresser.

Almost all of them smelled like flowers!

"Can you be more specific?" I asked, trying not to hurt his feelings.

"The one you wore the day I brought you the box of stuff."

I moved them around until I found the one I thought he wanted. It was sweet pea scented. One of my favorites. "This one?"

I opened it and held it to his nose. He closed his eyes. "Yeah, that's the one."

I tossed him the lotion and changed into a pair of sleep shorts and a tank top. I wasn't worried about getting cold because sleeping next to Luke was like having my own personal furnace. Plus, it meant I just had to burrow myself closer to him. That was never a bad thing.

I hurried to the bed and crawled in. Stacking the pillows behind my back into a comfortable half-sitting, half-laying back position, I lifted my eyebrows and wiggled my toes.

"I'm ready when you are."

He walked over without an ounce of trepidation and sat facing me at the foot of the bed. Lifting my feet, he rested them in his lap.

He squirted lotion into the palm of his hand and rubbed his palms together before covering my feet with his hands. I closed my eyes under his ministrations. His touch eased my stress. His fingertips were light. My leg automatically twitched and pulled back at the tickle and he gripped my foot in his hands.

"Are you ticklish?"

"Just on my feet and don't even think about it," I told him in a warning tone.

I *hated* being tickled.

He began massaging me again, not lightly, but since he had tickled me already, my body was stiff with anticipation.

"Harder," I told him through gritted teeth.

He laughed. "That's not the *first* time you've told me that."

"Perv."

His fingers deepened and kneaded the arch of my foot until I relaxed again.

"Only with you, Sweetheart."

By the time he was finished rubbing both feet, I was in a state of euphoria. I could feel his body shift and I opened my eyes. He had the bottle of nail polish in his hand, shaking it. He knew to shake it?

Hilarious!

"Do you have one of those things that keeps your toes apart?" he asked seriously.

"Yes, there's one in the drawer below the nail polish." I bit my lip to keep from laughing again.

This had to be the strangest experience of my life.

Finding what he needed, he settled himself back on the bed. He worked my toes into the foam contraption before looking up at me.

"Be still," he ordered.

I obeyed.

The sounds of Jacob's snoring infiltrated the air and our eyes locked before we started laughing.

Luke pulled the brush from the nail polish and started on my pinky toe.

"How long where you with the dickhead?" Luke asked.

I let out a breath, not really wanting to ruin the good mood with thoughts of someone not worth thinking about.

"A little less than two years," I answered flatly.

"That's a long time," he answered tightlipped.

"Yes and no," I said. "I was a typical college student and when I wasn't partying, I was studying, so we really didn't spend that much time together."

Luke nodded and I saw his jaw clinch before he asked, "What happened that ended with him laying his hands on you?"

"I wanted to stay in for once and study and he wanted to go out. It started a fight and he had already been drinking and the fight escalated and he hit me," I said and shrugged, "then like I said, he went down like a house of cards."

He didn't say anything, but I could feel the waves of anger rolling from his body as he worked his way through the toes on my right foot. When I looked down, I was surprised at what I saw. It looked great. There wasn't any on my skin and *I* couldn't even manage that feat.

"Are you sure you didn't spend your weekends dressed as a woman? You're awful good at this."

He grinned and shook his head. "No, but I used to work with bombs a lot and it takes a steady hand and that just so happens to come in handy when applying toenail polish."

"Bombs?" My eyes widened. "You worked with bombs?"

"Uh, yeah? I told you I was Special Forces." His eyebrows drew together.

"I know. I just didn't think about it in detail, I guess. That's terrifying."

And it was. Even though I knew Special Forces were the badass of the badass, the thought of him being near real life bombs made my stomach hurt.

"It was part of the job," he said in a matter of fact tone.

"Thank God you don't have that job anymore." I noticed him stiffen slightly.

I hadn't thought that maybe he *liked* being in the Army and missed it. I felt an uncomfortable air surround us. Clearing my throat, I looked at my finished toes. My feet looked soft and my toes looked polished to perfection. I felt quite feminine and pampered. I hadn't felt pampered in more than two years and it was all at the hands of a six-foot-three, two hundred five pound, Special Forces badass.

"I know what you should do after the world gets its shit back together," I said enthusiastically.

He looked at me with a half-grin that zapped all the solemnness from the room. "What would that be?"

"Open a day spa. You're damn good and I feel absolutely fabulous."

He growled as he hurled a pillow at my head.

"What?"

"You're such an ass."

I winked. "You seem to like my ass."

Like a predatory cat, he crawled up my body, his face inches from mine as he reached around and grabbed a handful of said ass.

"It *is* a nice ass."

CHAPTER FOURTEEN

Jacob Allen, I'm so going to kick your ass!" I yelled through the open kitchen door.

It was snowing heavy. So heavily I had a hard time seeing Jacob across the yard. He wasn't wearing gloves. I only knew this because I held his gloves in my hand. Irritated, I yanked a pair of boots over the new pink toenail polish Luke had painted on me the night before–something he had done once a week for four weeks now. He painted my toes, I gave him backrubs.

We had a *great* relationship.

I was just about to head out into the bitter cold when Luke's hand wrapped around my upper arm. I looked over my shoulder at him. He was wrapped in a sweater, covered in a thick coat and had the red beanie on his head. I had tried to give him multiple different beanies and caps, but he refused them all. He wanted to wear what I made him. It melted my heart.

Good thing he liked it because that's what I made for him and Jacob for Christmas. At least these looked much better than my first attempt. He *did* look cute in it though. He would look cute in a paper sack.

"I'll take them. I'm heading out there." He pulled the gloves from my hand and stuffed them in his pockets.

"Got your gloves?" I felt so much like my mother right then it hit me like a punch in the gut.

"Yes, ma'am." He patted his back pocket.

"Okay, well, hurry back and I'll have some hot cider ready."

He dipped for a quick kiss that ended up turning into a not so quick kiss before he stepped out into the throes of winter.

I closed the door behind him, trying not to worry about them freezing to death out there. Hopefully, getting more wood from the barn and refueling the generator wouldn't take that long. I started a pot of water to boil and looked around the house. It was a mess. The three of us had been cooped up and bored, yet not bored enough to pick up after ourselves.

I started with the kitchen, doing the dishes and cleaning the counters before I swept and mopped the floors. Working my way through the living room, I made a pile in the middle of the floor of random dirty clothes I had found all over the place. I found three shirts, a pair of one of the guys' shorts, and a bra (I have no idea how it got there). I swear I found five of Jacob's socks in between the couch cushions.

Yuck!

I did a quick dusting and fluffed pillows before placing another log on the fire and heading upstairs. Scrubbing the bathtub all three of us had to share now since it was just too cold to even try to take a quick shower, I realized I *really* hated sharing a bathroom with boys. However, I had denied them the right to use the toilet in my bathroom. They each had their own and they could clean it themselves.

Once I finished the bathroom, I straightened up our bedroom and organized the few things Luke had left around the room. He didn't know I called it "our" room, but that's what it was. He hadn't slept away from me since the night the guys came to the house six weeks ago. Or was it seven? It was so hard to keep track of time anymore.

I wasn't positive we were even going to celebrate Christmas on the twenty-fifth. We would be close enough, though.

Sex only seemed to get better as time passed and we got to know what each other liked and didn't. I hadn't actually found anything I didn't like for him to do and he found more than enough that he liked for me to do to him. We only had so many condoms, and the slick roads kept the guys from making many supply runs, so we were trying to spread the sex out and make the condoms last. It wasn't an easy thing to do, but we found ways to enjoy each other on the nights we didn't actually have sex. I smiled to myself. I couldn't even think of his mouth without getting worked up. And his hands. Oh, his hands were amazing.

I loved him.

L.O.V.E.D him.

Every night as we lay in bed, his arms wrapped protectively around me, I had to bite my tongue to keep from letting the words slip out. Telling him I loved him could end up bad and I for sure wasn't going to be the first one to say it. Yes, I was almost positive he felt the same way, but if he was holding back from saying it, there had to be a reason.

I wasn't ready for a nose dive into unknown waters just yet.

For now, showing it would have to be enough for the both of us. He showed me all the time in just about everything he did and how he spoke to me. I tried to do the same. I wanted him to feel it more than hear it.

On that thought, I decided it was time to officially move his sweet ass into our room. They would be back any minute and it would be a nice surprise for him if I had all of his things transferred over and in their place. I could even empty a drawer in the dresser for him. For me, that was like giving him a kidney.

If that didn't say, "Hey, I love you," I didn't know what did.

Decision made, I walked to my parents' door and turned the knob. The door swung open with an eerie creak before it lightly bounced against the doorstop next to the wall. My heartbeat kicked up a notch and my body felt stiff. I felt like at any second a ghost of a memory was going to jump out and slap me in the face. *It's just a room*, I reminded myself.

This was where you said goodbye, another voice said.

I stood in the doorway trying to keep my focus on the mission: get Luke's shit and get out. I really needed to move past it and just get it over with. My head said go, but my body wasn't responding.

Luke hadn't really changed anything. I could see his clothes here and there, but other than that it looked exactly the way it did the day Mom and Dad died.

Survive

Mom's dresser still held a jewelry box and a framed photo of Jacob and me at his graduation. They were so proud of us and I had been so proud of Jacob. I wished they could have seen the man he had become. He was a great man. Just like his father.

I closed my eyes and slowly let out a breath as I walked across the threshold. Opening my eyes, I unclenched my hands. Okay, I was in the room now. See, I could do this. I just needed to hurry.

I picked up the first shirt that was on the foot of the bed and tossed it over my shoulder. Instead of concentrating on one particular area, I let my eyes skim everything quickly so they didn't have the time to process much of what they were seeing. It was working, too. Finding Luke's things wasn't difficult considering they were so out of place. As I grabbed clothing, I tossed them into the hallway. I knew if I walked out that door, the hounds of hell weren't going to get me back in, so, I forced my body to stay.

I did hope they didn't come back while all of his clothes were flung all over. He would either think I had gone a little crazy or I was kicking him out.

I did a quick glance at the closet and grabbed what was Luke's hangers and all. I brushed away a tear that fell as I saw my mom's sundresses and my dad's button-up shirts.

Cut that shit out!

I took a breath and turned around. Noticing a pair of jeans and a sock next to the bed; I bent and picked them up. Looking around the floor for the other sock, I got on my knees and pulled up the bed skirt and found the missing sock along with the duffel bag he had been carrying the first night he arrived.

220

I smiled at the thought of how nervous I was when he first showed up and pulled on the bag. To my surprise, it rattled. Picking it up, I set it on the bed, staring at it. *Okay, do I open it? Surely he wouldn't care.* I did want to get all of his stuff put away in the room.

Who was I kidding? I knew there was something in that bag he didn't want us to see. What if what was in the bag was the thing he had been hiding from us? Did I really want to see it if it could change everything? How could I *not* look if it *could* change everything?

Taking a deep breath, I said a little prayer that the bag was full of skittles making all that noise and he hid them because he didn't want to share.

If I had skittles, I wouldn't share.

I slowly unzipped the bag, the theme song of *Indiana Jones* playing in my head as it fell open. My eyebrows came together and my heart pounded heavy against my ribcage. I was trying to process what I was looking at, but didn't quite understand what it was I was actually seeing.

Why would Luke be carrying a duffel bag full of prescription pill bottles?

My legs felt shaky and my head dizzy. My body was understanding the seriousness of this more than my head was. I squinted my eyes at the bottles and forced myself to focus.

Was he a drug addict? Placing my fingers on my temples, I tried to think back on any instances where he may have looked like he was high or not exactly present, but none came to mind. Just as that thought slipped away, another popped in my head.

Oh my God, did he have all this medicine available while Jacob lay dying from infection? While we made the dangerous trip to town, met a crazy man, and had that same crazy man and his band of idiots come out to the farm only to force me to kill someone and almost get raped?

Anger packed every ounce of my body. I thought this must be what the Hulk felt during his change–like every cell was being torn apart and mutated into pure anger. I hadn't realized I was crying until I watched a teardrop splatter onto one of the bottles. Who the hell was I in love with?

I picked up one of the bottles and read the label. Hydrocortisone? Wasn't that something that was rubbed on the skin? I picked up more bottles and they were either hydrocortisone or something called fludrocortisone. Each one had a different name and address. The states ranged from Colorado to Arkansas. I shook my head and dug through the bag some more, hoping there was some sort of letter explaining what I was looking at.

Okay, so the majority of them were the hydrocortisone, only a few of the fludrocortisone. Nothing was making sense. What the hell was going on?

Freaked the hell out, I started unzipping any and every zipper on the bag until I found a journal-style notebook. Okay, maybe now I would get some answers.

Not trusting my shaking body to hold me up much longer, I sat on the edge of the bed and opened to the first page. There was a picture of a man who looked an awful lot like Luke, just much thinner and younger. I flipped the photo over but found it blank. There was another photo behind it. It was a family photo out of a regular camera. Obviously, this was pre-plague days and it was clearly

Luke's family because he stood in the middle of them as they all smiled back to the camera. They all had the same hair and smile.

Luke had his arm around the boy from the other photo and a little girl in his arms. I closed my eyes and tried to catch my breath. He looked so natural carrying that toddler and so content surrounded by his family.

The guy in the photo by himself had to be Adam.

I pulled the photo closer to my face since the waterworks coming from my eyes were making it hard to see. Adam was really attractive. He looked almost identical to Luke, their only visible differences were their size and eyes. Adam's eyes were a deep green to Luke's silver-blue. He was maybe nineteen or twenty in the photo. He looked happy with his wide smile that matched the one Luke had begun to show more and more as time went by.

More tears rolled down my face. I hated that Luke hadn't trusted me or cared for me enough to show me these photos before. I wanted to punch him in the face.

I set the photos to the side and took a deep breath as I opened the notebook again. Well, if I thought I would get answers from this, I was wrong. I didn't understand any of it. It held page after page of letters and numbers listed in rows. There had to be a way to decipher this obvious code, but I had no clue how to do it. I wasn't good at puzzles; I couldn't even manage a Sudoku puzzle.

I flipped through the pages–each the same as the last– and about ten pages in it went blank. I went back until I found the last page. It was only half full. I read the last line.

ACW J AR WS2

Figuring that the last entry would be the most recent, I stared at the code trying to make sense of it. ACW. ACW. What could ACW mean? Air conditioning weights? Allergy climate weather? That made no sense either. Why did it feel so familiar?

I glanced up and looked around knowing I was missing something and that's when I saw it. A monogramed towel I had gifted my parents on their twenty-fifth wedding anniversary.

Allen. Carol. Williams. No. It couldn't be, could it?

A cold chill ran up my spine. My breathing began picking up pace as I tried to think of what the other part meant if it was indeed the initials to my parents. J AR.

Jasper freaking Arkansas.

Holy shit!

I didn't know what it ; I just knew it was bad. This was all *very* bad and I was terrified. I didn't want to be terrified, so I replaced that feeling with anger. Lots and lots of anger.

Placing the photos back into the front page of the notebook, I closed it and tossed it into the bag. I didn't bother zipping it up. How could he do this to us? I didn't know what he had done to us just yet, but come hell or high water I was going to find out.

The anger and pain fueled my body as I stood and yanked the bag off the bed and carried it out of the room. I glared at Luke's clothes splayed out across the hallway and took the extra time to dig my heel in and twist. If only he were *in* the clothes I might actually feel better. With a final kick to his favorite sweater, I stomped to my nightstand and grabbed the 9mm gun and carried it downstairs.

He was going to tell me what I wanted to know. I was done playing nice guy and waiting for him to tell me what secrets he was hiding.

I did my best to choke down the heartbreak of knowing the man I was in love with and sleeping with was either a fucked up drug lord for people with skin ailments or something else so explicitly bad, I couldn't wrap my head around it.

All I knew was he had better have a very rational explanation or he was out on his ass.

My heart plummeted at the thought of really losing Luke. Losing who I thought he was and what I thought we had. My entire body quaked with the force it was taking to hold myself together. I would not break in front of him. He would *not* see the hurt he caused. If he was not who he said he was then he didn't deserve to see me hurt.

I heard the sound of laughter before the sound of stomping feet on the porch. I stood, preparing myself inside and out as I held the 9mm in my trembling hand. The door opened and Luke walked through with Jacob right behind him. As soon as they saw me, the smiles fell from their faces and they were both on immediate alert. They scanned the room before looking back at me.

Luke took a step forward, his hands raised slightly. "Roni, what happ…"

"Stop! Don't you dare come any closer!" I yelled.

Jacob sidestepped him and slowly walked toward me. His eyes flicked to the gun in my hand and back to my face. I saw fear in his eyes. There was no telling what he saw

225

when he looked at me. I knew I was a mess, but couldn't have cared less what I looked like.

"Sissy, what's wrong? Did something happen?"

I bent and grabbed the duffel bag with my free hand and threw it at Luke. His eyes went wide and his face paled as he caught the bag at his chest. "That's what fucking happened."

"Roni, I can explain." He set the bag gingerly on the floor and took another step toward me, his eyes filled with pain. Could he see the pain he was causing me? How badly he was hurting me?

"You bet your ass you're going to explain," I spat out.

"Hold up," Jacob said, looking between the bag and Luke. "Let's all sit down and talk out whatever the hell is going on."

I glared at Luke as he took a step back and sat on the edge of the recliner. His eyes pleaded with me. I looked just over his shoulder so I didn't have to feel anything except anger. Jacob pried my fingers from the gun and pushed on my shoulder until I sat on the couch.

"What are the pills, Luke?" I couldn't keep my voice from cracking. My *heart* was cracking. I looked at him and could see the guilt for whatever was going on all over him.

"What pills?" Jacob asked sitting next to me and rubbing the middle of my back.

"He has a bag literally full of hydrocortisone."

"It's for my brother," Luke said, dropping his gaze.

My eyebrows shot up and I shook my head. "What, does he have like the most severe case of psoriasis *ever* or something?"

Luke pinched his lips together at my sarcasm. Was that an annoyed look on his face? No. Freaking. Way. I could show him annoyed if he wanted it.

"Isn't that a steroid?" Jacob asked, his hand stilling in the middle of my back.

"Steroid?" I laughed. "Is *that* how you stay so big? You take freaking *steroids*? Or do you want Adam to be as big as you so you're saving them for him?"

"Damn it, Roni. You know me better than that!" His voice was filled with not only annoyance, but a bit of anger.

"Really, Luke? I'm not sure I know you *at all*!" I threw anger back at him and saw the hurt in his eyes.

Good.

Now I wasn't the only one hurting.

Jacob held up a hand. "Okay. Sis, calm down for a few minutes and let him explain."

I whipped my head to face Jacob, who looked at me with what he thought was a reassuring nod. I could not believe this shit. Jacob was always the one flying off the handle and here he was, calm as a cucumber while I was falling apart. I crossed my arms over my chest and shoved my back against the back of the couch like a petulant child.

He didn't know about the notebook yet, either. I bet his attitude would change when he found out about that.

Jacob nodded to Luke and Luke took a deep breath.

"My brother, Adam, has Addison's Disease." He ran a hand over his face, his features turned emotionless. "It was a very rare disease before the plague and he may be the only person left in the world with it now."

"I think I've heard of it." Jacob nodded slowly. "Didn't President Kennedy have it?"

"Yeah." Luke took another breath before continuing. "Adam is Primary Addison's Disease which means his adrenal glands just don't work. At all."

I averted my eyes to the wall. I didn't want to see the hurt on Luke's face and start feeling sorry for him. If it were just the fact that Adam had a disease and he had to have the medication for him, why would Luke hide it? There was way more to the story and I would find out one way or another.

I turned to Jacob for explanation. "What's the adrenal glands?"

"They're two glands that sit on the kidneys that release adrenaline." Jacob shrugged. "Luke could probably tell you better."

"They release cortisol," Luke piped in. I listened, but refused to look at him. Instead, I looked at anything except him. "Cortisol supplies the body with fuel to do basically anything and everything. He has to take hydrocortisone three times a day, every day, to *live*. If he doesn't take the medicine, he wouldn't survive long. If he happens to get sick, or God forbid, break a bone, he only has minutes to get an emergency dose of hydrocortisone or his body would go into shock. It could cause him to have a heart attack or go into a coma. Even emotional stress can affect him."

"Oh, shit, man. That's rough," Jacob said, his voice low and heartfelt.

Luke stayed silent for what felt like forever. I let it sink in. Adam had a disease. A very *serious* disease. Something that sounds like it was difficult to manage *before* the plague and I couldn't imagine how hard he has had it since.

"He was diagnosed at nine and it took forever to diagnose him. There were so many misdiagnoses. First we were told he may have leukemia, but they ruled that out pretty quick. Then we were told heart failure because his blood pressure was so low. After that, it was lung failure. He had lost so much damn weight and his little body was so worn out, he couldn't *walk* much less pass the fucking lung test."

I took a peek at Luke then and he was staring at nothing, no doubt looking into the past. I wanted to go to him and hold him, but I couldn't. He lied to us. He closed his eyes, shaking his head before beginning again.

"They did one test that told us he had Cystic Fibrosis. With Addison's, your body releases salts all the time. Salt is essential to everyone's body. That's what the fludrocortisone pills are for. They're a salt replacement," he explained. "Once they realized it wasn't CF, we were all worn down. Even the doctors. It ended up being an intern who tested him for Addison's on a whim.

"We really thought we were going to lose him for months, but he's a fighter." His voice dipped almost into a whisper as if he were talking to himself. "He's always been a fighter. You couldn't imagine the fight he's had every damn day, just to *breathe*. Sure, he can have a perfectly normal life if he has the right meds and nothing drastic has happened, but life has been nothing *but* drastic for years now."

I dropped my head so he couldn't see the tears in my eyes for the boy with the wide smile in the photos. I didn't want him to see the pain I felt knowing all this time he had to worry if Adam was okay while he was there protecting me. If that were Jacob, I would have already gone crazy.

I couldn't be cold to him. Not about this.

I lifted my head until my eyes met his. His were glassy and red. *God, please don't cry.* I don't think I could take it if he cried. "Luke, I'm so sorry about Adam. Why didn't you tell us before now?"

Why didn't you tell me? I wanted to scream.

His jaw turned to stone and his eyes hardened. "Because if I screw up, he's the one who pays the price, not me."

Okay, the pills had been explained. I could live with that, but he hadn't explained everything and I had a burning in the pit of my stomach that we weren't even *close* to hearing the whole story.

"It has something to do with the notebook doesn't it?" I asked, cold again. "Why are my parents' initials inside of that notebook?"

I felt Jacob go still beside me. "What notebook? And what the *fuck* do you mean if you screw up? Screw up what?"

"Explain it to us, Luke. Explain what all those pages with code are in your notebook." All the anger left my voice and I tried, but failed, to hide the hurt.

Luke ran a hand over his face and took off his coat, tossing it to the floor. Jacob followed suit, looking a lot more alert than he had when we first sat down, but not threatened. I looked up to find Luke's eyes tracing my whole body like he was trying to memorize me. Just like he used to do when we first met.

"I'm going to start from the beginning."

"Okay, considering I have no idea what the hell is going on, it's probably the best place to start," Jacob said.

I remained silent, not trusting myself to speak again.

Jacob's continuing calm was surprising. Wasn't he the one who had warned me so many times that Luke was hiding something and to be careful? What had changed?

They became best friends and Jacob trusted him now. That's what changed.

"As you both know, I was Special Forces when the plague started." Jacob nodded, but I didn't move. "I was based in Colorado Springs so I could be close to my family, but mainly to be close to Adam. He wasn't old enough to remember our father and I've basically been that person for him since he was born. Mom had to work all the time to keep a roof over our heads so Rebecca and I were in charge of the little ones. Adam had clung to me since he could walk.

"When he got sick, I was the only person he wanted, the only one who could comfort him. I was the person who lay in bed with him every night and swore to him I wasn't ever going to let anything hurt him." He paused, his face going slack and a single tear ran down his face. "I went into the Army just to have the money to pay for his medical bills and help mom with bills at home.

"When the plague hit Colorado Springs, I was on base preparing for a mission. I had been getting calls from Adam, but I couldn't answer them because we were in full out Code Red. When I was finally able to call him, he was in a complete panic. It's what they call Addison's Crisis. I couldn't understand anything he was saying because he was so upset.

"The twenty minutes it took for me to get to Mom's house were the longest twenty minutes of my life. The streets were complete chaos. When I got there, thankfully, Adam had already tripled his dose and was *physically* okay, but not emotionally. My mom, my sister, Rebecca, and her two *beautiful* babies were all dead. My baby brother, the one I had sworn to protect, had been sitting there alone with his dead family all day, waiting for me to call him back to tell him what to do."

My hands went to my face in horror just thinking of what they both must have gone through. I glanced up at Jacob and found his nose red and his eyes welling up with tears. We hurt *for* him because we knew what it felt like. Except we never had to lose a child. They had to go through losing two.

I leaned my body into my brother's and wiped away tears that were flowing out of control. Jacob wrapped an arm around my shoulder and tucked me in tight. Luke wasn't looking at us. I guessed he was doing everything in his power to keep from breaking down while he told us of the devastation the plague had on them.

"I loaded him and all the medicines we had for him in my truck and barely made it to my sister, Mary's, apartment to find she was alive, but barely. We stayed with her throughout the night, doing everything we could to help her,

232

but nothing worked. By the next morning she was gone too." He took a moment before continuing. "It was just me and Adam left. So, I did the only thing I knew to do to get him the medicine he needed and to keep us safe, I went back to the military base. And, it was the worst decision I had ever made in my life."

CHAPTER FIFTEEN

A sizzling sound came from the kitchen and I knew exactly what it was and couldn't be more thankful for the break. "Hold on, I need to put more water in the pot."

I took slow steps away from the men and into the kitchen. Setting a pitcher in the sink, I turned the water on, letting it fill. Leaning down, I rested my elbows on the countertop and placed my face in my hands. I needed a few minutes to try to process everything I just heard before I could bear to hear more.

The more would be worse.

How could anything be worse than what he already told us?

I shook my head at the thought.

They had gone through so much. Jacob and I had lost people, but not like that. At least we got to say goodbye. At least our losses didn't include children.

I straightened my back and dumped the pitcher of water into the pot, causing the pot to hiss. Putting the pitcher back under the water, I spotted a jar of apple cider I had put on the countertop a few hours ago. They had to be cold and thirsty. I let out a huff at my softening resolve to kick Luke out on his ass.

I heated the cider while I finished filling the pot of water and pulled out three mugs from the cabinet. The entire time I was asking myself if Luke could really be some evil mastermind. After everything I had heard, did I think he meant us harm?

No matter how I turned it in my head, the answer kept coming back as no.

I bit back the guilt I felt for holding a gun on him when he walked through the door. Sure, I still didn't know what the notebook was about, and it was bad, but I also knew he would never do anything to intentionally hurt me. Whether I liked it or not, he loved me.

Before I did any more judging, I needed to hear the rest of the story.

Taking the pot and cups, I went back to the living room to find two very quiet men. I poured all three mugs and set the pot on a towel at the coffee table. As I handed Jacob a mug, his eyes looked tired with worry. I picked up another mug and turned until I faced Luke and held out the mug to him. He leaned forward and held it with two hands, brushing his fingers across mine.

My eyes flew to his and I wished they hadn't. His beautiful silver eyes were filled with so much longing and regret it made my soul ache. Releasing the cup, I maintained eye contact, not sure what to do. I wanted to comfort him so badly, but I wanted to hear it all first so I didn't end up making a fool of myself and trusting him again just yet.

"Thank you," he said, his voice soft. The *thank you* seemed like it was for more than just the cider.

Instead of replying, I turned and sat back down next to Jacob and picked up my mug.

"So, you were about to tell us about the base?" Jacob prompted taking a sip.

"Before I go on, I want you both to know how much I appreciate everything you've done for me. I can't remember the last time I felt a sense of home or even laughed." He paused and looked at his mug before staring straight at me. "And, Roni, I've never felt for anyone the way I feel for you. Ever."

My breathing quickened and I placed my mug onto the coffee table. I said the only thing I could. "I believe you."

His shoulders slumped and he closed his eyes with a slight smile like that was the most important thing he had to say and my reply was the only thing that mattered.

I wasn't sure what I felt right then. Every emotion I could think of was taking its turns being front and center. I might be the most ignorant person left alive, but I *did* believe him. He didn't have to say he loved me for me to know. I just did. He had spent weeks showing me just as I had spent weeks showing him. On the other hand, I was so scared and angry that I had a hard time looking at him.

"When I took Adam back to the base it was chaos there too. About half of the base was dead or dying and all I could think about was keeping Adam safe. I knew that if we hadn't gotten the plague by then, we were most likely not going to get it at all.

"Just so happens that a Four Star General was at the base when the shit hit the fan and Marshall Law had been implemented right before communications went down."

"I remember when we were put on Marshall Law, but no one around here was around to do anything to enforce it," Jacob said placing his mug on the coffee table.

Luke nodded. "That's how it was there, so General Wells decided to take power and call in a draft of sorts."

"Meaning?" I asked. If he didn't hurry up with his explanation I was going to scream.

"Meaning, he began drafting any men he came across to the Army." Luke's top lip curled with disgust.

"He drafted Adam?" I asked breathlessly. Hadn't Adam been through enough yet? How could he even fight in the army when he would no doubt use up so much more adrenaline?

"No," Luke shook his head, "he didn't draft Adam. He did *use* Adam against me though. If I didn't do exactly what was asked of me, Adam wouldn't get his medicine."

"What the hell? Are you kidding me?" Jacob asked, sitting up and resting his hands on his thighs. Jacob was angry. I was angry. General Wells was a dickhead.

I closed my eyes and rubbed my temples with my thumbs. How could someone use a person like that? How could they hold a person's life over another's head to get what they wanted? It was disgusting.

Jacob's body was hard as a rock next to me. I rubbed the center of his back with the palm of my hands. Slowly, he began to relax. I would do anything for Jacob. *Anything.*

Just as I knew Jacob would do for me. Knowing that, I had to ask my next question.

"What did they tell you to do?" I asked gripping my mug. Whatever it was, I didn't blame him anymore. How could I when I would do whatever it took to protect Jacob.? Hell, I didn't even know Adam and I wanted to protect him. I also wanted to kick General Wells in the nuts.

Luke swallowed. His face was set like granite. His eyes dark like onyx. He was steeling himself for what he was about to say. I wanted to hold him–to tell him it would be okay–but I knew in my heart that it wouldn't. Things would probably never be okay again.

"I was turned into a scout. I'm supposed to go out ahead of them and find places for them to stay, food to eat, and men they want to draft."

"They're traveling?" Jacob asked as my heart kicked into hyper gear.

"Yes. They want to get to Atlanta. I leave them coded messages to follow so they know where to go." Luke couldn't look either of us in the eye, instead he stared into his mug.

My mind reeled. *Coded messages. Coded messages. He had to leave them a trail to follow of places to stay, food, and men. Allen. Carol. Williams. WS2. Water. Shelter. Two people.* My hands shook and Jacob took the mug from me and turned to face me.

"Veronica?" he asked, his voice shaky. I was sure I looked like death because I felt like it.

"The code. The code in the notebook." I looked up to find Luke's pained expression. At least he was looking me in the eyes, but those beautiful eyes held so much guilt. He knew I knew. "You were leading them here. To us."

"God, Luke, please say that isn't true," Jacob said, running a hand through his hair.

"That *is* why I was here the first night, but I swear to you, I would *never* lead them to you," Luke begged for us to believe him. "Roni, I promised you I would never let anything hurt you and I meant it. I will *never* let anyone hurt you!"

My face was wet and my eyes were swollen from the repeated bouts of sobbing over the past few hours. How is my body not shriveled into a heap on the floor with the amount of fluids I had lost already? My heart already felt like it had been turned to dust.

"You've been here almost two months now. How far behind are they?" Jacob stood and started pacing the floor before walking to the window and looking out.

"They are probably a month out, but you have nothing to worry about. I've made sure they won't know about this place or that the two of you exist."

"How did you manage that Luke? How can you be so sure they aren't going to show up here?" I asked, a chill running up my spine at the thought of more men coming to our home.

"I destroyed any trace of this farm, your parents, or you from the courthouse. This farm and house doesn't exist anymore. I've been scouting different locations further north of Jasper to keep them from seeing the smoke from the chimney." I let out a defeated breath and laid back on the couch. "I know what I'm doing, baby. They won't find you."

Jacob pushed himself from the windowsill to face Luke. "I don't understand why you have all that medicine if you're doing all this for General Wells so your brother can keep getting medicine."

"Because I want to get my brother the hell out of there and the only way I can do that safely is to stockpile as much of his meds as I can before we run. And I *will* get him out," he said flatly. Determination was set hard in his eyes. He looked like a warrior. Nothing and no one would keep him from his path of freeing his brother.

De Oppresso Liber.

Free the Oppressed.

"What can I do to help?" Jacob asked, shoving his hands in his front pockets while looking down at Luke.

"Jacob," I warned while Luke shook his head.

"The only thing you need to do is protect your sister," Luke said turning to look directly at me. "And maybe protect *me* from her."

Jacob snorted and looked in my direction. "You're right. Thought she was going to blow your head off when you came in."

"The day is still young," I said dryly and they both laughed at me. Laughed at me! I glared at Jacob. "There's more than one bullet in that gun, so I would shut up."

They threw their heads back and laughed again. I glared so hard I could barely see between my lids as Luke stood and shook Jacob's hand.

"Seriously, man, I'm sorry I didn't say anything sooner. I wanted to keep you guys clear of it all."

"I understand. I would probably do the same thing in your position, but I don't know how you've kept your head all this time." Jacob clapped Luke on the shoulder, which seemed to say something in man code because Luke thinned his lips and nodded to him. "I'm going to make us all something to eat and you two can talk. Yell if you need help."

Jacob looked down at me and winked. "Go easy on him, Tiger."

I tilted my head and gave him a sarcastic grin as he walked across the room and out of view. Feeling Luke's eyes on me, I swallowed hard and took my time moving my eyes until they found him. When I finally did, I was forced to swallow hard again. His eyes were soft and filled with something that looked like fear, but I wasn't sure the man feared anything.

"Can we go upstairs and talk alone?" he asked, his voice low.

I nodded, although I took my time refilling our mugs with warm cider. Luke began shifting his weight from foot to foot trying to keep his patience, but knowing full well what I was up to. I finally gave in and stood, handing Luke his mug without looking at him and started upstairs. Knowing he usually put his strong hands on the small of my back when we walked together, I hurried myself taking two steps at a time until I reached the top of the stairs.

Luke's clothes were still strewn all over the hallway floor. I was looking down at the mess when Luke came up behind me and looked over my shoulder. I turned my head toward him and he wasn't looking at the clothes, he was watching me. My stomach fluttered, so I stepped over the clothes, shoving a few with my foot as I opened my bedroom door and stepped inside.

I stood in the middle of the room, twisting my hands, not knowing what to do, but knowing I sure as hell didn't want to sit on the bed. That bed no longer evoked memories of childhood; it reminded me of Luke holding me in his arms and the way he would wake me every morning with a kiss at the base of my neck before he made love to me. Now, I didn't know what was happening between us, I just knew it wasn't the same.

Luke came in and shut the door before walking to me and stopping just shy of touching his chest to mine. My breath came in short pants which I miserably failed to control. When his hands cupped my face, my eyes stung with unshed tears.

"Sweetheart."

That one word pushed me over the edge and I went tumbling down. I leaned in and rested my forehead on his chest and cried. His arms encompassed me and I gripped his shirt in my fists. Anger, hurt, and fear rippled through my body in waves. I cried and cried as Luke held on tight.

"I'm so sorry, baby. So sorry," he whispered as he kissed the top of my head.

Taking a cleansing breath, I pulled away from Luke. His arms reluctantly loosened to give me movement, but he didn't let go. I wiped my eyes and looked up at him. He was so tall and big. My neck was tilted and his was bent, but there were still at least six inches between us. Was everything I had thought we had between us a lie? Was it all to get from point A to point B? If we were laying it all out on the table, I wanted to know the truth. No matter how much it hurt. I had to know.

"What was real with us and what wasn't? Was this," I waved a hand in the short distance between our chests, "just a way to get off on our mission? I know I basically threw myself at you, so was it a way to keep me off your back and on mine so I wouldn't wonder about what you were really doing?"

After my line of questioning, his grip on me became tighter, but not enough to be painful. "Are you fucking serious?"

I pushed back from him. Well, I tried, but didn't make any progress because pushing against him was like pushing against a brick wall. "Yes, I'm dead serious."

"Let's get one thing fucking straight right now." His voice was a growl. "Not a goddamned thing you and I have is a fucking lie. No, I sure as hell don't need this shit."

At those words my eyes went to slits and I placed both hands to his chest and pushed. I was beyond getting pissed that he wasn't letting me go. "Oh, you don't *have* to have *any* of this shit. And trust me, I don't need this shit, either! It may be the end of the world, but you sure as hell aren't the *last* man alive."

When his eyes went to slits, mine widened, because I *knew* I didn't look anywhere near that scary when I had tried a few moments earlier. He finally released me. Unfortunately, it was only to put his hands on both my hips, lift me, and toss me on the bed, coming down with me.

243

"What are you doing?"

"Shut up," his voice wasn't loud, but held enough anger to make me go still and shut the hell up.

I looked into his beautiful eyes. Eyes which had made my insides melt from the first moment I looked into them, and even though they were darkened with anger, they still made me melt. This pissed me off, but I kept it to myself.

He bent his head down until his forehead touched mine. "You drive me insane sometimes. You *never* do as you're told. You jump to conclusions, not to mention act before you think when you're pissed off."

I struggled to move, but he held me tighter and lifted his head.

"You always smell good. Like sweat peas. You're beautiful. So damn beautiful that sometimes it makes my chest hurt to look at you. You laugh and make me laugh. I can't remember the last time I laughed before I found you. You dream about the future and you make me dream about a future and I *never* did that. Not even *before* the end of the world. You're my future, baby. You, Adam, and Jacob."

I stilled. "Luke."

"Shut up. I'm not done."

Luke–big, brooding Luke–with his quiet demeanor and never failing calm was not calm and was *definitely* not quiet. I wasn't sure how to take it. I just knew the words coming from his mouth were beyond anything I would have assumed he thought.

"I didn't want to, I knew better, but I fell in love with you. Fell so damn hard and I couldn't stop it. Not after seeing the look in your eyes when I'm inside you. And as

244

far as *you're* concerned, I *am* the last man on earth because you're mine and I'm not giving you up."

"What did you just say?" My body went stock-still under him. I didn't even try to breathe.

"I said you're mine," he growled.

"You," I pushed my head further into the pillow, so I could look into his eyes, "*love* me?"

For some reason only he knew, he grinned devilishly. "Sweetheart, how could I not?"

My eyes widened and my mouth opened in shock and he took that opportunity to cover my mouth with his. I couldn't help but kiss him back. When Luke Greslon was kissing you, you kissed back.

He loved me.

Loved me!

Okay, so I continued kissing him as I pondered how to handle the epic news. *I would be stupid not to continue kissing the sexiest man alive*, I told myself as his hands started to roam. Why did I believe him? Yes, damn it to hell, I did. I loved him. I'd loved him for a long time and it was because of the person he was *regardless* of what he had kept from us. If I were honest with myself, his reasons for keeping all the secrets made me love him even more. He was trying to keep the ones he loved safe even if that meant carrying that burden alone.

He was a hero.

"Luke," I panted as his mouth moved from mine and to my neck.

He didn't stop kissing me.

"Luke," I said, again.

He looked up, waiting for me to speak as he pushed his erection into my pelvis before returning to my neck. I pushed against his shoulders until he raised up to his elbows.

"I need you to promise me something." When he watched me, I continued. "Don't be the hero with me."

His eyebrows came together. "What?"

"You can't be this one-man-against-the-world guy with me. If we're in this, we're in it together. No more keeping secrets just because you think you're protecting the guys or me. If we're going to do this, then we are partners. I'm not a weakling that will fall apart at the first sign of danger."

He leaned back until he was on his knees, repositioning my legs until they were wrapped around his hips before leaning back down to his elbows. This was a position we seemed to be in a lot. Only this time we both had clothes on.

"You're my woman, which makes me your man. It's my job to protect you and I will." I opened my mouth to protest, but he stopped me with a hard look that told me he wasn't finished. "I am highly trained. I'm used to getting things done and that normally doesn't include telling my family details about an operation. I've told you everything there is to tell, so I'm not hiding anything from you, but when I tell you to do something, you have to do it. No questions asked. Just do it."

Family? We're his family. Oh my God.

I said the first thing that came to my mind. "I love you."

His body went still before his mouth broke out into a full, wide smile that showed his dimples. Man, I loved his dimples.

I raised my head as I wrapped a hand around the back of his neck and pulled his mouth to mine. The kiss started gentle, loving, but quickly turned heated. I loved this man so damn much it hurt. I loved the taste of him, the feel of him. I loved that he was stockpiling medicine for his brother, so he could get him out of a terrible situation. I loved that he thought of us as family. I loved that I wasn't the only one doing the loving.

I tugged at the hem of his shirt until he lifted up enough for me to pull it off. When my hands went to his jeans to unbutton them, he halted them with his. I growled at him. He smiled again. I wasn't ready to stop, and thankfully, he wasn't ready, either, because he took his time pulling off my shirt and unhooking my bra. His mouth covered my nipple and my back arched into him as I dug my fingers into his hair.

I couldn't count the amount of times he had done the exact same thing, but every time felt like the first time. It never got old. Not with Luke. So when his hands slid down my bare stomach and unsnapped my jeans, I shivered. He broke contact with my nipple as he leaned back and pulled my jeans and underwear down my legs, tossing them on the floor.

"Why do I always end up naked first?"

"Because that's the way I like it," he replied, unbuttoning his own jeans and pulling himself free of them.

Survive

Seeing his gorgeous, naked body over mine was mouthwatering. I bit my lip in sweet anticipation. And knowing that he loved me and wanted a life with me made it so much sweeter.

"Luke," I did my best to growl. "Hurry up."

He gave a small chuckle with a grin, before leaning over me to grab a condom on the nightstand. He slowly opened it, and with shaking hands, I grabbed it from him. He full out laughed at this and I glared at him. Quickly sliding the condom onto his oversized cock, I pulled him down on me.

He kissed me and I wrapped my legs around his hips when he didn't enter me. I was getting annoyed–I wanted him inside me so badly, I was starting to shake. At this point he could blow on me and I was bound to come. I felt the head of him just at my entrance, but he still didn't enter me.

"Luke," I panted and gripped his upper arms.

He looked at me and ran his thumb over my chin, his eyes dark with heat. "I want you to say it again."

"Say what?" I asked, out of breath.

"Say it, Sweetheart." He pushed in not even an inch then backed up.

"Say what?" I asked, getting increasingly impatient.

"Tell me you love me."

His eyes held a desperate need–a need he wanted me to fill. He had been so strong and independent throughout his life, so seeing that weakness in him right then broke my heart. My loving him was important to him. Not just him loving me. He wanted me to love him back.

I lifted my hands and cupped his face as I looked into his eyes. "I love you, Luke."

Then at the same time his mouth covered mine, he plunged into me, muffling my cry. My hands gripped the hard muscles of his smooth back, as he repeatedly drove into me.

"You feel so good, Sweetheart," he said pulling my left leg up higher to my chest, giving him more access to go deeper.

It was building. I could feel the coils in my stomach begin to tighten with every stroke of him. Breaking my mouth from his, I pulled his body hard against mine, wrapping my arms around his back and shoulder. He kissed my neck and just below my ear, sending me straight over the edge. My body went to stone just before it turned to liquid. Once he felt my body pulsating around him, he moved faster and harder.

Finding someone like Luke in any lifetime would have been a dream, but finding him through all that the world was, was a miracle. He was *my* miracle. I loved him. He loved me. How did I ever deserve to have someone as beautiful and wonderful as Luke making love to me right then? I really didn't know. The one thing I *did* know was I would fight for it. I would do whatever I had to do to keep him safe. I wasn't going to give him up.

"I love you. I love you," I whispered between pants. "I love you so damn much."

Still holding my leg, he used his other arm to wrap around the small of my back. I loved when he would do that. He made me feel so tiny and feminine with him wrapped around me. Within seconds his body tightened and his hips dug in before he let out a long breath and relaxed on me. His forehead rested on the pillow next to me, as I stroked his hair. Tilting his head just an inch, he kissed my neck.

"You're unbelievable," he murmured against my skin.

I smiled. "You're pretty unbelievable yourself."

He slowly removed himself from inside me and kissed the top of my nose. "Stay here."

I watched his back as he picked up his clothes and went to the door. He peeked out before hurrying across the hall, all without making a sound. That had to be part of that training he was talking about. The man was like a ghost.

Without Luke's body heat keeping me nice and cozy, the chill in the air settled on my skin and made me shiver. I moved and picked up my clothes. I threw on my panties and bra and was pulling up my jeans when Luke walked back in and gave me a look of disappointment.

"It's cold," I explained.

He shook his head. "No, it's not that, though I *do* like to see you waiting on me naked."

I pulled my shirt over my head and stood. "What's wrong then?"

"My clothes," he said pointing toward the door, "in the hallway?"

"Yeah, well, I was going to surprise you with moving you in here with me, but, well, you know…" My words fell away as Luke stepped in front of me. I bit my bottom lip.

He put both palms on the sides of my face and tilted it up until I was looking at him. He took his time looking at me before he grinned and kissed me softly.

"I'll make a deal with you."

I raised my eyebrows.

"I'll pick up my clothes, but you have to go tell Jacob he can take the pink ear muffs off his head now. I just saw him wearing them as he walked by the staircase."

I closed my eyes and listened to Luke chuckle as he released me.

Shit! I had never missed fans, television, or any kind of noise more than I did right then.

CHAPTER SIXTEEN

"Good morning," I heard through the fog of sleep. I felt the warmth of his breath close to my ear, but didn't feel his body next to mine. Not liking the feeling of him being gone, I reached out for him only to find empty space where he should be. I groaned because I just wanted to sleep and I wanted that sleep to be while wrapped in Luke's arms. "Wake up, Sweetheart. It's Christmas."

The sound of a click and hum penetrated the fuzziness in my head. I opened one eye to investigate when I found Luke with a wide smile while waving something in his hand and a Polaroid camera hanging from a strap around his neck. I jerked up, fully awake.

"How did you…" I pushed the hair from my face and popped up to my knees. "Where did you… Oh my gosh!"

Grinning ear to ear, Luke pulled the strap over his head and handed me the camera. He leaned in and kissed my forehead. "Merry Christmas, Baby."

I held the camera on my thighs, looking it over. It was black and silver and old, but seemed to be in good shape for its age. A camera. He got me a freaking camera! He knew

252

I wanted one and he got it. How he managed it, I didn't know, but it was probably the best gift anyone had ever given me. I was in shock, not sure what to say.

I couldn't believe this caring, thoughtful man who painted my toenails and remembered things like me wanting a camera was mine. My eyes filled with tears, but I blinked them back.

"But I thought you gave me my present last night?"

He sat on the bed next to me, the heat from his skin radiating to mine, warming me to the soul. "Baby, I love that you call it a present, but I give you that all the time."

Getting to undress Luke was a lot like unwrapping a present. A really freaking hot present. My mind went to the night before and how I had climbed on top of him and rode him until I couldn't breathe, before he took over.

"I was talking about the perfume," I said, nudging his shoulder with mine.

"My family gave one present on Christmas Eve, but the good one always came on Christmas morning," he explained.

"I can't believe you got me a camera. *How* did you get me a camera?" I shook my head and picked it up, looking through the view finder to see a clear lens before setting it back down.

"Jasper is full of antique shops." It was more like flea markets, but I didn't correct him. "I went through them until I found one and a shit load of film."

I reached over and squeezed his hand. I didn't think anyone had ever done something so sweet for me. He went out and searched for the one thing I kept saying I wanted. How the hell did I get so lucky? "I have Jacob's and your present downstairs, but you're probably not going to be as thrilled about it as I am about this."

He chuckled and kissed my bare shoulder. "You bring joy into my life and you make me smile. That's a present no one in this world could give me except you."

I groaned and tilted my head back to face the ceiling. "Why do you have to be so freaking *amazing*?"

He laughed and I noticed the photo in his hand of me sleeping. I tried to snatch it from him, but he held it out of my reach. "You gotta throw that away."

"Oh, no. It's mine." He stared down at the photo. "I like watching you sleep and now I can anytime I want."

My nose crinkled. "You watch me sleep?"

"Yes. Every morning." He didn't sound the least bit embarrassed about his confession.

I tried not to think too much about him watching me as I drooled. I had seen myself in the mirror after waking up and there wasn't anything attractive about it, but if that's what he wanted to do, I wasn't going to complain. Especially considering most mornings ended with him giving me an orgasm.

"Let's get downstairs and I'll make us breakfast. Then presents and pictures!" I said, jumping from the bed and bouncing to my dresser to get clothes for the day. "We should all dress up for the pictures!"

"Oh God," Luke moaned as he stood.

I pulled a pair of jeans out of the dresser and pushed the drawer closed with my knee. "What?"

"You're not going to make us wear matching sweaters and pose in front of the fireplace, are you?"

"We don't *have* matching sweaters," I replied sarcastically.

"But if we did, you'd make us wear them, wouldn't you?" One side of his mouth went up.

Yes! "No."

He crossed his arms over his chest and watched as I pulled my nightgown off and slipped into jeans, and yes, a sweater. It was cold. I needed to stay warm. Plus, it was red and he liked me in red.

"Sure," he smirked as he turned to the door and opened it. "I'm going to head downstairs and help Jacob gather more wood."

"Wait," I said, moving until I was pressed against him. "Thank you for the camera. It's really the best present I've ever gotten, and well, thank you for just being you."

"I love you, Sweetheart," he said pushing my hair behind my ear. "There's nothing I wouldn't try to give you if you wanted it."

"I love you, too." I smiled and kissed him.

"Okay, I've had more touchy feely moments with you in the last month than I've had my entire life. I need to go do something manly, like break something."

I laughed and patted him on the butt as he walked away. Making my way to the bathroom, I took extra time putting on makeup and brushing my long, natural waves. I no longer worried what I would find when I looked into the mirror, because every time I saw happiness. I was happy. The world might be demolished and just about everyone I knew was gone, but I had never been so happy in my life.

Was that wrong of me? I had lost many hours of sleep, staring into the night, contemplating my right to feel so much joy. This is what I came up with. If my parents could speak to me right then, I know they would want me to be happy. Death, no matter if it was a single person or the mass majority of the world, was devastating to the ones who cared for them. But those left behind, the ones who made it another day, had to live.

I was going to be happy and live. For my father, for my mother, for my co-workers, and for all of their children. I was going to bask in the love surrounding me that so many people could live a lifetime not finding.

No, it wasn't wrong of me.

I ran a tube of lip gloss over my lips and went back to the bedroom to get the camera and slip my feet into house shoes since the house was cold. It hadn't snowed in nearly a week, but the wind was brutal. We were doing great on wood, but our food supply was dwindling like I knew it would, so we were all being careful with what we ate. It helped that we all thought it would be best to only eat breakfast and dinner and skip lunch. Luckily, Luke and Jacob's traps caught enough rabbits every day to make dinner a filling meal.

As soon as the ice on the roads cleared enough to be drivable, Luke would be back on them looking for supplies and making sure the Army wasn't on its way. That was a whole other fear that I wasn't going to think about. It was Christmas and I planned on enjoying every second of it.

Feeling good inside and out, I walked downstairs to find my family. I guess I had taken too long because the men already had breakfast made and smiles on their faces. It was a beautiful thing.

"Don't you look pretty today," Jacob said, surprisingly. Taken aback for a moment, I looked at him sideways before leaning down and giving him a peck on the cheek. "Merry Christmas."

"Thank you," I said, sitting down next to Luke. "Merry Christmas to you, too. Did you see what he got me?"

Jacob smiled. "Yeah, I've been told to be prepared for torture at some point today."

Luke chuckled and I glared. "It's not torture, it's capturing memories."

"Torture," they said in unison.

I choose to ignore them and put apple chutney on my oatmeal instead. "Did you two work out again this morning? Now, that's what *I* call torture."

Over the past few weeks the men had taken at least two hours each day to get their bodies in shape. I already thought both were in shape, but was informed--lectured--on the importance of keeping the body fit. It did seem to help the movement in Jacob's shoulder and he looked like he was getting bulkier. Luke just looked like Luke. Which was good.

Luke had also been teaching Jacob moves he had learned in the Special Forces. I hoped Jacob never had to apply them, but in the world we lived in it was more than likely he would.

"No, we took the day off. Figured you would have us singing Christmas carols all day," Jacob said.

I picked up a hand towel that was on the table and tossed it at him, missing by a good two feet. I really needed to work on my aim. "Just for that, we *are* going to sing all day and I know how much you love to hear me sing."

Jacob looked at Luke with mock fear and Luke laughed.

"It can't be *that* bad."

It was Jacob's and my turn to laugh. I could do a lot of things in life, but singing wasn't one of them. That and throwing anything with any sort of accuracy.

"It really *can* be that bad." Jacob took a bite, swallowed, then said. "You know the sound of nails on chalkboard?"

Luke nodded.

"It's like that with a thousand nails at the same time."

Luke turned to me and I shrugged my shoulders. Okay, I probably wasn't *that* bad, but even my sweet mother wore earplugs when I went through the whole wanting-to-be-a-rock-star stage as a pre-teen. And then there was that time my college friends took me to a karaoke bar and I got booed offstage. I swear if they would have had tomatoes, I would have walked away looking like a bottle of ketchup.

"One day I'll find something you're not good at, either," I said to Luke before taking a bite and smiling as I chewed.

"Gag," Jacob said, but Luke and I stayed looking at one another.

We finished breakfast while we chatted about nothing in particular. The three of us did the dishes together. I washed, Jacob rinsed, and Luke dried and put them away. I warmed a pot of apple cider and we made our way into the living room.

Jacob made himself comfortable on the recliner while Luke sat on the couch. I sat on the floor next to our artificial tree. For obvious reasons, the tree didn't have lights, but I had worked hard decorating it with ornaments and bows Luke had found in the closet of my parents' room. I thought it looked great and both guys helped decorate it, so it was special.

And even though they didn't act like they cared, I knew they liked having it up just as much as I did.

I handed Luke and Jacob their gifts. They were wrapped in newspaper I had found in the pantry. It wasn't pretty, but it served its purpose. They opened their gifts and tried to act surprised about the beanies. They were surprised to find the insides of the beanies filled with candy I had been hiding for months. I was pretty proud of myself for not eating it when I had the chance.

We opened Jacob's gifts next. I say *opened* loosely. We pulled them out of the old Wal-Mart bags he had put them in. He had found me five romance novels and gave Luke a brand new pair of work gloves. They were fantastic gifts.

"I already put yours in your room this morning," Luke said to Jacob.

Jacob looked surprised and so was I. Luke hadn't told me what he got for Jacob and I was very curious. We all stood and followed Jacob to his room. I walked in behind Luke to find Jacob in the center of his room, staring at the wall with a slack jaw. I turned to see what he was staring at and rolled my eyes.

"I think I love you," Jacob said. I wasn't sure if he was talking to Luke or to the posters of bikini clad women tacked to the wall flanking his previous poster. He was probably talking to the girls. He gave Luke a hard pat on the back and said, "I approve. You may continue seeing my sister."

Luke laughed. "Glad you like it."

I lifted the camera that was still strapped on my neck and snapped a photo of the two most important people in my world. Pulling the picture out of the slot, I watched as their smiling faces came into view while they both grumbled.

"So it begins," Luke said quietly to Jacob.

"Hey man, you do realize this is *your* fault, right?"

260

CHAPTER SEVENTEEN

C an't you wait one more day?" I asked, shoving a bag of apple chips into Luke's backpack. I kept my eyes down and reached over to grab a bottled water and shoved it inside, hearing the crunch of crushed apple chips. *Damn it.* "I mean, it's like a sheet of ice out there."

I stuck my hand out to snatch a can of soup to toss into the backpack when Luke's hand wrapped around my forearm and spun me around to face him. I stared at his chest. I was too afraid if I looked at his face, I would burst into tears.

When I woke that morning, I had a gnawing feeling in my gut that wouldn't go away. Luke hadn't been in bed with me, which was highly unusual, but wasn't the reason for the feeling. I had gotten up and started my day with a boulder of fear and foreboding resting heavy in the pit of my stomach.

It was a feeling I really didn't like.

At breakfast, Luke announced he was going to do a run into town for supplies and fuel. I had to grip my hands in my lap to keep them from shaking. Something bad was coming and I wasn't sure there was anything I could do to stop it. I just had to try.

Unfortunately, Luke wasn't having any of it.

He released my arm and put a hand on each side of my face. He lifted until I was looking into his eyes. What was staring back at me was a set of soft, silver eyes. Eyes that could make me do just about anything without even having to ask.

"Sweetheart, what's up?" he asked, running a thumb across my cheek as he studied my face. "Why are you upset?"

Not wanting to tell him I had an icky feeling I didn't know how to explain, I went with my prior argument. "I'm worried about you on the roads."

"Sweetheart, I'll be fine. The sky is clear and the suns out. The ice will be melted in no time." He lowered his chin until he was at my level and kissed my lips.

After his lips left mine, I turned my head and rested it on his chest, wrapping my arms around his back.

"I love you, Luke," I murmured against his chest.

"I love you, too, Sweetheart." He kissed the top of my head and pulled me back a few inches. "I need to get going so I can hurry and get back."

I gave him a quick nod since there really wasn't anything I could say to keep him there. Well, unless I wanted to tell him my womanly intuition was telling me something was up, yet I wasn't sure what that something was or if it even had to do with him. I had a feeling that unless

I had a reasonable explanation of why I wanted him to stay, he wouldn't.

I turned, grabbed the can of soup and a travel can opener, and tossed them in the bag. Zipping it up, I handed the backpack to him.

"Hurry home."

****

"Would you sit your ass down?" Jacob asked in a low but firm voice.

I released the curtain, letting it fall back into place, and turned to Jacob. I wasn't sure how long I had been standing at the window, but it wasn't long enough. Luke wasn't home. It was late. And by late, I mean *really* late. The sun had set hours ago and nothing.

No sounds.

No Luke.

Nothing.

"Sit, Roni," Jacob said again, but this time pointed to the couch.

I crossed my arms over my chest, stomped to the couch, and planted my ass down. My eyes went to the door, thinking if I stared at it hard enough Luke would walk through.

Where the hell was he? What if he slid off the road and straight into a tree? What if he was hurt, alone, and waiting for us to go find him?

"Get out of your head, Roni," Jacob said. My eyes flicked to him before they found their way back to the door.

 the the the

"I think we should go look for him," I said.

"We can't do that and you know it." Jacob leaned forward in the recliner, resting his forearms on his thighs.

I crossed my legs at the knees and my foot was moving back and forth ninety to nothing. I realized I was biting my thumb nail, so I yanked it out of my mouth and rolled my fingers into a ball in my lap.

"Calm down, there's no need to panic."

My foot halted mid-swing and my eyes widened. "No need to panic? No need to panic?"

"Roni," he gave a low warning.

"No! Do you know what happened the last time you guys were late? Do you remember getting shot and almost dying? Well, I do. I *freaking* do! I remember sitting here, just like this, wondering if you were going to come back, and if it wasn't for Luke you wouldn't have."

I slammed the side of my fist onto the coffee table when Jacob opened his mouth. I wasn't sure when I uncrossed my legs and moved to the edge of the couch, but there I was. Fear had turned my spine into an iron rod.

"He's alone, Jacob. *A-freaking-lone!* And *no one* to bring him back if he's hurt."

Jacob moved and was at my side in seconds, wrapping his arms around me. I tucked my face into his shoulder and fisted my hands into his shirt. I didn't cry, though. Not one drop.

I was too terrified to cry.

"He's okay, Sis. He's okay." He gave my shoulders a squeeze and pulled back until he was facing me. "He's the freaking Hulk."

"The Hulk?" *Where did that come from?*

He gave a low laugh. "Yeah, the Hulk. The man's a beast. Trust me, nothing is going to happen to him."

"But. . ." I shook my head.

"No, Roni, no buts. You're not hearing me, so listen," he said, exasperated. I clamped my lips together and glared. He shifted his feet and looked away, clearly trying to figure out how to say whatever it was he wanted to say. "Remember last week when we had the snowball fight?"

How could I forget? It was Jacob and me on a team against Luke. Luke picked the teams. I wanted it to be each man, or in my case woman, for themselves, but Luke tilted his head and I ended up caving to his wishes. By the end, it wasn't really a fight, it was more like a massacre.

"Yeah, I remember."

"Do you remember what happened?"

I couldn't help a shaky grin. I nodded.

"I've never seen anything like it," he said, shaking his head at the memory. "He was so damn fast. No matter what we cooked up we couldn't hit him for shit, but he never missed, and we were soaking wet by the time we waved the white flag."

Jacob has right. By the end, we looked like drowned rats and Luke was dry as a bone. What I remembered most about that day was how much and how hard Luke laughed.

My body might have been frozen, but my soul had been warm and cozy.

"He's a beast, Roni. Even more so when it comes to you. He'll be back because I don't think anything on this planet would keep him from coming back to you." He squeezed my knee before patting it and standing up. "Now, you're going to calm your ass down while I make something to eat. Then I'm going to let you win at a board game and wait it out."

I took a long breath and blew it out slowly before resting my back against the couch. I gave Jacob a nod and sent him on his way with a wave of my hand. He gave me a cheesy grin and made his way out of the living room.

I got it. I listened and I got what Jacob was saying. Luke wasn't like us mortals. He was quicker, stronger, and smarter than the average person. So, if he happened to have run off the road and wrecked the truck, he would run home. If there were bad guys out there, he would make quick work of incapacitating them and come home. No matter what could possibly be wrong out there, he would come home. Because of me.

I was his home.

He would come back.

With the thoughts Jacob cleverly embedded in my mind, I ate the soup he brought me and beat him at four games of Yahtzee. I tried to keep from looking at the clock or the door, but every now and then I couldn't help it. Especially when the hours kept ticking by and he still wasn't there. Jacob did his part by distracting me with a joke or something equally as juvenile any time he noticed my calm weaning. But it worked.

He would make a great husband and father someday. That was for certain.

It was one o'clock in the morning and I was yawning on the couch with one of my mother's crocheted afghans draped across my legs, while Jacob had the feet of the recliner up and the back of the chair leaned back. Both of us were laid back and the only sounds were coming from the crackling of the fireplace.

"Jacob?"

"Yeah," he said sleepily. He was struggling to stay awake. I had tried to get him to go to bed, but he refused, wanting to stay close to me. Maybe to be supportive and maybe to make sure I didn't make a mad dash out of the house on a rescue mission. Either way, it was sweet.

"Who's Laura?"

The slow, steady breathing Jacob had lulled himself into came to a halt. I turned onto my side with a hand under my head to watch him. He didn't move, but I could see his eyes open, staring at the ceiling. Maybe I shouldn't have said anything and wasn't sure why I waited until then to ask, but I did. And I really wanted to know.

"How do you know about Laura?" he asked, still not moving an inch. His voice was low, just above a whisper, and full of pain.

Okay, so maybe I didn't want to know who Laura was. "I...uh...you brought her up one night when you were drunk."

The room was silent for so long I gave up on him saying more, so I moved to my back and closed my eyes. *Damn it.*

I should have used a little more tact. I could have hinted around about Laura beforehand, so he could have been more prepared. Now, I felt like a predator waiting in the weeds for my prey to get nice and comfy.

I was a jackass sister.

"Laura," Jacob said, making me jump a little. I closed my eyes and listened. "Laura was beautiful. She was always smiling. Always happy. Her smile was one of those that made other people smile just by watching her. I met her the first week of med school. She wanted to be an Oncologist, and she would have made a damn good one, too." He paused, took a deep breath, and continued. "You would've loved her."

"Did *you*?" I asked, already knowing the answer.

"Yeah," another heavy breath, "I did. She was the one."

The one? Holy shit! Maybe there were people out there who said that about every person they dated, but not Jacob. No, Jacob wasn't the kind of man to throw words like that around. Not even in high school when he dated all the prettiest girls in school.

My baby brother had been, and still looked to be, in love. *How had I missed it? Had my head been stuck that far up my own ass for the past two years not to see that?* I thought over the last two years trying to remember any indication he was in love and there just wasn't any. We had lost our parents and everyone we knew, so, yeah, we were both devastated. I thought back even further, trying to remember if he ever brought her up before the world went nuts. He had been happy. But when had Jacob *not* been happy?

"She may have made it. *We* did."

He shook his head and laced his fingers over his stomach, his jaw clenched and his eyes closed.

"Seriously, Jacob. She co…"

"No, Roni! *She's dead!*" The words came out hard, making it clear he wanted me to shut the hell up.

So I shut the hell up.

"She was already quarantined at the hospital by the time I made it home. She's dead. I've dealt with it. So leave it alone."

"Okay," was the only word I uttered. There wasn't anything left to be said. I might want to do my usual thing and try to talk it out or find hope when there was none, but not this time. No. I was going to let him have the peace of knowing the woman he loved was gone and not out there alone, fighting to survive without him.

I couldn't do that to Jacob.

All the questions and answers were masked with the sounds of the popping of the fireplace and the heartbreak of the two people remaining in the room. I didn't look at the clock to know it was too late for Luke to walk through the door. He wouldn't risk being followed or his headlights seen to even try to come home. I just had to believe and know he would come home. That was something Jacob didn't have. His Laura wouldn't be back.

My Luke would.

CHAPTER EIGHTEEN

Jacob came through the kitchen door, kicking the sides of his boots against the door jamb to knock off the freshly fallen snow. I crossed my arms over my chest and leaned a hip on the counter and braced myself.

"So?"

"Sorry, Sis. I couldn't get it started. The battery is dead and even if it wasn't, all four tires are flat."

I closed my eyes and let my head fall forward. Mom's old Buick was our best option to go look for Luke and now that wasn't an option at all. We could walk, but even I thought that wasn't smart. That would be as safe as holding an apple on my brother's head and me shooting it off with a bow and arrow. I actually attempted that once as a preteen until Dad saw what I was about to do and grounded me from the phone for a week.

When we woke that morning and Luke hadn't made it back yet, I tried my best to stay positive, but it was difficult. As the day went on, my calm began to dissolve. It didn't help that I had repeatedly caught Jacob looking out the window with worry in his eyes that more than likely mirrored my own. At noon, we both remained uncomfortably silent. I figured the previous night's conversation about Laura and the growing concern for Luke was weighing on both our minds.

"What now?" I asked, not willing to give up.

He put his hands on his hips and shook his head. "No freaking clue."

I pulled out a chair from the kitchen table and dropped down, defeated. "There has to be something. . ."

"Listen," Jacob said, holding up his hand, palm facing me, his head turned toward the door.

I couldn't hear anything, but I jumped up and moved to the kitchen door and swung it open. Then I could hear it. It was an engine. Leaving the door open, I ran to the living room and yanked on my boots and coat. Jacob closed the kitchen door and walked up next to me holding a shotgun.

"Wait, Roni," he said. "It might not be him. Don't go running out there until we know for sure."

"Of course it's him." It was. I could *feel* it. I opened the front door and stood on the porch. As the sounds grew louder, so did my smile. Jacob stood next to me, the gun at the ready when the front of the truck became visible. Within seconds the truck was parking in the drive way and I was running to him.

He barely had time to get out and shut the truck door before I threw myself into his arms. Wrapping his arms around me, he lifted me to him, crushing his mouth to mine. I wrapped my legs around his waist and leaned back.

"You scared the shit out of me."

"I know, Sweetheart, I'm sorry," he said, kissing my forehead.

"What happened?" I asked, still clinging to him.

"Let's go in and we'll talk," he said next to my ear. There were warning bells going off in my head. Something in his voice that was screaming trouble. He began walking with his arms still wrapped around me and my legs wrapped around his waist like I didn't weigh more than a toddler.

At the top of the stairs, I let my legs go and stood on my own two feet. His arm held me tightly to him, so I wrapped my arms around his waist and reveled in the warmth of him next to me. He shook Jacob's hand with his free hand and we all walked inside.

"What the hell, man?" Jacob asked laughing and clapped Luke on the shoulder.

"Let's sit down," Luke suggested.

I wasn't ready to hear whatever he was about to say. It wasn't going to be good and I just wanted a few more minutes of normal—a few minutes to enjoy knowing Luke was alive and right where he belonged.

"Are you hungry?" I asked.

"Not right now. We have to talk." He didn't look down at me. Instead, he was looking at Jacob.

Jacob sat in the recliner while Luke and I sat close together on the couch. He wrapped his arm around my shoulder and pulled me even closer. Guess he missed me, too.

"So, what happened?" Jacob asked.

"They're close," he announced. We knew who "they" were. This was not good.

That feeling I had in my gut yesterday now has a name. General Wells.

"How close?" Jacob asked, now leaning forward in his seat.

"About a day, maybe two, out," Luke answered. "I ran into one of the scouts. I had to hunker down with him at the place north of town and he went back to lead them that way."

"So, what's that mean?" I asked even though I was terrified I already knew the answer.

He must have heard it in my voice because he squeezed my upper arm and kissed my forehead. "It means I'm going to have to go for a while."

"What do I need to do here?" Jacob asked. He was all business and ready to go.

"Stay at the house for the next week at least. No supply runs. Don't use the fireplace during the day just in case they have more people scouting. Other than that, just take care of Roni 'til I get back."

I wasn't ready. Not yet. Not when it hurt so bad to be without him for one night. I knew this day would come, but not yet. I closed my eyes and took a deep breath. If General Wells was close, that meant Adam was close too. He had to get Adam away from that crazy man. No matter how bad I hurt, I had to be strong for Luke. After everything he had done for us, it was the least we could do for him.

"When are you leaving?" I asked, swallowing the pain rising in my throat.

"Sun up tomorrow morning." He looked at Jacob. "Would you mind taking me up north tomorrow? That way I can be there in plenty of time and you will still have time to get back here before they arrive."

"Sure thing, brother," Jacob told him. "You going to be alright?"

Jacob called him brother and was worried about him. Luke was a part of us. Luke must have felt it, too, because he took a minute before answering.

"Sucks leaving man, but I miss Adam like you wouldn't believe," he said, shaking his head.

Jacob and I looked at one another and I imagined we were thinking the same thing. We could believe it. It would be torture if we were separated and not knowing where the other was or if we were okay. For that reason, I was happy for Luke. He and Adam both deserved a better hand than they were dealt, and hopefully, life would give them a break.

"I can't wait to meet him," I said, doing my best to put cheer in my voice.

"Get him and both of you get your asses back home," Jacob told him. That was Jacob's way of telling Luke this was home. I freaking loved my brother. "I bet you're starving, so I'm going to be a kickass kind of guy and make you something to eat."

Luke nodded at him. His next words had more meaning than just about getting fed. "Appreciate it, man."

Jacob went to the kitchen and I turned to Luke. He was so damn beautiful. He hadn't shaved in the last week because I had mentioned that I bet he looked sexy in a beard. Luke being Luke and trying to make me happy, started

274

growing a beard the next morning. I was right. He *did* look sexy with a beard.

"How long do you think you'll be gone?"

He twisted his upper body, put his hands under both my arms, and pulled me until I was cradled on his lap. He brushed a loose strand of hair from my face and tucked it behind my ear. "I don't know, Baby. It's going to be a while. I have to make sure we're far enough away when I do get Adam out that they won't think to look for us around here."

"I don't get it. Why does he want you so bad? I mean, doesn't he have plenty of other men than to go through all the trouble of hunting you down if you ran?"

He squeezed my hip. "Because I'm the best. He knows that. He knows if he didn't have my brother to hold over my head that I would take him out. And he has something planned. Not sure what it is. Maybe he wants to become the leader of the former free world. The man is a nutcase. There's really no telling what his end game is."

That didn't give me any warm and fuzzy feelings. In fact, it creeped me the hell out. Thinking of him out there doing the biddings of a madman wasn't how I wanted to spend my days.

"Can you maybe give an estimate on how long 'til you're back?" I needed a time frame. Without that, how would I know if he changed his mind about us? What if the madman decided he didn't need Luke anymore and killed him? How would I know when to start dealing with the fact that he wasn't coming back? Was this how military spouses felt sending their loved ones off to war? Not knowing what was to come? Not knowing how long it would be or if they would come home at all? It was a terrible feeling I didn't wish on anyone.

"Wish I could, but it could be weeks and it could be months, but, Sweetheart, I *swear* to you, I'm coming home." He put a hand to the back of my head and pulled me to him until our lips met. My arm wrapped around his neck and I kissed him. His lips were warm and soft against mine, his tongue gently caressing mine. He leaned back and looked into my eyes intently. "Nothing or no one on this god damned planet will keep me from coming back to you."

"I love you, Luke Greslon."

He put a hand to his chest. "'Til I die, Sweetheart."

"Foods up," Jacob called from the kitchen. "Come get it while the gettin's good."

Luke kissed the top of my nose and we both stood. He held my hand until we got to the table. Neither one of us wanted to let go, but seriously, we weren't ridiculous enough to cuddle through lunch. Plus, Jacob just might hang himself if he had to watch one more kiss.

I pushed all thoughts of impending gloom and doom from my mind and focused on the fact that Luke was safe right then and I had the day with him.

"Wow, Jacob, you managed this all on your own?" I teased.

"Yes, opening a jar of vegetable soup and heating it up takes talent," Luke chimed in.

"Okay, assholes," Jacob said, pointing a ladle at us, "shut it or you can heat up your own food."

"Oh no, you mean you'd make me open my own jar?" I mocked. Jacob slowly raised his middle finger while he sat down.

We each dished up our bowls and began to eat. Jacob and Luke talked about what supplies Luke was going to need and Luke reiterated we were not to use the fireplace for at least a week. It might get cold, but it wouldn't be unbearable. I tried not to think about Luke being out there in the elements, going without meals, or being cold. Luke was trained and he would be fine. I had to trust that. The man had made it from Colorado to Arkansas by himself and was in great shape when he got here.

"It's time for the three," Jacob said, pulling me from my thoughts. "You first, Roni."

I let the handle of my spoon fall to the side of the bowl and tried to think. I know what I wanted to say, but I didn't want to verbalize the depression I was feeling inside. Instead, I said. "I need a vacation somewhere warm. I want Skype." I winked at Luke and he gave me a wide smile. "I don't miss my apartment in Tulsa."

"Luke?" Jacob asked.

"No, brother," he said, still looking at me. "You go."

"Okay." Jacob sat back and crossed his arms in great contemplation. "Well, I've been thinking I need to find some books on how to make hydrocortisone and how to treat Addison's."

Luke's head whipped to Jacob. "Really? Can you do that?"

"I was in med school, so I know about the endocrine system and I know how to mix chemical components. I just need to know what goes in it and if we can find it. I can't make any promises, but I want to try."

"Holy shit, man. That's incredible. I'll do what I can to find books for you while I'm gone." Luke slapped Jacob on his good shoulder. "Thanks, man."

That would be amazing. I know it had to be weighing on Luke's mind on how to keep Adam in medicine indefinitely and if Jacob could possibly help would be huge. For all of Jacob's country boy façade, there was an exceptionally smart man in there. Jacob hadn't told me he had been thinking about trying to help it with Adam. Of course, it seemed Jacob kept a lot of important things to himself. Namely, Laura.

"So, little brother. What are you going to bombshell us with on your other two?"

"Well, my want is to build another house out here so I don't have to wear earmuffs to bed," he said with raised eyebrows.

Warmth crept up my face and I picked up my spoon and started eating again. Luke laughed and squeezed my thigh under the table.

"And I don't miss rush hour traffic."

"Guess it's my turn," Luke said. "I need for all this to be over and have Adam with us. My want is more of Roni's apple pie. My don't miss is walking through Kansas. That place is hot as hell in the summer."

He may have meant all three things, but I could tell by the way he still squeezed my knee that it wasn't what he *wanted* to say. Maybe he wanted to wait until we were alone or maybe it was the fact that Jacob just rocked his world and he didn't know how to respond.

If it wasn't clear already, Jacob had made it crystal clear that day that Luke was a part of our family and that meant Adam was, too. This was their home. Right here, with us.

CHAPTER NINETEEN

S o beautiful," Luke said as he took his time entering me inch by inch. My hands gripped the tight muscles of his upper back as I tried to pull him down on me to no avail. He shook his head *no* as he leisurely moved his hips back and forth. "No, baby. I want to look at you."

The single candle lighting the darkened bedroom danced on his skin, making the dips of his muscles shadowed and highlighting the ridges of his skin. He looked surreal, like a perfectly painted image of what a man *should* look like. He was the beautiful one. Honestly, I thought he looked like a superhero.

Considering this was the third time that night that we had made love—the first two being vigorous and passionate—I was beginning to wonder if he actually was, in fact, a superhero.

"I want you close," I said between labored breaths.

He laced his fingers with mine on each hand, hauling them up until my hands were resting over my head. His chest was pressed heavily against my breast, his face inches from mine. I wrapped my legs around his hips and leaned

280

forward to kiss him as he moved inside me. Nothing in this world had ever made me feel as good as I did at that very moment. His mouth covered mine, taking long, slow kisses before lifting his head. He studied my face like he used to when he first came here. Like he was trying to memorize me.

Every touch of his lips, every movement of his body, told me just how much he loved me without him saying a word.

How did I get this fortunate? Unshed tears filled my eyes, threatening to spill over if I so much as blinked.

"Don't cry, Sweetheart," he said releasing my hands and wrapping them around his shoulders before he wrapped his around mine. "I can't take it when you cry."

We held on to each other for dear life. His movements getting faster, but not rough and with every movement my orgasm built. I wasn't sure if it was all the emotions I was keeping bottled up or the pace he was keeping, but every second he was inside me felt like the best second of my life.

Seconds I could spend a lifetime wanting back.

Just as my orgasm came full force and my body clenched his, Luke whispered in my ear, "Remember this. Every night before you go to sleep, remember me inside you."

My muscles only marginally relaxed as I came down from my orgasm, but my hold on him didn't loosen. Tears I could no longer hold back were falling from my face in a silent plea for this night to never end.

"Say it, Sweetheart."

"I promise. Every night," I said just before his lips crashed into mine, his tongue no longer gentle. His hips moved faster and, the muscles in his arms grew tighter just before he leaned his head forward to my shoulder and came.

We laid with him still inside me and me running my fingers through his hair for a few more minutes before we both cleaned up, crawled back into bed and settled in normally with me on my side and his body wrapped behind me. He moved my hair and kissed the base of my neck and pulled me even closer.

"Everything is going to be okay," he told me. "You believe that, right?"

I nodded as I prayed he was right.

"What are you thinking?" he asked, running his thumb just below my breast.

"Just. Well, do you think Adam will like it here? With us?"

I could feel Luke's smile against my shoulder just before he kissed my neck again. "Sweetheart, he's going to love it *and* the two of you."

That made me smile. Adam meant the world to Luke and it would be extremely awkward and wearisome if Adam didn't care for us or the orchard. At least he would have Jacob around and they were basically the same age. Jacob could make *anyone* like him.

"I'm already ready for you to be back," I admitted. He hugged me to him.

"We'll be back before you know it."

That I doubted. I had a feeling I would know and remember every minute he was gone. Him being gone the night before felt like an entire lifetime. I didn't want to think of what I would be feeling until they were home.

"Goodnight, Beautiful," he whispered when we both went silent in our thoughts.

I laid my hand over his and whispered back. "Goodnight."

I didn't sleep a wink.

****

"Hey, can you grab a few bottles of the meds for Adam and throw them in the bag? Just two or three," Luke asked as he sat on the edge of the bed getting dressed to leave.

Luke had only been awake for maybe ten minutes, but I had already been out of bed for an hour. I was doing my best to control my shit before I lost it and turned into a lunatic. I had packed his backpack with a change of clothes, a few cans of food, and an envelope containing a letter and one of the Polaroid photos of the three of us together. He didn't know about the envelope. I would rather he waited until he wasn't here to read the letter.

"Are you leaving the rest here?" I asked, stunned that he wouldn't want to keep them with him at all times. I picked up the backpack from the floor and held it tightly to my chest.

"Yeah, I don't want them to find me carrying tons of meds. They'll know what I'm up to." He stood and gave me a quick kiss. "I need to wake Jacob up and get the truck ready."

"Okay," I whispered before biting my top lip. He eyed me closely. I was pretty sure he was checking to see if I was about to lose it, but I managed to give a weak smile. "Go wake Jacob."

He nodded, his jaw clenching before turning and walking out the door. I closed my eyes and took a deep breath, praying I didn't start crying until after he was gone. I needed to be strong. He needed me to be strong for him and I didn't want to let him down. Therefore, I opened my eyes and started moving. Keeping myself busy was going to be the only way I was going to hold it together.

Going to the back of the closet, I dug out three bottles of the one thing I couldn't pronounce and one bottle of the other stuff I couldn't pronounce. One night he explained it in terms I could understand. The main bottles were what Adam had to have to function at all. The other was to keep salt in his body. If he didn't take it, his body would dehydrate, amongst other things.

I unfastened the backpack and stuffed them inside, next to the envelope. I looked around for anything else I thought he might need before slinging the backpack on my shoulder and heading downstairs. If I packed everything I thought he might need, he would end up having to lug around an enormous suitcase. Luke pulling a suitcase on wheels behind him just wasn't something I could seriously picture happening.

By the time I made it downstairs, Jacob and Luke were already in the living room in quiet conversation near the fireplace. When they both straightened and stopped talking, I figured it was probably something to do with me.

I imagined it was somewhere along the lines of keep me in line or protect me at all costs kind of talk. Like I was some damsel in distress. Had they even one time witnessed me pulling a Scarlet O'Hara and fainting when there was danger? No. As a matter of fact, I had shot multiple men to protect them.

Of course they wouldn't see it that way. I had boobs; therefore, I wasn't as strong.

Men.

"What's wrong with you?" Jacob asked at my scowl.

"Nothing," I answered. I had to let it go. Luke was leaving any minute and I didn't want to spoil the last few minutes we had together for I wasn't sure how long. How they were acting was ingrained in them since birth. "Let me make you guys breakfast before you go."

"We don't have time, Sweetheart. There's food at the other place and Jacob can eat something when he gets back." Luke came up behind me, wrapped his arms around me, and nuzzled my neck. I closed my eyes and filed the moment and the feeling of him wrapped around me for the cold lonely nights to come. "You okay?"

I nodded, not trusting myself to speak. He leaned in and kissed my cheek before moving back to Jacob's side and leaving my body feeling cold and bare. I inhaled deeply, held it a few extra seconds and slowly let it go.

We would make it through this.

We were survivors.

Right then was the time to show them how strong I *really* was. My mother once said a woman could handle more pain than a man. She was right. I was feeling so many emotions right then that my core was crumbling, and no matter how badly it hurt, I had to fold it up and tuck it deep inside. I had to be strong for Luke. Strong enough that he didn't worry about me while he was gone. Strong enough to take care of myself and my brother without falling apart with him gone. I could be that strong.

I *would* be that strong.

I forced a smile as Luke lifted the backpack and Jacob pulled the truck keys out of his pocket.

"Time to go, Baby," Luke said, his silver eyes deepened with worry.

"Yeah," I said on an exhale. "I'll walk you out."

Jacob hurried to the truck and started it up to get the engine warm. I pulled on a pair of boots and enveloped myself in one of the coats Luke wore to work around the house. He reached down and held out his hand until I put mine in his. I averted my eyes from his face while he led me down the stairs and toward the truck.

When he reached the passenger door, he tossed the backpack in and closed it. He turned to face me. Cupping each side of my face with his hands, he looked down at me with those beautiful silver eyes. *Shit, this was the hard part. This was it. This was goodbye. Woman up, Veronica.*

I grabbed his hands and kissed each palm before wrapping my hands around the back of his neck and pulling him down only inches from my face. God, he was beautiful. I didn't think I could ever get used to what I saw and felt when I looked at him. And not just his clear hotness. His entire being was beautiful, and against all odds, he was mine. I planned on keeping it that way.

286

"I love you. Hurry your ass home."

With that, he bent the rest of the way and kissed me hard. His arms wrapped around my shoulders and mine wrapped around his waist. He broke away and kissed my forehead before opening the truck door. I only had to keep it together a few more minutes. Just a few minutes. *God, please, let me hold it together a few more minutes.*

"Keep a gun with you until Jacob comes back. Stay inside," he said, getting into the truck. I nodded with an eye roll and a smile. "Love you, Roni."

He shut the door and they started down the drive. I waited until they were no longer visible before walking up the steps and finding my way to the porch swing and dropping into it. I did it. I made it the entire goodbye without shedding one tear. I still wasn't crying, though I didn't know why. I felt like I *should* be crying. My body hurt like it did when I cried, yet I just didn't.

I stared at the limp hands resting on top of my lap. The hands that were no longer smooth and soft like they used to be. I had working hands. Hands like my mother's. Hands that took care of her family like I was taking care of mine. My mom raised a resilient woman and she would be proud.

Standing, I made my way into the house, inhaling the inside of Luke's coat before hanging it on the hook behind the door. I made my way up the stairs and toward my parents' room. Adam would need a room that was for him and made him feel at home. I had a lot of stuff to get in order before my family came home.

Without an ounce of trepidation, I opened the door and walked through. I put my hands on my hips and did a visual inventory of the space. The room was kind of crammed. Mom was not exactly a hoarder, but she did have issues with letting anything go that she thought she might be able to use later. Luckily mom had an allergy problem—not so lucky for her then—so almost all of her quilting and crafts were already boxed into plastic totes.

I walked back to the hallway and jumped until I was able to reach the chain hanging from the ceiling. As I pulled, the stairs to the attic slowly came down. I made my way up the stairs and poked my head through just enough to see if there would be enough room to store all of Mom and Dad's belongings. There was plenty of room from what I could see. It looked like there was just the Christmas tree and a few boxes of decorations and that was it.

Making my way back down the stairs and into the room, I picked up the first tote. Once I got it back to the stairs, I set it down and looked between the stairs and the tote. *Okay, I can do this.* I hefted the tote up to my shoulder and turned it sideways until the bottom was against the stairs and the side was resting on my shoulder. I slowly marched up each step, praying I didn't fall and break my neck. *Maybe I should have waited for Jacob to do this part?*

I reached the top and pushed the tote over the side into the attic. I made it up waist high before pushing the tote to slide it as far as I could without having to actually be *in* the attic. Visions of spiders, mice, and bats ran through my head and I gave an involuntary shutter.

On the third trip, I was halfway up the steps when I heard the truck come up, turn off, and the front door open and close. I closed my eyes and tried not to think about the fact that Luke was now on his own and instead concentrated on the fact that it only meant I wouldn't be waiting on the day for him to leave and now I could look forward to the day he would be coming home.

"Roni?" Jacob called.

"Upstairs," I called back to him. I could hear him coming up the steps and muttering under his breath until he reached the bottom of the attic stairs.

"What the hell are you doing?" Jacob demanded to know.

I kept going up the stairs until I made it to the top and pushed the tote over. I was probably in for an earful when I made it down, so I took my time situating the tote in the right position to push it out of the way without hitting the other totes. I made my way back down until I stood in the hallway facing my very exasperated little brother. "I'm cleaning out Mom and Dad's room."

He frowned at me. He was most likely debating on if he should go easy on me because he knew the issues I had with going into their room or if he should throttle me for being productive while he wasn't here.

Apparently, throttling won out.

"Why wouldn't you wait to risk your life until I got back so I could actually *help* you?" He ran a hand through his hair. "Dammit, Roni. Seriously. You *have* to stop doing this. We can't be worrying that every time we turn our backs, you're going to do something you shouldn't. If our minds are on rather or not you're in danger, instead of what we're doing, someone is going to end up hurt."

"I'm sorry. I didn't think it. . ." I was going to say I didn't think it was that big of a deal, but he stopped me.

"Exactly. You *didn't* think." I jerked back like I had been slapped. I supposed verbally, I had. Jacob rested both hands on his hips and let his head fall before looking back up at me, his eyes much softer. "Listen, I'm not trying to be a dick. I know you're independent. You always have been. But you're the glue. Mine *and* Luke's. If something happened to you, everything would just fall apart. So from now on, just try to think to yourself, would Jacob or Luke want me to do this? If the answer is no or even a maybe, just wait. Simple as that. Wait."

"Okay," I said quietly, tugging on the hem of my shirt. If my waiting meant giving Jacob some peace of mind, I would be more cautious in my actions. Well, for a while, at least.

"Okay," he repeated, obviously shocked I gave in so quickly. "Okay. Now, let's get the rest of those boxes into the attic."

CHAPTER TWENTY
SIX WEEKS LATER

I laid on my side, my head resting on my pillow, feeling the same dull ache I woke with every morning since Luke left. I couldn't move. Not yet. All I could do after my hellish night of terrible dreams was to simply stare at the photo of Luke and me that I had propped on top of my nightstand against the useless lamp, waiting for me to realize it was only nightmares.

Luke had not changed his mind.

Luke was not dead.

Luke was coming home.

It was the same mantra I repeated in my head over and over until I could convince myself of what was real and what wasn't.

Weeks ago, when the dreams started, I had put the photo of us nearby so it would be the last thing I saw at night and the first thing I saw when I opened my eyes. It was one Jacob had taken one night of Luke smiling brightly at the camera, his arms wrapped around me and my head resting on his chest having just laughed at something he had just said.

I couldn't remember the last time I really laughed. Sure, Jacob would tell a joke or story that would be funny and I might chuckle, but not laugh. Not really.

The photo brought me both happiness and agony.

Happiness of what we shared and the agony of not knowing if we would ever have that again.

Stop it! I warned myself. It would happen again. He would be coming home any day.

A knock came at the door. "Roni, breakfast is ready."

"Be down in a minute," I answered, not ready to use my voice, but kowing from experience if I didn't reply, he would come in the room to check on me. Occasionally, I wondered if he thought I was about to hurt myself. He watched me closely now. Closer than he ever did before.

The thought of hurting myself never crossed my mind. Not when I was still bleeding from the wounds the world had already inflicted.

Killing myself would mean I gave up and the world won. I refused to let that happen. Not when my guys needed me.

Sometimes, I would imagine Luke coming home in the middle of the night and panicking because I wasn't where I was supposed to be. I could see him walking into our old room and freaking out because nothing was the same. At first, I had a hard time sleeping in the master bedroom because I worried he would walk in, find all of my things gone, and walk back out. Then I would remind myself it was Luke and he would find me.

I sat up and rubbed the hem of the t-shirt I was wearing of Luke's between my fingers. I didn't try to inhale him like I had the first few weeks. His scent had left his shirts a long time ago and it would only depress me more to try.

Standing, I walked to the door of the balcony. I put my hand to the glass and leaned in, letting my breath fog the window. A heart appeared where I had traced it in the same place every time I looked out. I wasn't sure why I did this. Tracing the same line once more, I stepped away.

I pulled on a pair of jeans and a long sleeved t-shirt before going to the master bathroom and brushing my teeth and hair. I twisted my hair into a messy bun before stepping away from the mirror.

"Roni?" I heard muffled through the door.

"I'm coming." I yelled as I rolled my eyes.

"Hurry up. Food's getting cold."

"'K," I replied and stood still until I heard his steps fading away.

His constant checking and worry was irritating. It wasn't like I stayed in bed all day. Sure, if he didn't make breakfast I probably would skip the meal, but I wasn't starving myself. I was eating plenty. Plus, it didn't hurt him to help out around the kitchen more. I tended the house, the yard, and the chickens just like I always had. I functioned normally every day just like he did. Yeah, I didn't like to talk about Luke or Adam much, but he couldn't blame me for that.

Maybe it was because I hadn't cried yet. Like, at all. Not one tear. Not when I was alone. Not when I laid in bed at night and kept my promise to Luke to remember him inside me. Not even when I had nightmares of Luke's body lying dead in a ditch. I still wasn't sure what stopped me from crying, but it just didn't happen. More than likely, that's what had Jacob so worried. I had always been overly sensitive and cried way more than a grown woman should. Not anymore, though.

I just assumed I had womaned up like I should have a long time ago.

I made my way downstairs and sat across from a waiting Jacob. He gave me a weak smile and bent his head to take a bite of the oatmeal. A lock of hair fell across his forehead and over his eye and he moved it out of his view. I hadn't realized his hair had gotten so long. Why hadn't he said anything?

"Want a haircut tonight?" I asked him before taking a large bite. Not bothering to add brown sugar or apple chutney to it, I just wanted to get the task of eating over with so I could get to work.

Jacob's eyebrows shot up and he nodded. "Yeah, I would appreciate it."

I tilted my head slightly, watching him this time. *Why did he look so surprised I had asked?* He had always been a stickler about his hair. I couldn't remember the last time he let his hair get so long. Actually, I couldn't *ever* remember a time he let it get this long. "Why haven't you asked me to cut your hair?"

He hesitated before shrugging his shoulders and taking a bite.

"Jacob," I said, my voice stern, "why haven't you asked?"

294

He was midway to his mouth with another spoonful before he set it back in the bowl. Sitting back with his shoulders slumped and his hands in his lap, he looked me straight in the eyes. His eyes looked sad. The look wasn't just *in the moment*, but more like the sadness had settled in and been there for some time. *How did I not see this before?*

"Because," he said then stopped to take a breath before continuing. "Because I didn't want to bother you."

Huh? I thought. It hurt that he thought it would be bothering me, but that wasn't what he was going to say. I wasn't sure what had stopped him from saying what he wanted to, but I wasn't letting it go. This wasn't like him. The hair. The eyes. This wasn't Jacob.

"Bullshit, try again." I said and when he rolled his eyes, I pushed, "Why? The *real* reason."

He nodded, his lips pursed. "Okay, you want the real reason? I'll give you the real reason. I walk around on damn eggshells all the time, thinking something I do or say will be the thing that makes you crack. You walk around with the lights on, but nobody's home."

Stunned, I sat back in my chair with widened eyes. Okay, so I had been distant. I wasn't going to crack. Was I? Maybe I was, but I was still me. He wasn't done yet. I wanted the reason and he sure as hell was giving it to me.

"I try to talk to you, but you stare at walls like you don't even hear me. It's like I'm not even here. I get it. I really do. You miss him. *I* fucking miss him, Roni. But you know what? I missed Laura, but did I turn into a zombie? No, I didn't. I didn't, because you needed me."

"Jacob, I . . ." I tried to tell him I didn't mean to ignore him, but he couldn't hear me. He was right, though. I didn't know about Laura because he kept his head together for me. Obviously, he had been sitting on these thoughts for a while and needed to get it out, so I was going to sit back and let him.

"Well, I am here and I still need you and you act like you couldn't care less if I'm even here if he's not. You didn't even remember my birthday." With that, he stood forcefully, causing the chair to tilt back and clatter to the floor. He didn't bother to pick it up before he stomped out of the room.

His birthday? His birthday was in January and it was… it was February and I had seriously forgotten his birthday! I was a horrible sister. I was *beyond* horrible. I was a shit sister.

I jumped up and ran in front of him, blocking his path. He didn't deserve for me to treat him this way. Having taken advantage that he would always be there, I allowed his feelings be pushed to the wayside because I was drowning in my own sorrows. I hadn't taken care of him. I hadn't done my part. I hadn't even bothered to remember to tell him happy birthday.

"Jacob. Oh God, Jacob, I'm so sorry." I slammed myself into him and wrapped my arms around him. "I need you, Jacob. I need *you*. I'm so sorry."

He tugged his arms free from my hold and hugged me tightly.

"I've just been so scared. I didn't think . . . If you weren't here, I wouldn't make it. I love him so much it's killing me inside, but you're my world. Without you, I would already be dead."

He swayed from side to side, rocking me. He ran a hand over my hair and patted my back. "About damn time, Sis."

I leaned back and looked up at his amused face. His hair was still covering his dark green eyes that were so much like my own. I was so going to cut his hair and then I was going to make him an amazing dinner for having to put up with me the way I had been.

"What do you mean, about damn time?"

"You're back. You're still alive in there." He hugged me again and let me go. Slipping a cap hat on his head and turning back to me. "You coming out soon?"

"Yeah, I'll be out in a few."

His face beamed, making me feel like shit for not taking into account how he must be feeling all this time. He said he missed Luke too. Luke and he had gotten close, like brothers, before he left. I really hadn't thought about that at all. I really was an idiot.

He opened the door and stepped out, closing it behind him before immediately opening it and sticking his head through with a childish grin. "Love you, Sissy."

I felt the first real smile that I had had in weeks spread across my face. "Love you, too, butthead."

"It's warm out, so you don't need to bundle up," he said before closing the door again.

With that, he closed the door and I stood staring at it, thinking about what he said. Warm out? My eyes slid to the living room windows and bright light shined through. How could that happen already? It had been a mild winter, but warm? It felt too early for that.

I walked to the makeshift calendar Jacob and I had made to keep track of the days once our calendars went out. I rolled my eyes. *Valentine's Day? For fuck's sake. Come on.* I looked up to the ceiling, speaking to whoever was listening up there.

"Seriously, when's enough, enough?"

CHAPTER TWENTY-ONE

I t took close to an hour to finally make my way outside and find Jacob. He was pulling the tarp off the chicken coop so I went to help him. We had moved the chickens from the barn back to their home a few weeks earlier because it had warmed up some and they preferred to be in their normal environment. The chickens jumped around the fenced area, excited to see us. At least, that's how I liked to think of it. They probably just knew us being there meant it was time to eat.

"Thought they could use some sun today. If it turns cold, I'll put the tarp back up."

I turned my face toward the sun and closed my eyes, hoping Luke was feeling the same warmth I was. My chest tightened. Sometimes he felt so close. Like I would turn around and see him standing there. I opened my eyes and put those thoughts away.

"What are your plans for today?" I asked, digging a handful of feed out of the bag Jacob had out and tossing it to the eager chickens before looking at him.

"I need to get some gas from the cellar and check on the generator since it's been making some noise. The fireplace needs cleaned out since it looks like we could probably get away with not using it anymore." He ran a hand over the back of his neck as he checked off his list. "Then I need to get on the stack on the stove. I think there's a block in there or something, and the sink is dripping, so I have to figure that out. After that, I figured I could load up the rest of the firewood on the side of the house and take it to the barn so it'll be ready for next winter."

I raised my eyebrows. "Impressive. Okay. How about I go to the cellar and get the gas and I can clean out the fireplace." He gave me that look, so I said, "Come on, I could use a walk to clear my head and it's the cellar, not a trip to town. I'll take a gun if that makes you feel better."

He pulled off the cap and ran a hand over his hair, reminding me again of what a horrible sister I had been for weeks, and put the cap back on. "Okay, how about we do the stuff inside and then, if you take the gun, you can go down to the cellar while I start on the wood. Deal?"

"Deal," I agreed with a grin and a raised fist. He rolled his eyes and fist bumped me before he put an arm around my shoulder and walked us back to the house.

As soon as we hit the door, we got to work. I found the tin ash bucket and used a little sorry excuse for a shovel to clean the fireplace while Jacob worked on the stove. I filled the tin and lifted to take it outside when my eyes found a Polaroid photo of the three of us posing for cheesy Christmas photos resting on the mantle. My chest tightened.

Come home, Luke.

I ripped my eyes away from the photo and numbly carried the bucket of ashes to the burn barrel. He felt so close, but so damn far away. It drove me crazy. I leaned my head back with closed eyes, soaking in the sun's energy to pull myself back out of that place I had been in for so long. Most of the time, I felt like sanity and insanity were playing an evil game of tug of war in my head. And sanity's arms were starting to wear out.

A cool wind blew over me and I opened my eyes to find Jacob standing on the porch, watching me with hands in his front pockets. I gave myself a mental shake and smiled at him.

"Did you get it fixed?" I walked toward him and stopped at the bottom of the stairs and looked up at him. I really wasn't in the mood to talk, but apparently that was a going trend for me, but I sucked it up for Jacob's benefit.

He shook his head. "Good as it's going to get until I can hunt down another stack. Sink's fixed, though. Well, for now."

I snickered and pointed to him. "If we end up with the downstairs flooded, you're cleaning it."

"Sure! But don't ask for my help next time you want hot water lugged up the stairs." He gave a gotcha grin and some of the sadness in his eyes from earlier eased away.

I stuck my tongue out at him and smiled. "What's next?"

"Go get your gun and a flashlight. That generator is getting louder, so I want to take a look at it while you get the gas."

Survive

I hurried past him and up the stairs, picked up my handgun, and secured it in the waistband at the back of my jeans. Going to the cellar would be the furthest I had been away from the house since Luke and I had to hunt down antibiotics for Jacob. It was a sad day when a walk to the cellar felt like an adventure.

As time went by, my world seemed to be getting smaller and smaller.

I stopped by the kitchen and retrieved a flashlight, flicking it on and off to make sure the batteries were still working. I lucked out and they were, but doubtfully for too much longer. Jacob was still waiting on the porch when I made it back outside. "I got it."

Concern etched the corners of his mouth, but he nodded. "Be careful and pay attention to everything."

I was proud of myself for not rolling my eyes. Instead, I held two fingers up in a peace sign. "Scouts honor."

"You're such a dork," he said.

"I know," I said and leaned in and kissed him on the cheek before trotting down the steps. "I'm going to walk *very* slow!"

"Roni," he called in warning. "Don't make me come after you."

I started toward the row of trees and looked over my shoulder to him. "Love you!"

I slowed my pace once I hit the tree line. It was so peaceful out there. The bare apple trees had an eeriness I had always found beautiful. Not even one leaf lingered, just a thick stock of branches refusing to give in to winter. *I was refusing, too,* I thought.

302

I made it past the orchard and about fifty feet into an open field to the cellar that was tucked in the ground. If I didn't know where it was, I would have never guessed it was there, which made it a perfect hiding place. I reached down and opened the metal door that once was my playhouse while the adults were tending to the orchard. Turning on the flashlight, I pointed it down the dark steps. The air rising up was musty, but not moldy. That was a good sign that all the contents had made it through the winter unscathed.

I took a deep breath, probably my last of fresh air for a few minutes, and made my way down the stairs. When I hit the bottom, I scanned the metal floor of the entire cellar with the light, checking for any mice that might have made this place their home. There were none! *Thank God.*

My next inspection was of the bench on one side and the cot sized bed on the back wall. Everything looked good, so I set the flashlight pointed toward the ceiling, illuminating the room, so I could have both hands free. I checked the row of gas cans and all seven of them were still full. I quickly checked the plastic tote holding a shitload of those military meals that were not exactly appetizing, but had enough calories to make it through a day on one package. Everything seemed to be just fine. Those meals even had a few more years before they, too, would expire.

I lifted a plastic container of gas in each hand and walked them to the top of the stairs and set them down. When I raised up, I could faintly hear something, but couldn't quite make it out. I closed my eyes and tilted my head trying to decipher the sound, but the sound of the fallen leaves in the wind was keeping the sound from being clear. I waited another second before deciding it was my imagination and went back into the cellar. I straightened the room the best I could and decided I would come back later with a few rags and cleaning supplies. Just leaving the door open for an hour or two would do a lot to get the smell out.

I picked up the flashlight and moved up the stairs, stopping when I was far enough up that my head was above ground. My pulse jumped, my arms shook. That was the sound of engines. Not just one, but multiple engines, and they were at the house. My only thought was for Jacob.

I ran up the remaining steps in such a rush, I tripped and hit my shin on the lip of the entrance. Cursing and biting back the pain, I kept moving. I didn't bother closing the door to the cellar or picking up the gas. I needed to get back to Jacob. Yanking the handgun out of my waistband, I gripped the handle as I took off in a run toward home.

I stayed on the edge of the last row just in case I needed to make a quick dash for the woods. About halfway there, multiple voices filled the air, but were still far enough away that I couldn't make out any words. One thing was for sure, they were all male. I stopped in my tracks and squatted down, low to the ground, and crawled until I could see the house through the trees. I was still too far away, but I needed to make smart choices and not jump in guns blazing, making things worse.

Jacob could be hiding somewhere safe, and if I went into the fray I would be putting not only myself, but him in danger because I didn't use my head. I would never forget the lesson Jacob taught me the day he dropped Luke off. If they couldn't trust that I wouldn't do something risky then they were in danger, constantly worrying what I would do. That wouldn't happen this time.

I didn't see our truck, but I could see four other vehicles in the drive. Two were trucks, one older four door car, and one military looking truck. My heart skipped a beat. Could it be Luke? *No*, I quickly dismissed the idea. Luke would never risk bringing anyone else here other than Adam. Where was Jacob? Did he go somewhere or know that people were coming and hide the truck?

I looked around me, trying to determine my best plan of action. I was still a good ways from the house and about a hundred yards from the barn. The barn would probably be my best bet. I could go through the back entrance and climb into the loft so I could see better. Heck, Jacob was probably up there right then, hoping I didn't walk right up to the house and tell the people to leave.

Gun in hand, I crawled toward the barn, taking my time and stopping from time to time to check if anyone had spotted me. The sun was warm on my back, but the ground was still cold and damp, causing the knees of my jeans to soak through to my skin. The house was much closer now and I could clearly see two men, probably in their twenties, standing on the porch talking to each other. The two men were carrying large automatic guns and held them like they knew their way around a gun.

Who the hell were these people and why were they there?

I started moving again. About twenty feet from the barn and the most dangerous part because there wasn't any cover, I heard Jacob's voice coming from beside the house with another voice that I prayed I had not imagined. I whipped my head around and every muscle in my body turned to liquid.

Luke.

It was Luke.

Oh my God, it was really him. He was alive. He was home!

I was just about to raise to a stand and run to him when I noticed the mood of the men begin to change from relaxed to alert. Jacob looked pissed off. Luke had a hard set in his jaw and was surveying the surroundings like he was waiting for someone. Like he was waiting for me. Something was not right. Maybe he wanted to warn me to stay out of the way until he could get the other men away.

Three more men came from the side of the house. All the men turned to the man in the center like they were waiting for his instructions. He was obviously the leader. This was strange to me. It was hard for me to imagine any scenario where Luke wasn't the leader. Unless... Unless it was General Wells. I squinted my eyes to look at the leader. It couldn't be him. Luke had said the general was in his fifties and this man was probably in his mid-thirties at the oldest. Whoever he was, he was clearly in charge.

"Has he agreed?" the leader called, his raised voice carried with the wind and bit into my ears.

Luke shook his head no. The leader moved closer, his voice normal and he said something, but all I could hear was the word *inside* before both of the men behind Jacob pushed him forward hard enough that Jacob's feet stumbled before he caught himself and walked inside. All but two of the men followed them in. That left two men guarding the front door.

While the men were still distracted, I used that time to dash across the open area and to the back of the barn. The truck was back there. The tailgate was down and the majority of the wood had been removed.

Luke had this. He wouldn't let anything happen to Jacob. Jacob was like a brother to him. Thinking of brothers, none of the men looked like they could be Adam.

Where was Adam?

I stepped into the dark barn, careful to only open the door just enough to slide in before closing it behind me. I got myself oriented to the darkened room, letting my eyes adjust before I started moving. Last thing I needed to do was trip over something and make noise. I tucked the gun into my waistband and used both arms stretched out in front of me to feel for the ladder that would take me to the loft and the window facing the house.

Finding the ladder, I slowly made my way up the whole time hoping Luke had a handle on whatever the hell was going on and that the two of them were safe. I had to believe they would be safe.

Luke was home.

At the top of the loft, I crouched low just in case someone happened to look up and see me through the window. I didn't think it was possible, but I didn't want to make any mistakes. Not when the love of my life and my brother were here and we were so close to all of this being over. I really wanted to know why they were all here, why they were pushing my brother around and what they wanted him to agree to. I hoped Luke beat their asses for treating Jacob like that.

I peeked through the window to the men by the door. They were facing each other, talking again, so I took that opportunity to find a wooden apple crate and situated it in front of the window to sit down. I pulled the gun out of my waistband and leaned forward until my forearms were on my thighs and the gun was gripped with both hands. This would make it easier for me to raise my gun and shoot if whatever was going on down there came to that.

I hoped it didn't.

I had only sat for a few minutes when three of the men were coming out of the house and down the stairs carrying boxes of food. *Our* food. I pinched my lips tight and my finger twitched on the trigger. I had to let it go. If this was the agreement they had made to possibly let Luke go and give him his brother, then they could clean the house out. I just wanted them gone and to wrap my arms around my man so I could feel that this was real.

The men continued making trips back and forth from the house, carrying supplies to the back of the trucks. Well, they were for sure cleaning us out. The three men stopped at the trucks, relaxing against it and laughing to one another. That's when a shot rang out from inside the house. My body jumped in the seat and I pulled the gun up. Luke was making his move. He had waited to get most of the men outside so he could take them one by one. Except… my eyebrows scrunched together, the men outside didn't seem alarmed. They were still lounging around the truck. The two at the door were looking inside, but were leaned into the door frame like nothing big just happened.

My breaths got shorter and my pulse thudded in my chest. This felt all wrong. Something was *very* wrong. I heard two more shots before the men at the door stood up straighter and moved down the stairs and toward the trucks.

They spoke to the other men and they all loaded in the vehicles and waited.

My eyes darted back and forth from the men in the trucks to the house. *God, please don't let what I think just happened have happened. God, please! They can't be dead. They can't.*

The leader walked out calmly, his arms crossed over his large frame. He looked over his shoulder, back inside the house before moving down the stairs and into the passenger side of the military vehicle.

Luke was next to come out and when he did, my world went cold and dark.

He held a handgun in one hand and the other was under the arm of Jacob's limp body. The last guy with them held Jacob's other arm as they pulled his lifeless body from the house to the back of the car. He slammed the door of the backseat, said something to the leader, and went back inside. He wasn't in the house long before coming out and getting into the driver's side of the car.

Pain seared through my body, engulfing every ounce of what was me. Or more, the shell of what was left of me. Jacob was dead and Luke had killed him.

Jacob was dead!

And the love of my life had killed the only thing I had left.

Everything was a lie.

The vehicles started to move, the car being the last to start the engine. I could have sworn I saw Luke look up to the barn and straight at where I was sitting before he, too, drove away.

I was alone.

Jacob was gone.

Jacob was gone!

My body was numb. My lips tingled and all I could hear was ringing in my ears. I closed my eyes, and with a shaking hand raised the gun to my head and pulled the trigger. I let out an ear piercing scream when nothing happened. The pain of seeing Jacob's lifeless body still burned in my soul. I was still alive.

I did not *want* to be alive!

I opened my eyes and looked at the gun. The barrel was jammed. I screamed again and threw the gun in a rage. I jumped from the apple crate, picked it up and threw it as hard as I could against the wall and fell to my knees, using my fist to beat the wood planks beneath me.

Jacob was dead.

Luke killed Jacob.

Luke lied to us.

Luke deserved to die. And I was going to be the one to make that happen.

I didn't remember moving, but somehow I was walking through the door of the house. A kitchen chair was placed in the middle of the living room floor, spots of blood on the carpet beneath it. Sweat beaded my forehead as I looked around the room, my mind not quite seeing anything anymore. I walked to the mantle where the photo of the three of us had been sitting just that morning. It was face down. I didn't lift it. I *couldn't* lift it.

The next time I ever saw Luke's face was going to be when I was about to put a bullet in it.

I scanned the room when a piece of paper on the table caught my eye. I walked on shaking legs and picked it up. Two words. Two words from the man who had given us life then ripped it away. Two words that no longer meant anything to me. The two words would be the last he would ever hear coming from my mouth before I made sure he never lied again.

Trust me.

Everything inside me turned weightless and still, as if I was underwater. Except there was no water, just rage saturating every part of me. I was drowning, but wouldn't stop grasping for breath until I killed the man I loved.

ACKNOWLEDGEMENTS

The biggest thank you in the world goes to Paula LaFevers. I don't know how many calls, texts, and conversations we had during the writing of this book. You have no idea what that has meant to me. One day, years from now, we will be on our porch, in rocking chairs, arguing about this book. You are my best friend and my biggest fan and I seriously couldn't have done this without you.

Carrie Sanders, Katie Jetton, Penney Davis, Teresa Morris thank you for reading the book for me and all the work you put into making this a better story. You ladies are amazing!

Some Indies to Lean On for being the best group of writer's willing to help another author along the way.

John Sullivan for being a fantastic photographer and putting up with Paula and me at the photo shoot, not the mention the vast amount of emails and text I sent you. Thank you for not charging by the hour.

Danyeil Covington for being the best, prettiest, model in the world and not complaining when we told you to lay down on the cold, wet grass during the winter. You will go far.

About The Author

A mber R Polk was born and raised in a small town in Eastern Oklahoma. Since then, she moved to Colorado, back to Oklahoma, and now resides in Western Arkansas. Although her husband disagrees, she will always consider herself an Okie and proud of it. She is a great cook (don't fact check with her children) and loves spending her time getting kicked off go-cart tracks for aggressive driving. If you have any questions or comments you can find her on Facebook (she's always there).

Made in the USA
San Bernardino, CA
28 February 2015